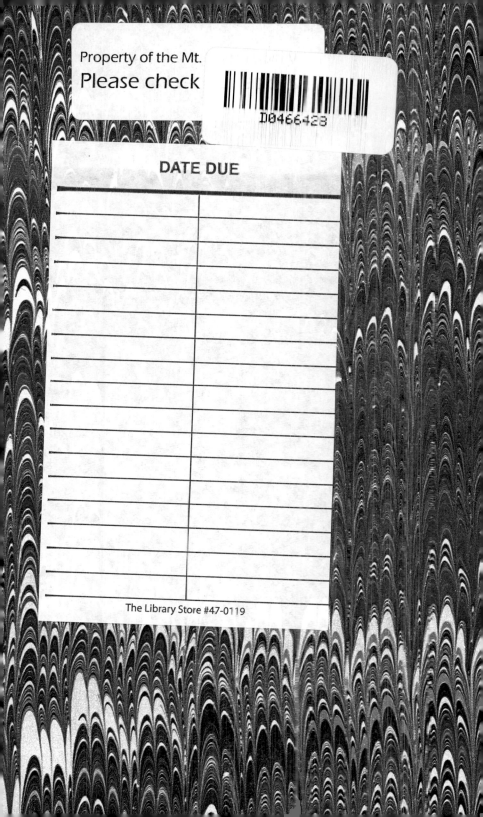

# THE TUESDAY
# CLUB MURDERS

# THE TUESDAY CLUB MURDERS

## AGATHA CHRISTIE

**BANTAM BOOKS**

TORONTO • NEW YORK • LONDON • SYDNEY • AUCKLAND

To Leonard and Katharine Woolley

THE TUESDAY CLUB MURDERS
*A Bantam Book / published by arrangement with
Dodd, Mead & Company*

*The Agatha Christie Mystery Collection / July 1986*

*If you would be interested in receiving bookends for
The Agatha Christie Mystery Collection,
please write to the following address for information:*

*The Agatha Christie Mystery Collection
Bantam Books
P.O. Box 957
Hicksville, New York 11802*

ISBN 0-553-35048-X

*Published simultaneously in the United States and Canada*

---

*Bantam Books are published by Bantam Books, Inc. Its trademark, consisting of the
words "Bantam Books" and the portrayal of a rooster, is Registered in U.S. Patent and
Trademark Office and in other countries. Marca Registrada. Bantam Books, Inc., 666
Fifth Avenue, New York, New York 10103.*

---

PRINTED IN THE UNITED STATES OF AMERICA

0 9 8 7 6 5 4 3 2 1

# CONTENTS

# THE TUESDAY
# CLUB MURDERS

# CHAPTER I

# THE TUESDAY
# NIGHT CLUB

"UNSOLVED mysteries."

Raymond West blew out a cloud of smoke and repeated the words with a kind of deliberate self-conscious pleasure.

"Unsolved mysteries."

He looked round him with satisfaction. The room was an old one with broad black beams across the ceiling and it was furnished with good old furniture that belonged to it. Hence Raymond West's approving glance. By profession he was a writer and he liked the atmosphere to be flawless. His Aunt Jane's house always pleased him as the right setting for her personality. He looked across the hearth to where she sat erect in the big grandfather chair. Miss Marple wore a black brocade dress, very much pinched in round the waist. Mechlin lace was arranged in a cascade down the front of the bodice. She had on black lace mittens, and a black lace cap surmounted the piled-up masses of her snowy hair. She was knitting—something white and soft and fleecy. Her faded blue eyes, benignant and kindly, surveyed her nephew and her nephew's guests with gentle pleasure. They rested first on Raymond himself, self-consciously debonair, then on Joyce Lemprière, the artist, with her close-cropped black head and queer hazel-green eyes, then on that well-groomed man of the world, Sir Henry Clithering. There were two other people in the room, Dr. Pender, the elderly clergyman of the

1

parish, and Mr. Petherick, the solicitor, a dried-up little man with eyeglasses which he looked over and not through. Miss Marple gave a brief moment of attention to all these people and returned to her knitting with a gentle smile upon her lips.

Mr. Petherick gave the dry little cough with which he usually prefaced his remarks. "What is that you say, Raymond? Unsolved mysteries? Ha—and what about them?"

"Nothing about them," said Joyce Lemprière. "Raymond just likes the sound of the words and of himself saying them."

Raymond West threw her a glance of reproach at which she threw back her head and laughed.

"He is a humbug, isn't he, Miss Marple?" she demanded. "You know that, I am sure."

Miss Marple smiled gently at her but made no reply.

"Life itself is an unsolved mystery," said the clergyman gravely.

Raymond sat up in his chair and flung away his cigarette with an impulsive gesture.

"That's not what I mean. I was not talking philosophy," he said. "I was thinking of actual bare prosaic facts, things that have happened and that no one has ever explained."

"I know just the sort of thing you mean, dear," said Miss Marple. "For instance, Mrs. Carruthers had a very strange experience yesterday morning. She bought two gills of picked shrimps at Elliot's. She called at two other shops and when she got home she found she had not got the shrimps with her. She went back to the two shops she had visited but these shrimps had completely disappeared. Now that seems to me very remarkable."

"A very fishy story," said Sir Henry Clithering gravely.

"There are, of course, all kinds of possible explanations," said Miss Marple, her cheeks growing slightly pinker with excitement. "For instance, somebody else——"

"My dear Aunt," said Raymond West with some amusement, "I didn't mean that sort of village incident. I was thinking of murders and disappearances—the kind of thing that Sir Henry could tell us about by the hour if he liked."

"But I never talk shop," said Sir Henry modestly. ' No, I never talk shop."

Sir Henry Clithering had been until lately Commissioner of Scotland Yard.

"I suppose there are a lot of murders and things that never are solved by the police," said Joyce Lemprière.

"That is an admitted fact, I believe," said Mr. Petherick.

"I wonder," said Raymond West, "what class of brain really succeeds best in unravelling a mystery? One always feels that the average police detective must be hampered by lack of imagination."

"That is the layman's point of view," said Sir Henry dryly.

"You really want a committee," said Joyce, smiling. "For psychology and imagination go to the writer——"

She made an ironical bow to Raymond but he remained serious.

"The art of writing gives one an insight into human nature," he said gravely. "One sees, perhaps, motives that the ordinary person would pass by."

"I know, dear," said Miss Marple, "that your books are very clever. But do you think that people are really so unpleasant as you make them out to be?"

"My dear Aunt," said Raymond gently, "keep your beliefs. Heaven forbid that I should in any way shatter them."

"I mean," said Miss Marple, puckering her brow a little as she counted the stitches in her knitting, "that so many people seem to me not to be either bad or good, but simply, you know, very silly."

Mr. Petherick gave his dry little cough again.

"Don't you think, Raymond," he said, "that you attach too much weight to imagination? Imagination is a very dangerous thing, as we lawyers know only too well. To be able to sift evidence impartially, to take the facts and look at them as facts—that seems to me the only logical method

of arriving at the truth. I may add that in my experience it
is the only one that succeeds."

"Bah!" cried Joyce, flinging back her black head indig-
nantly "I bet I could beat you all at this game. I am not
only a woman—and say what you like, women have an
intuition that is denied to men—I am an artist as well. I
see things that you don't. And then, too, as an artist I have
knocked about among all sorts and conditions of people. I
know life as darling Miss Marple here cannot possibly
know it."

"I don't know about that, dear," said Miss Marple.
"Very painful and distressing things happen in villages
sometimes."

"May I speak?" said Dr. Pender, smiling. "It is the
fashion nowadays to decry the clergy, I know, but we hear
things, we know a side of human character which is a
sealed book to the outside world."

"Well," said Joyce, "it seems to me we are a pretty
representative gathering. How would it be if we formed a
Club? What is to-day? Tuesday? We will call it The Tuesday Night Club. It is to meet every week, and each member
in turn has to propound a problem. Some mystery of which
they have personal knowledge, and to which, of course,
they know the answer. Let me see, how many are we? One,
two, three, four, five. We ought really to be six."

"You have forgotten me, dear," said Miss Marple, smiling brightly.

Joyce was slightly taken aback, but she concealed the
fact quickly.

"That would be lovely, Miss Marple," she said. "I didn't
think you would care to play."

"I think it would be very interesting," said Miss Marple,
"especially with so many clever gentlemen present. I am
afraid I am not clever myself, but living all these years in
St. Mary Mead does give one an insight into human nature."

"I am sure your co-operation will be very valuable,"
said Sir Henry, courteously.

"Who is going to start?" said Joyce.

"I think there is no doubt as to that," said Dr. Pender,

"when we have the great good fortune to have such a distinguished man as Sir Henry staying with us——"

He left his sentence unfinished, making a courtly bow in the direction of Sir Henry.

The latter was silent for a minute or two. At last he sighed and recrossed his legs and began:

"It is a little difficult for me to select just the kind of thing you want, but I think, as it happens, I know of an instance which fits these conditions very aptly. You may have seen some mention of the case in the papers of a year ago. It was laid aside at the time as an unsolved mystery, but, as it happens, the solution came into my hands not very many days ago.

"The facts are very simple. Three people sat down to a supper consisting, amongst other things, of tinned lobster. Later in the night, all three were taken ill, and a doctor was hastily summoned. Two of the people recovered, the third one died."

"Ah!" said Raymond approvingly.

"As I say, the facts as such were very simple. Death was considered to be due to ptomaine poisoning, a certificate was given to that effect, and the victim was duly buried. But things did not rest at that."

Miss Marple nodded her head.

"There was talk, I suppose," she said, "there usually is."

"And now I must describe the actors in this little drama. I will call the husband and wife Mr. and Mrs. Jones, and the wife's companion Miss Clark. Mr. Jones was a traveller for a firm of manufacturing chemists. He was a good-looking man in a kind of coarse, florid way, aged about fifty. His wife was a rather commonplace woman, of about forty-five. The companion, Miss Clark, was a woman of sixty, a stout cheery woman with a beaming rubicund face. None of them, you might say, very interesting.

"Now the beginning of the troubles arose in a very curious way. Mr. Jones had been staying the previous night at a small commercial hotel in Birmingham. It happened that the blotting paper in the blotting book had been put in

5

fresh that day, and the chambermaid, having apparently nothing better to do, amused herself by studying the blotter in the mirror just after Mr. Jones had been writing a letter there. A few days later there was a report in the papers of the death of Mrs. Jones as the result of eating tinned lobster, and the chambermaid then imparted to her fellow servants the words that she had deciphered on the blotting pad. They were as follows: 'Entirely dependent on my wife ... when she is dead I will ... hundreds and thousands ...'

"You may remember that there had recently been a case of a wife being poisoned by her husband. It needed very little to fire the imagination of these maids. Mr. Jones had planned to do away with his wife and inherit hundreds of thousands of pounds! As it happened, one of the maids had relations living in the small market town where the Joneses resided. She wrote to them, and they in return wrote to her. Mr. Jones, it seemed, had been very attentive to the local doctor's daughter, a good-looking young woman of thirty-three. Scandal began to hum. The Home Secretary was petitioned. Numerous anonymous letters poured into Scotland Yard, all accusing Mr. Jones of having murdered his wife. Now I may say that not for one moment did we think there was anything in it except idle village talk and gossip. Nevertheless, to quiet public opinion an exhumation order was granted. It was one of these cases of popular superstition based on nothing solid whatever, which proved to be so surprisingly justified. As a result of the autopsy sufficient arsenic was found to make it quite clear that the deceased lady had died of arsenical poisoning. It was for Scotland Yard working with the local authorities to prove how that arsenic had been administered, and by whom."

"Ah!" said Joyce. "I like this. This is the real stuff."

"Suspicion naturally fell on the husband. He benefited by his wife's death. Not to the extent of the hundreds of thousands romantically imagined by the hotel chambermaid, but to the very solid amount of £8000. He had no money of his own apart from what he earned, and he was a man of somewhat extravagant habits with a partiality for the society of women. We investigated as delicately as possible the rumour of his attachment to the doctor's daughter; but while it seemed clear that there had been a strong friendship between them at one time, there had been a most abrupt break two months previously, and they did not appear to have seen each other since. The doctor himself, an elderly man of a straightforward and unsuspicious type, was dumbfounded at the result of the autopsy. He had been called in about midnight to find all three people suffering. He had realised immediately the serious condition of Mrs. Jones, and had sent back to his dispensary for some opium pills, to allay the pain. In spite of all his efforts, however, she succumbed, but not for a moment did he suspect that anything was amiss. He was convinced that her death was due to a form of botulism. Supper that night had consisted of tinned lobster and salad, trifle and bread and cheese. Unfortunately none of the lobster remained—it had all been eaten and the tin thrown away. He had interrogated the young maid, Gladys Linch She was terribly upset, very tearful and agitated, and he found it hard to get her to keep to the point, but she declared again and again that the tin had not been distended in any way and that the lobster had appeared to her in a perfectly good condition.

"Such were the facts we had to go upon. If Jones had feloniously administered arsenic to his wife, it seemed clear that it could not have been done in any of the things eaten at supper, as all three persons had partaken of the meal. Also—another point—Jones himself had returned from Birmingham just as supper was being brought in to table, so that he would have had no opportunity of doctoring any of the food beforehand."

"What about the companion," asked Joyce—"the stout woman with the good-humoured face?"

Sir Henry nodded.

"We did not neglect Miss Clark, I can assure you. But it seemed doubtful what motive she could have had for the crime. Mrs. Jones left her no legacy of any kind and the net result of her employer's death was that she had to seek for another situation."

"That seems to leave her out of it," said Joyce thoughtfully.

"Now one of my inspectors soon discovered a significant fact," went on Sir Henry. "After supper on that evening Mr. Jones had gone down to the kitchen and had demanded a bowl of corn-flour for his wife, who had complained of not feeling well. He had waited in the kitchen until Gladys Linch prepared it, and then carried it up to his wife's room himself. That, I admit, seemed to clinch the case."

The lawyer nodded.

"Motive," he said, ticking the point off on his fingers. "Opportunity. As a traveller for a firm of druggists, easy access to the poison."

"And a man of weak moral fibre," said the clergyman.

Raymond West was staring at Sir Henry.

"There is a catch in this somewhere," he said. "Why did you not arrest him?"

Sir Henry smiled rather wryly.

"That is the unfortunate part of the case. So far all had gone swimmingly, but now we come to the snags. Jones was not arrested because on interrogating Miss Clark she told us that the whole of the bowl of corn-flour was drunk not by Mrs. Jones but by her.

"Yes, it seems that she went to Mrs. Jones' room as was her custom. Mrs. Jones was sitting up in bed and the bowl of corn-flour was beside her.

" 'I am not feeling a bit well, Milly,' she said. 'Serves me right, I suppose, for touching lobster at night. I asked Albert to get me a bowl of corn-flour, but now that I have got it I don't seem to fancy it.'

" 'A pity,' commented Miss Clark—'it is nicely made too, no lumps. Gladys is really quite a nice cook. Very few girls nowadays seem to be able to make a bowl of corn-flour nicely. I declare I quite fancy it myself, I am that hungry.'

" 'I should think you were, with your foolish ways,' said Mrs. Jones.

"I must explain," broke off Sir Henry, "that Miss Clark,

alarmed at her increasing stoutness, was doing a course of
what is popularly known as 'banting.'

" 'It is not good for you, Milly, it really isn't,' urged
Mrs. Jones. 'If the Lord made you stout he meant you to be
stout. You drink up that bowl of corn-flour. It will do you
all the good in the world.'

"And straight away Miss Clark set to and did in actual
fact finish the bowl. So, you see, that knocked our case
against the husband to pieces. Asked for an explanation of
the words on the blotting book, Jones gave one readily
enough. The letter, he explained, was in answer to one
written from his brother in Australia who had applied to
him for money. He had written, pointing out that he was
entirely dependent on his wife. When his wife was dead he
would have control of money and would assist his brother
if possible. He regretted his inability to help but pointed
out that there were hundreds and thousands of people in
the world in the same unfortunate plight."

"And so the case fell to pieces?" said Dr. Pender.

"And so the case fell to pieces," said Sir Henry gravely.
"We could not take the risk of arresting Jones with nothing
to go upon."

There was a silence and then Joyce said, "And that is
all, is it?"

"That is the case as it has stood for the last year. The
true solution is now in the hands of Scotland Yard, and in
two or three days' time you will probably read of it in the
newspapers."

"The true solution," said Joyce thoughtfully. "I wonder. Let's all think for five minutes and then speak."

Raymond West nodded and noted the time on his watch.
When the five minutes were up he looked over at Dr.
Pender.

"Will you speak first?" he said.

The old man shook his head. "I confess," he said, "that
I am utterly baffled. I can but think that the husband in
some way must be the guilty party, but how he did it I
cannot imagine. I can only suggest that he must have given
her the poison in some way that has not yet been discov-

9

ered, although how in that case it should have come to light after all this time I cannot imagine."

"Joyce?"

"The companion!" said Joyce decidedly. "The companion every time! How do we know what motive she may have had? Just because she was old and stout and ugly it doesn't follow that she wasn't in love with Jones herself. She may have hated the wife for some other reason. Think of being a companion—always having to be pleasant and agree and stifle yourself and bottle yourself up. One day she couldn't bear it any longer and then she killed her. She probably put the arsenic in the bowl of corn-flour and all that story about eating it herself is a lie."

"Mr. Petherick?"

The lawyer joined the tips of his fingers together professionally. "I should hardly like to say. On the facts I should hardly like to say."

"But you have got to, Mr. Petherick," said Joyce. "You can't reserve judgment and say 'without prejudice,' and be legal. You have got to play the game."

"On the facts," said Mr. Petherick, "there seems nothing to be said. It is my private opinion, having seen, alas, too many cases of this kind, that the husband was guilty. The only explanation that will cover the facts seems to be that Miss Clark for some reason or other deliberately sheltered him. There may have been some financial arrangement made between them. He might realise that he would be suspected, and she, seeing only a future of poverty before her, may have agreed to tell the story of drinking the corn-flour in return for a substantial sum to be paid to her privately. If that was the case it was of course most irregular. Most irregular indeed."

"I disagree with you all," said Raymond. "You have forgotten the one important factor in the case. *The doctor's daughter.* I will give you my reading of the case. The tinned lobster was bad. It accounted for the poisoning symptoms. The doctor was sent for. He finds Mrs. Jones, who has eaten more lobster than the others, in great pain, and he sends, as you told us, for some opium pills. He does not go

10

himself, he sends. Who will give the messenger the opium pills? Clearly his daughter. Very likely she dispenses his medicines for him. She is in love with Jones and at this moment all the worst instincts in her nature rise and she realises that the means to procure his freedom are in her hands. The pills she sends contain pure white arsenic. That is my solution."

"And now Sir Henry, tell us," said Joyce eagerly.

"One moment," said Sir Henry. "Miss Marple has not yet spoken."

"Dear, dear," she said. "I have dropped another stitch. I have been so interested in the story. A sad case, a very sad case. It reminds me of old Mr. Hargraves who lived up at the Mount. His wife never had the least suspicion—until he died, leaving all his money to a woman he had been living with and by whom he had had five children. She had at one time been their housemaid. Such a nice girl, Mrs. Hargraves always said—thoroughly to be relied upon to turn the mattresses every day—except Fridays, of course. And there was old Hargraves keeping this woman in a house in the neighbouring town and continuing to be a Churchwarden and to hand round the plate every Sunday."

"My dear Aunt Jane," said Raymond with some impatience. "What have dead and gone Hargraves got to do with the case?"

"This story made me think of him at once," said Miss Marple. "The facts are so very alike, aren't they? I suppose the poor girl has confessed now and that is how you know, Sir Henry."

"What girl?" said Raymond. "My dear Aunt, what *are* you talking about?"

"That poor girl, Gladys Linch, of course—the one who was so terribly agitated when the doctor spoke to her—and well she might be, poor thing. I hope that wicked Jones is hanged, I am sure, making that poor girl a murderess. I suppose they will hang her too, poor thing."

"I think, Miss Marple, that you are under a slight misapprehension," began Mr. Petherick.

But Miss Marple shook her head obstinately and looked across at Sir Henry.

"I am right, am I not? It seems so clear to me. The hundreds and thousands—and the trifle—I mean, one cannot miss it."

"What about the trifle and the hundreds and thousands?" cried Raymond.

His aunt turned to him.

"Cooks nearly always put hundreds and thousands on trifle, dear," she said. "Those little pink and white sugar things. Of course when I heard that they had had trifle for supper and that the husband had been writing to someone about hundreds and thousands, I naturally connected the two things together. That is where the arsenic was—in the hundreds and thousands. He left it with the girl and told her to put it on the trifle."

"But that is impossible," said Joyce quickly. "They all ate the trifle."

"Oh, no," said Miss Marple. "The companion was banting, you remember. You never eat anything like trifle if you are banting; and I expect Jones just scraped the hundreds and thousands off his share and left them at the side of his plate. It was a clever idea, but a very wicked one."

The eyes of the others were all fixed upon Sir Henry.

"It is a very curious thing," he said slowly, "but Miss Marple happens to have hit upon the truth. Jones had got Gladys Linch into trouble, as the saying goes. She was nearly desperate. He wanted his wife out of the way and promised to marry Gladys when his wife was dead. He doctored the hundreds and thousands and gave them to her with instructions how to use them. Gladys Linch died a week ago. Her child died at birth and Jones had deserted her for another woman. When she was dying she confessed the truth."

There was a few moments' silence and then Raymond said:

"Well, Aunt Jane, this is one up to you. I can't think how on earth you managed to hit upon the truth. I should never have thought of the little maid in the kitchen being connected with the case."

"No, dear," said Miss Marple, "but you don't know as much of life as I do. A man of that Jones' type—coarse and jovial. As soon as I heard there was a pretty young girl in the house I felt sure that he would not have left her alone. It is all very distressing and painful, and not a very nice thing to talk about. I can't tell you the shock it was to Mrs. Hargraves, and a nine days' wonder in the village.'

# CHAPTER II

# THE IDOL HOUSE
# OF ASTARTE

"And now, Dr. Pender, what are you going to tell us?"
The old clergyman smiled gently.

"My life has been passed in quiet places," he said.
"Very few eventful happenings have come my way. Yet
once, when I was a young man, I had one very strange and
tragic experience."

"Ah!" said Joyce Lemprière encouragingly.

"I have never forgotten it," continued the clergyman.
"It made a profound impression on me at the time, and to
this day by a slight effort of memory I can feel again the
awe and horror of that terrible moment when I saw a man
stricken to death by apparently no mortal agency."

"You make me feel quite creepy, Pender," complained
Sir Henry.

"It made me feel creepy, as you call it," replied the
other. "Since then I have never laughed at the people who
use the word atmosphere. There is such a thing. There are
certain places imbued and saturated with good or evil
influences which can make their power felt."

"That house, The Larches, is a very unhappy one,"
remarked Miss Marple. "Old Mr. Smithers lost all his
money and had to leave it, then the Carslakes took it and
Johnny Carslake fell downstairs and broke his leg and Mrs.
Carslake had to go away to the south of France for her
health, and now the Burdens have got it and I hear that

poor Mr. Burden has got to have an operation almost immediately."

"There is, I think, rather too much superstition about such matters," said Mr. Petherick. "A lot of damage is done to property by foolish reports heedlessly circulated."

"I have known one or two 'ghosts' that have had a very robust personality," remarked Sir Henry with a chuckle.

"I think," said Raymond, "we should allow Dr. Pender to go on with his story."

Joyce got up and switched off the two lamps, leaving the room lit only by the flickering firelight.

"Atmosphere," she said. "Now we can get along.'

Dr. Pender smiled at her, and leaning back in his chair and taking off his pince-nez, he began his story in a gentle reminiscent voice.

"I don't know whether any of you know Dartmoor at all. The place I am telling you about is situated on the borders of Dartmoor. It was a very charming property, though it had been on the market without finding a purchaser for several years. The situation was perhaps a trifle bleak in winter, but the views were magnificent and there were certain curious and original features about the property itself. It was bought by a man called Haydon—Sir Richard Haydon. I had known him in his college days, and though I had lost sight of him for some years, the old ties of friendship still held, and I accepted with pleasure his invitation to go down to Silent Grove, as his new purchase was called.

"The house party was not a very large one. There was Richard Haydon himself, and his cousin, Elliot Haydon. There was a Lady Mannering with a pale, rather inconspicuous daughter called Violet. There was a Captain Rogers and his wife, hard riding, weather-beaten people, who lived only for horses and hunting. There was also a young Dr. Symonds and there was Miss Diana Ashley. I knew something about the last named. Her picture was very often in the Society papers and she was one of the notorious beauties of the Season. Her appearance was indeed very striking. She was dark and tall, with a beautiful skin

15

of an even tint of pale cream, and her half-closed dark eyes set slantways in her head gave her a curiously piquant oriental appearance. She had, too, a wonderful speaking voice, deep-toned and bell-like.

"I saw at once that my friend Richard Haydon was very much attracted by her, and I guessed that the whole party was merely arranged as a setting for her. Of her own feelings I was not so sure. She was capricious in her favours. One day talking to Richard and excluding everyone else from her notice, and another day she would favour his cousin, Elliot, and appear hardly to notice that such a person as Richard existed, and then again she would bestow the most bewitching smiles upon the quiet and retiring Dr. Symonds.

"On the morning after my arrival our host showed us all over the place. The house itself was unremarkable, a good solid house built of Devonshire granite. Built to withstand time and exposure. It was unromantic but very comfortable. From the windows of it one looked out over the panorama of the Moor, vast rolling hills crowned with weatherbeaten Tors.

"On the slopes of the Tor nearest to us were various hut circles, relics of the bygone days of the late Stone Age. On another hill was a barrow which had recently been excavated, and in which certain bronze implements had been found. Haydon was by way of being interested in antiquarian matters and he talked to us with a great deal of energy and enthusiasm. This particular spot, he explained, was particularly rich in relics of the past.

"Neolithic hut dwellers, Druids, Romans, and even traces of the early Phoenicians were to be found.

" 'But this place is the most interesting of all,' he said. 'You know its name—Silent Grove. Well, it is easy enough to see what it takes its name from.'

"He pointed with his hand. That particular part of the country was bare enough—rocks, heather and bracken, but about a hundred yards from the house there was a densely planted grove of trees.

" 'That is a relic of very early days,' said Haydon. 'The

16

trees have died and been replanted, but on the whole it has
been kept very much as it used to be—perhaps in the time
of the Phoenician settlers. Come and look at it.'

"We all followed him. As we entered the grove of trees
a curious oppression came over me. I think it was the
silence. No birds seemed to nest in these trees. There was
a feeling about it of desolation and horror. I saw Haydon
looking at me with a curious smile.

" 'Any feeling about this place, Pender?' he asked me.
'Antagonism now? Or uneasiness?'

" 'I don't like it,' I said quietly.

" 'You are within your rights. This was a stronghold of
one of the ancient enemies of your faith. This is the Grove
of Astarte.'

" 'Astarte?'

" 'Astarte, or Ishtar, or Ashtoreth, or whatever you
choose to call her. I prefer the Phoenician name of Astarte.
There is, I believe, one known Grove of Astarte in this
country—in the North on the Wall. I have no evidence, but
I like to believe that we have a true and authentic Grove of
Astarte here. Here, within this dense circle of trees, sacred
rites were performed.'

" 'Sacred rites,' murmured Diana Ashley. Her eyes
had a dreamy far-away look. 'What were they, I wonder?'

" 'Not very reputable by all accounts,' said Captain
Rogers with a loud unmeaning laugh. 'Rather hot stuff, I
imagine.'

"Haydon paid no attention to him.

" 'In the centre of the Grove there should be a Tem-
ple,' he said. 'I can't run to Temples, but I have indulged
in a little fancy of my own.'

"We had at that moment stepped out into a little
clearing in the centre of the trees. In the middle of it was
something not unlike a summer-house made of stone. Diana Ashley looked inquiringly at Haydon.

" 'I call it The Idol House,' he said. 'It is the Idol
House of Astarte.'

"He led the way up to it. Inside, on a rude ebony

pillar, there reposed a curious little image representing a woman with crescent horns, seated on a lion.

" 'Astarte of the Phoenicians,' said Haydon, 'the Goddess of the Moon.'

" 'The Goddess of the Moon,' cried Diana. 'Oh, do let us have a wild orgy to-night. Fancy dress. And we will come out here in the moonlight and celebrate the rites of Astarte.'

"I made a sudden movement and Elliot Haydon, Richard's cousin, turned quickly to me.

" 'You don't like all this, do you, Padre?' he said.

" 'No,' I said gravely. 'I don't.'

"He looked at me curiously. 'But it is only tomfoolery. Dick can't know that this really is a sacred grove. It is just a fancy of his; he likes to play with the idea. And anyway, if it were——'

" 'If it were?' "

" 'Well—' he laughed uncomfortably. 'You don't believe in that sort of thing, do you? You, a parson.'

" 'I am not sure that as a parson I ought not to believe in it.'

" 'But that sort of thing is all finished and done with.'

" 'I am not so sure,' I said musingly. 'I only know this: I am not as a rule a sensitive man to atmosphere, but ever since I entered this grove of trees I have felt a curious impression and sense of evil and menace all around me.'

"He glanced uneasily over his shoulder.

" 'Yes,' he said, 'it is—it is queer, somehow. I know what you mean but I suppose it is only our imagination makes us feel like that. What do you say, Symonds?'

"The doctor was silent a minute or two before he replied. Then he said quietly:

" 'I don't like it. I can't tell you why. But somehow or other, I don't like it.'

"At that moment Violet Mannering came across to me.

" 'I hate this place,' she cried. 'I hate it. Do let's get out of it.'

"We moved away and the others followed us. Only Diana Ashley lingered. I turned my head over my shoulder

18

and saw her standing in front of the Idol House gazing earnestly at the image within it.

"The day was an unusually hot and beautiful one and Diana Ashley's suggestion of a Fancy Dress party that evening was received with general favour. The usual laughing and whispering and frenzied secret sewing took place and when we all made our appearance for dinner there were the usual outcries of merriment. Rogers and his wife were Neolithic hut dwellers—explaining the sudden lack of hearth-rugs. Richard Haydon called himself a Phoenician sailor, and his cousin was a Brigand Chief, Dr. Symonds was a chef, Lady Mannering was a hospital nurse, and her daughter was a Circassian slave. I myself was arrayed somewhat too warmly as a monk. Diana Ashley came down last and was somewhat of a disappointment to all of us, being wrapped in a shapeless black domino.

" 'The Unknown,' she declared airily. 'That is what I am. Now for goodness' sake let's go in to dinner.'

"After dinner we went outside. It was a lovely night, warm and soft, and the moon was rising.

"We wandered about and chatted and the time passed quickly enough. It must have been an hour later when we realised that Diana Ashley was not with us.

" 'Surely she has not gone to bed,' said Richard Haydon.

"Violet Mannering shook her head.

" 'Oh, no,' she said. 'I saw her going off in that direction about a quarter of an hour ago.' She pointed as she spoke towards the grove of trees that showed black and shadowy in the moonlight.

" 'I wonder what she is up to,' said Richard Haydon, 'some devilment, I swear. Let's go and see.'

"We all trooped off together, somewhat curious as to what Miss Ashley had been up to. Yet I, for one, felt a curious reluctance to enter that dark foreboding belt of trees. Something stronger than myself seemed to be holding me back and urging me not to enter. I felt more definitely convinced than ever of the essential evilness of the spot. I think that some of the others experienced the same sensations that I did, though they would have been loath to

19

admit it. The trees were so closely planted that the moonlight could not penetrate. There were a dozen soft sounds all round us, whisperings and sighings. The feeling was eerie in the extreme, and by common consent we all kept close together.

"Suddenly we came out into the open clearing in the middle of the grove and stood rooted to the spot in amazement, for there, on the threshold of the Idol House, stood a shimmering figure wrapped tightly round in diaphanous gauze and with two crescent horns rising from the dark masses of her hair.

" 'My God!' said Richard Haydon, and the sweat sprang out on his brow.

"But Violet Mannering was sharper.

" 'Why, it's Diana,' she exclaimed. 'What has she done to herself? Oh, she looks quite different somehow!'

"The figure in the doorway raised her hands. She took a step forward and chanted in a high sweet voice.

" 'I am the Priestess of Astarte,' she crooned. 'Beware how you approach me, for I hold death in my hand.'

" 'Don't do it, dear,' protested Lady Mannering. 'You give us the creeps, you really do.'

"Haydon sprang forward towards her.

" 'My God, Diana!' he cried. 'You are wonderful.'

"My eyes were accustomed to the moonlight now and I could see more plainly. She did, indeed, as Violet had said, look quite different. Her face was more definitely oriental, and her eyes more of slits with something cruel in their gleam, and the strange smile on her lips was one that I had never seen there before.

" 'Beware,' she cried warningly. 'Do not approach the Goddess. If anyone lays a hand on me it is death.'

" 'You are wonderful, Diana,' cried Haydon, 'but do stop it. Somehow or other I—I don't like it.'

"He was moving towards her across the grass and she flung out a hand towards him.

" 'Stop,' she cried. 'One step nearer and I will smite you with the magic of Astarte.'

"Richard Haydon laughed and quickened his pace, when

20

all at once a curious thing happened. He hesitated for a moment, then seemed to stumble and fall headlong.

"He did not get up again, but lay where he had fallen prone on the ground.

"Suddenly Diana began to laugh hysterically. It was a strange horrible sound breaking the silence of the glade.

"With an oath Elliot sprang forward.

" 'I can't stand this,' he cried, 'get up, Dick, get up man.'

"But still Richard Haydon lay where he had fallen Elliot Haydon reached his side, knelt by him and turned him gently over. He bent over him, peering in his face.

"Then he rose sharply to his feet and stood swaying a little.

" 'Doctor,' he said. 'Doctor, for God's sake come. I—I think he is dead.'

"Symonds ran forward and Elliot rejoined us, walking very slowly. He was looking down at his hands in a way I didn't understand.

"At that moment there was a wild scream from Diana.

" 'I have killed him,' she cried. 'Oh, my God! I didn't mean to, but I have killed him.'

"And she fainted dead away, falling in a crumpled heap on the grass.

"There was a cry from Mrs. Rogers.

" 'Oh, do let us get away from this dreadful place,' she wailed, 'anything might happen to us here. Oh, it's awful '

"Elliot got hold of me by the shoulder.

" 'It can't be, man,' he murmured. 'I tell you it can t be. A man cannot be killed like that. It is—it s against Nature.'

"I tried to soothe him.

" 'There is some explanation,' I said. 'Your cousin must have had some unsuspected weakness of the heart. The shock and excitement——'

"He interrupted me.

" 'You don't understand,' he said. He held up his hands for me to see and I noticed a red stain on them.

21

" 'Dick didn't die of shock, he was stabbed—stabbed to the heart, and *there is no weapon.*'

"I stared at him incredulously. At that moment Symonds rose from his examination of the body and came towards us. He was pale and shaking all over.

" 'Are we all mad?' he said. 'What is this place—that things like this can happen in it?'

" 'Then it is true,' I said.

"He nodded.

" 'The wound is such as would be made by a long thin dagger, but—there is no dagger there.'

"We all looked at each other.

" 'But it must be there,' cried Elliot Haydon. 'It must have dropped out. It must be on the ground somewhere. Let us look.'

"We peered about vainly on the ground. Violet Mannering said suddenly:

" 'Diana had something in her hand. A kind of dagger. I saw it. I saw it glitter when she threatened him.'

"Elliot Haydon shook his head.

" 'He never even got within three yards of her,' he objected.

"Lady Mannering was bending over the prostrate girl on the ground.

" 'There is nothing in her hand now,' she announced, 'and I can't see anything on the ground. Are you sure you saw it, Violet? I didn't.'

"Dr. Symonds came over to the girl.

" 'We must get her to the house,' he said. 'Rogers, will you help?'

"Between us we carried the unconscious girl back to the house. Then we returned and fetched the body of Sir Richard."

Dr. Pender broke off apologetically and looked round. "One would know better nowadays," he said, "owing to the prevalence of detective fiction. Every street boy knows that a body must be left where it is found. But in these days we had not the same knowledge, and accordingly we carried the body of Richard Haydon back to his bedroom in

22

the square granite house and the butler was despatched on a bicycle in search of the police—a ride of some twelve miles.

"It was then that Elliot Haydon drew me aside.

" 'Look here,' he said. 'I am going back to the grove. That weapon has got to be found.'

" 'If there was a weapon,' I said doubtfully.

"He seized my arm and shook it fiercely. 'You have got that superstitious stuff into your head. You think his death was supernatural; well, I am going back to the grove to find out.'

"I was curiously averse to his doing so. I did my utmost to dissuade him, but without result. The mere idea of that thick circle of trees was abhorrent to me and I felt a strong premonition of further disaster. But Elliot was entirely pigheaded. He was, I think, scared himself, but would not admit it. He went off fully armed with determination to get to the bottom of the mystery.

"It was a very dreadful night, none of us could sleep, or attempt to do so. The police, when they arrived, were frankly incredulous of the whole thing. They evinced a strong desire to cross-examine Miss Ashley, but there they had to reckon with Dr. Symonds, who opposed the idea vehemently. Miss Ashley had come out of her faint or trance and he had given her a strong sleeping draught. She was on no account to be disturbed until the following day.

"It was not until about seven o'clock in the morning that anyone thought about Elliot Haydon and then Symonds suddenly asked where he was. I explained what Elliot had done and Symonds' grave face grew a shade graver. 'I wish he hadn't. It is—it is foolhardy,' he said.

" 'You don't think any harm can have happened to him?'

" 'I hope not. I think, Padre, that you and I had better go and see.'

"I knew he was right, but it took all the courage in my command to nerve myself for the task. We set out together and entered once more that ill-fated grove of trees. We called him twice and got no reply. In a minute or two we came into the clearing, which looked pale and ghostly in the early morning light. Symonds clutched my arm and I uttered a muttered exclamation. Last night when we had seen it in the moonlight there had been the body of a man lying face downwards on the grass. Now in the early morning light the same sight met our eyes. Elliot Haydon was lying on the exact spot where his cousin had been.

" 'My God,' said Symonds. '*It has got him too!*'

"We ran together over the grass. Elliot Haydon was unconscious but breathing feebly and this time there was no doubt of what had caused the tragedy. A long thin bronze weapon remained in the wound.

" 'Got him through the shoulder, not through the heart. That is lucky,' commented the doctor. 'On my soul, I don't know what to think. At any rate he is not dead and he will be able to tell us what happened.'

"But that was just what Elliot Haydon was not able to do. His description was vague in the extreme. He had hunted about vainly for the dagger and at last giving up the search had taken up a stand near the Idol House. It was then that he became increasingly certain that someone was watching him from the belt of trees. He fought against this impression but was not able to shake it off. He described a cold strange wind that began to blow. It seemed to come not from the trees but from the interior of the Idol House. He turned round, peering inside it. He saw the small figure of the Goddess and he felt he was under an optical delusion. The figure seemed to grow larger and larger. Then he suddenly received something that felt like a blow between his temples which sent him reeling back, and as he fell he was conscious of a sharp burning pain in his left shoulder.

"The dagger was identified this time as being the identical one which had been dug up in the barrow on the hill, and which had been bought by Richard Haydon. Where he had kept it, in the house or in the Idol House in the grove, none seemed to know.

"The police were of the opinion, and always will be, that he was deliberately stabbed by Miss Ashley, but in view of our combined evidence that she was never within

24

three yards of him, they could not hope to support the charge against her. So the thing has been and remains a mystery."

There was a silence.

"There doesn't seem anything to say," said Joyce Lemprière at length. "It is all so horrible—and uncanny. Have you no explanation yourself, Dr. Pender?"

The old man nodded. "Yes," he said. "I have an explanation—a kind of explanation, that is. Rather a curious one—but to my mind it still leaves certain factors unaccounted for."

"I have been to séances," said Joyce "and you may say what you like, very queer things can happen. I suppose one can explain it by some kind of hypnotism. The girl really turned herself into a Priestess of Astarte, and I suppose somehow or other she must have stabbed him. Perhaps she threw the dagger that Miss Mannering saw in her hand."

"Or it might have been a javelin," suggested Raymond West. "After all, moonlight is not very strong. She might have had a kind of spear in her hand and stabbed him at a distance, and then I suppose mass hypnotism comes into account. I mean, you were all prepared to see him stricken down by supernatural means and so you saw it like that."

"I have seen many wonderful things done with weapons and knives at music halls," said Sir Henry. "I suppose it is possible that a man could have been concealed in the belt of trees, and that he might from there have thrown a knife or a dagger with sufficient accuracy—agreeing, of course, that he was a professional. I admit that that seems rather far-fetched, but it seems the only really feasible theory. You remember that the other man was distinctly under the impression that there was someone in the grove of trees watching him. As to Miss Mannering saying that Miss Ashley had a dagger in her hand and the others saying she hadn't, that doesn't surprise me. If you had had my experience you would know that five persons' accounts of the same thing will differ so widely as to be almost incredible."

Mr. Petherick coughed.

"But in all these theories we seem to be overlooking one essential fact," he remarked. "What became of the weapon? Miss Ashley could hardly get rid of a javelin standing as she was in the middle of an open space; and if a hidden murderer had thrown a dagger, then the dagger would still have been in the wound when the man was turned over. We must, I think, discard all far-fetched theories and confine ourselves to sober fact."

"And where does sober fact lead us?"

"Well, one thing seems quite clear. No one was near the man when he was stricken down, so the only person who *could* have stabbed him was he himself. Suicide, in fact."

"But why on earth should he wish to commit suicide?" asked Raymond West incredulously.

The lawyer coughed again. "Ah, that is the question of theory once more," he said. "At the moment I am not concerned with theories. It seems to me, excluding the supernatural in which I do not for one moment believe, that that was the only way things could have happened. He stabbed himself, and as he fell his arms flew out, wrenching the dagger from the wound and flinging it far into the zone of the trees. That is, I think, although somewhat unlikely, a possible happening."

"I don't like to say, I am sure," said Miss Marple. "It all perplexes me very much indeed. But curious things do happen. At Lady Sharpley's garden party last year the man who was arranging the clock golf tripped over one of the numbers—quite unconscious he was—and didn't come round for about five minutes."

"Yes, dear Aunt," said Raymond gently, "but he wasn't stabbed, was he?"

"Of course not, dear," said Miss Marple. "That is what I am telling you. Of course there is only one way that poor Sir Richard could have been stabbed, but I do wish I knew what caused him to stumble in the first place. Of course, it might have been a tree root. He would be looking at the girl, of course, and when it is moonlight one does trip over things."

"You say that there is only one way that Sir Richard could have been stabbed, Miss Marple," said the clergyman, looking at her curiously.

"It is very sad and I don't like to think of it. He was a right-handed man, was he not? I mean to stab himself in the left shoulder he must have been. I was always so sorry for poor Jack Baynes in the War. He shot himself in the foot, you remember, after very severe fighting at Arras. He told me about it when I went to see him in the hospital, and very ashamed of it he was. I don't expect this poor man, Elliot Haydon, profited much by his wicked crime."

"Elliot Haydon," cried Raymond. 'You think he did it?"

"I don't see how anyone else could have done it," said Miss Marple, opening her eyes in gentle surprise. "I mean if, as Mr. Petherick so wisely says, one looks at the facts and disregards all that atmosphere of heathen goddesses which I don't think is very nice. He went up to him first and turned him over, and of course to do that he would have to have had his back to them all, and being dressed as a brigand chief he would be sure to have a weapon of some kind in his belt. I remember dancing with a man dressed as a brigand chief when I was a young girl. He had five kinds of knives and daggers, and I can't tell you how awkward and uncomfortable it was for his partner."

All eyes were turned towards Dr. Pender.

"I knew the truth," said he, "five years after that tragedy occurred. It came in the shape of a letter written to me by Elliot Haydon. He said in it that he fancied that I had always suspected him. He said it was a sudden temptation. He too loved Diana Ashley, but he was only a poor struggling barrister. With Richard out of the way and inheriting his title and estates, he saw a wonderful prospect opening up before him. The dagger had jerked out of his belt as he knelt down by his cousin, and almost before he had time to think, he drove it in and returned it to his belt again. He stabbed himself later in order to divert suspicion. He wrote to me on the eve of starting on an expedition to the South Pole in case, as he said, he should never

27

come back. I do not think that he meant to come back, and I know that, as Miss Marple has said, his crime profited him nothing. 'For five years,' he wrote, 'I have lived in Hell. I hope, at least, that I may expiate my crime by dying honourably.' "

There was a pause.

"And he did die honourably," said Sir Henry. "You have changed the names in your story, Dr. Pender, but I think I recognize the man you mean."

"As I said," went on the old clergyman, "I do not think that explanation quite covers the facts. I still think there was an evil influence in that grove, an influence that directed Elliot Haydon's action. Even to this day I can never think without a shudder of The Idol House of Astarte."

# CHAPTER III

## INGOTS OF GOLD

"I do not know that the story that I am going to tell you is a fair one," said Raymond West, "because I can't give you the solution of it. Yet the facts were so interesting and so curious that I should like to propound it to you as a problem, and perhaps between us we may arrive at some logical conclusion.

"The date of these happenings was two years ago, when I went down to spend Whitsuntide with a man called John Newman, in Cornwall."

"Cornwall?" said Joyce Lemprière sharply.

"Yes. Why?"

"Nothing. Only it's odd. My story is about a place in Cornwall, too—a little fishing village called Rathole. Don't tell me yours is the same?"

"No. My village is called Polperran. It is situated on the west coast of Cornwall; a very wild and rocky spot. I had been introduced to John a few weeks previously and had found him a most interesting companion. A man of intelligence and independent means, he was possessed of a romantic imagination. As a result of his latest hobby he had taken the lease of Pol House. He was an authority on Elizabethan times, and he described to me in vivid and graphic language the rout of the Spanish Armada. So enthusiastic was he that one could almost imagine that he had been an eye-witness at the scene. Is there anything in reincarnation? I wonder—I very much wonder."

29

"You are so romantic, Raymond dear," said Miss Marple, looking benignantly at him.

"Romantic is the last thing that I am," said Raymond West, slightly annoyed. "But this fellow Newman was chock-full of it and he interested me for that reason as a curious survival of the past. It appears that a certain ship belonging to the Armada, and known to contain a vast amount of treasure in the form of gold from the Spanish Main, was wrecked off the coast of Cornwall on the famous and treacherous Serpent Rocks. For some years, so Newman told me, attempts had been made to salve the ship and recover the treasure. I believe such stories are not uncommon, though the number of mythical treasure ships is largely in excess of the genuine ones. A company had been formed, but had gone bankrupt, and Newman had been able to buy the rights of the thing—or whatever you call it—for a mere song. He waxed very enthusiastic about it all. According to him it was merely a question of the latest scientific, up-to-date machinery. The gold was there, and he had no doubt whatever that it could be recovered.

"It occurred to me as I listened to him how often things happen that way. A rich man such as Newman succeeds almost without effort, and yet in all probability the actual value in money of his find would mean little to him. I must say that his ardour infected me. I saw galleons drifting up the coast, flying before the storm, beaten and broken on the black rocks. The mere word galleon has a romantic sound. The phrase 'Spanish Gold' thrills the schoolboy—and the grown-up man also. Moreover, I was working at the time upon a novel, some scenes of which were laid in the sixteenth century, and I saw the prospect of getting valuable local colour from my host.

"I set off that Friday morning from Paddington in high spirits, and looking forward to my trip. The carriage was empty except for one man, who sat facing me in the opposite corner. He was a tall, soldierly-looking man, and I could not rid myself of the impression that somewhere or other I had seen him before. I cudgelled my brains for some time in vain; but at last I had it. My travelling companion was Inspector Badgworth, and I had run across him when I was doing a series of articles on the Everson disappearance case.

"I recalled myself to his notice and we were soon chatting pleasantly enough. When I told him I was going to Polperran he remarked that that was a rum coincidence, because he himself was also bound for that place. I did not like to seem inquisitive, so was careful not to ask him what took him there. Instead, I spoke of my own interest in the place, and mentioned the wrecked Spanish galleon. To my surprise the inspector seemed to know all about it. 'That will be the *Juan Fernandez*,' he said. 'Your friend won't be the first who has sunk money trying to get money out of her. It is a romantic notion.'

" 'And probably the whole story is a myth,' I said. 'No ship was ever wrecked there at all.'

" 'Oh, the ship was sunk there right enough,' said the inspector—'along with a good company of others. You would be surprised if you knew how many wrecks there are on that part of the coast. As a matter of fact, that is what takes me down there now. That is where the *Otranto* was wrecked six months ago.'

" 'I remember reading about it,' I said. 'No lives were lost, I think?'

" 'No lives were lost,' said the inspector; 'but something else was lost. It is not generally known, but the *Otranto* was carrying bullion.'

" 'Yes?' I said, much interested.

" 'Naturally we have had divers at work on salvage operations, but—*the gold has gone, Mr. West.*'

" 'Gone!' I said, staring at him 'How can it have gone?'

" 'That is the question,' said the inspector. 'The rocks tore a gaping hole in her strong-room. It was easy enough for the divers to get in that way, but they found the strong-room empty. The question is, was the gold stolen before the wreck or afterwards? Was it ever in the strong-room at all?'

" 'It seems a curious case,' I said.

" 'It is a very curious case, when you consider what bullion is. Not a diamond necklace that you could put into your pocket. When you think how cumbersome it is and how bulky—well, the whole thing seems absolutely impossible. There may have been some hocus-pocus before the ship sailed; but if not, it must have been removed within the last six months—and I am going down to look into the matter.'

"I found Newman waiting to meet me at the station. He apologised for the absence of his car, which had gone to Truro for some necessary repairs. Instead, he met me with a farm lorry belonging to the property.

"I swung myself up beside him, and we wound carefully in and out of the narrow streets of the fishing village. We went up a steep ascent, with a gradient, I should say of one in five, ran a little distance along a winding lane, and turned in at the granite-pillared gates of Pol House.

"The place was a charming one; it was situated high up the cliffs, with a good view out to sea. Part of it was some three or four hundred years old, and a modern wing had been added. Behind it farming land of about seven or eight acres ran inland.

" 'Welcome to Pol House,' said Newman. 'And to the Sign of the Golden Galleon.' And he pointed to where, over the front door, hung a perfect reproduction of a Spanish galleon with all sails set.

"My first evening was a most charming and instructive one. My host showed me the old manuscripts relating to the *Juan Fernandez*. He unrolled charts for me and indicated positions on them with dotted lines, and he produced plans of diving apparatus, which, I may say, mystified me utterly and completely.

"I told him of my meeting with Inspector Badgworth, in which he was much interested.

" 'They are a queer people round this coast,' he said reflectively. 'Smuggling and wrecking is in their blood. When a ship goes down on their coast they cannot help regarding it as lawful plunder meant for their pockets.

There is a fellow here I should like you to see. He is an interesting survival.'

"Next day dawned bright and clear. I was taken down into Polperran and there introduced to Newman's diver, a man called Higgins. He was a wooden-faced individual, extremely taciturn, and his contributions to the conversation were mostly monosyllables. After a discussion between them on highly technical matters, we adjourned to the Three Anchors. A tankard of beer somewhat loosened the worthy fellow's tongue.

" 'Detective gentleman from London has come down,' he grunted. 'They do say that that ship that went down here last November was carrying a mortal lot of gold. Well, she wasn't the first to go down, and she won't be the last.'

" 'Hear, hear,' chimed in the landlord of the Three Anchors. 'That is a true word you say there, Bill Higgins.'

" 'I reckon it is, Mr. Kelvin,' " said Higgins.

"I looked with some curiosity at the landlord. He was a remarkable man, dark and swarthy, with curiously broad shoulders. His eyes were bloodshot, and he had a curiously furtive way of avoiding one's glance. I suspected that this was the man of whom Newman had spoken, saying he was an interesting survival.

" 'We don't want interfering foreigners on this coast,' he said somewhat truculently.

" 'Meaning the police?' asked Newman, smiling.

" 'Meaning the police—and others,' said Kelvin significantly. 'And don't you forget it, mister.'

" 'Do you know, Newman, that sounded to me very like a threat,' I said as we climbed the hill homewards.

"My friend laughed.

" 'Nonsense; I don't do the folk down here any harm.'

"I shook my head doubtfully. There was something sinister and uncivilised about Kelvin. I felt that his mind might run in strange, unrecognised channels.

"I think I date the beginning of my uneasiness from that moment. I had slept well enough that first night, but the next night my sleep was troubled and broken. Sunday dawned, dark and sullen, with an overcast sky and the threatenings of thunder in the air. I am always a bad hand at hiding my feelings, and Newman noticed the change in me.

" 'What is the matter with you, West? You are a bundle of nerves this morning.'

" 'I don't know,' I confessed, 'but I have got a horrible feeling of foreboding.'

" 'It's the weather.'

" 'Yes, perhaps.'

"I said no more. In the afternoon we went out in Newman's motor boat, but the rain came on with such vigour that we were glad to return to shore and change into dry clothing.

"And that evening my uneasiness increased. Outside the storm howled and roared. Towards ten o'clock the tempest calmed down. Newman looked out the window.

" 'It is clearing,' he said. 'I shouldn't wonder if it was a perfectly fine night in another half-hour. If so, I shall go out for a stroll.'

"I yawned. 'I am frightfully sleepy,' I said. 'I didn't get much sleep last night. I think that to-night I shall turn in early.'

"This I did. On the previous night I had slept little. Tonight I slept heavily. Yet my slumbers were not restful. I was still oppressed with an awful foreboding of evil; I had terrible dreams. I dreamt of dreadful abysses and vast chasms, amongst which I was wandering, knowing that a slip of the foot meant death. I waked to find the hands of my clock pointing to eight o'clock. My head was aching badly, and the terror of my night's dreams was still upon me.

"So strongly was this so that when I went to the window and drew it up, I started back with a fresh feeling of terror, for the first thing I saw, or thought I saw, was a man digging an open grave.

"It took me a minute or two to pull myself together; then I realised that the grave-digger was Newman's gardener, and the 'grave' was destined to accommodate three new rose trees which were lying on the turf waiting for the moment they should be securely planted in the earth.

"The gardener looked up and saw me and touched his hat.

" 'Good morning, sir. Nice morning, sir.'

" 'I suppose it is,' I said doubtfully, still unable to shake off completely the depression of my spirits.

"However, as the gardener had said, it was certainly a nice morning. The sun was shining and the sky a clear pale blue that promised fine weather for the day. I went down to breakfast whistling a tune. Newman had no maids living in the house. Two middle-aged sisters, who lived in a farmhouse near by, came daily to attend to his simple wants. One of them was placing the coffeepot on the table as I entered the room.

" 'Good-morning, Elizabeth,' I said. 'Mr. Newman not down yet?'

" 'He must have been out very early, sir,' she replied. 'He wasn't in the house when we arrived.'

"Instantly my uneasiness returned. On the two previous mornings Newman had come down to breakfast somewhat late; and I didn't fancy that at any time he was an early riser. Moved by those forebodings I ran up to his bedroom. It was empty, and, moreover, his bed had not been slept in. A brief examination of his room showed me two other things. If Newman had gone out for a stroll he must have gone out in his evening clothes, for they were missing.

"I was sure now that my premonition of evil was justified. Newman had gone, as he had said he would do—for an evening stroll. For some reason or other he had not returned. Why? Had he met with an accident? Fallen over the cliffs? A search must be made at once.

"In a few hours I had collected a large band of helpers, and together we hunted in every direction along the cliffs and on the rocks below. But there was no sign of Newman.

"In the end, in despair, I sought out Inspector Badgworth. His face grew very grave.

" 'It looks to me as if there had been foul play,' he said.

'There are some not over-scrupulous customers in these parts. Have you seen Kelvin, the landlord of the Three Anchors?'

"I said that I had seen him.

" 'Did you know he did a turn in gaol four years ago? Assault and battery.'

" 'It doesn't surprise me,' I said.

" 'The general opinion in this place seems to be that your friend is a bit too fond of nosing his way into things that do not concern him. I hope he has come to no serious harm.'

"The search was continued with redoubled vigour. It was not until late that afternoon that our efforts were rewarded. We discovered Newman in a deep ditch in a corner of his own property. His hands and feet were securely fastened with rope, and a handkerchief had been thrust into his mouth and secured there so as to prevent him crying out.

"He was terribly exhausted and in great pain; but after some frictioning of his wrists and ankles, and a long draught from a whisky flask, he was able to give his account of what had occurred.

"The weather having cleared, he had gone out for a stroll about eleven o'clock. His way had taken him some distance along the cliffs to a spot commonly known as Smugglers' Cove, owing to the large number of caves to be found there. Here he had noticed some men loading something from a small boat, and had strolled down to see what was going on. Whatever the stuff was it seemed to be a great weight, and it was being carried into one of the farthermost caves.

"With no real suspicion of anything being amiss, nevertheless Newman had wondered. He had drawn quite near them without being observed. Suddenly there was a cry of alarm, and immediately two powerful seafaring men had set upon him and rendered him unconscious. When next he came to himself he found himself lying on a motor vehicle of some kind, which was proceeding, with many bumps and bangs, as far as he could guess, up the lane which led from the coast to the village. To his great surprise the lorry turned in at the gate of his own house. There, after a whispered conversation between the men, they at length drew him forth and flung him into a ditch at a spot where the depth of it rendered discovery unlikely for some time. Then the lorry drove on, and, he thought, passed out through another gate some quarter of a mile nearer the village. He could give no description of his assailants except that they were certainly seafaring men, and, by their speech, Cornishmen.

"Inspector Badgworth was very interested.

" 'Depend upon it that is where the stuff has been hidden,' he cried. 'Somehow or other it has been salvaged from the wreck and has been stored in some lonely cave somewhere. It is known that we have searched all the caves in Smugglers' Cove, and that we are now going farther afield, and they have evidently been moving the stuff at night to a cave that has been already searched and is not likely to be searched again. Unfortunately they have had at least eighteen hours to dispose of the stuff. If they got Mr. Newman last night I doubt if we will find any of it there by now.'

"The inspector hurried off to make a search. He found definite evidence that the bullion had been stored as supposed, but the gold had been once more removed, and there was no clue as to its fresh hiding-place.

"One clue there was, however, and the inspector himself pointed it out to me the following morning.

" 'That lane is very little used by motor vehicles,' he said; 'and in one or two places we get the traces of the tires very clearly. There is a three-cornered piece out of one tire, leaving a mark which is quite unmistakable. It shows going into the gate; here and there is a faint mark of it going out of the other gate, so there is not much doubt that it is the right vehicle we are after. Now, why did they take it out through the farther gate? It seems quite clear to me that that lorry came from the village. Now, there aren't many people who own a lorry in the village—not more than two or three at most. Kelvin, the landlord of the Three Anchors, has one.'

" 'What was Kelvin's original profession?' asked Newman.

" 'It is curious that you should ask me that, Mr. Newman. In his younger days Kelvin was a professional diver.'

"Newman and I looked at each other. The puzzle seemed to be fitting itself together piece by piece.

" 'You didn't recognize Kelvin as one of the men on the beach?' asked the inspector.

"Newman shook his head.

" 'I am afraid I can't say anything as to that,' he said regretfully. 'I really hadn't time to see anything.'

"The inspector very kindly allowed me to accompany him to the Three Anchors. The garage was up a side street. The big doors were closed, but by going up a little alley at the side we found a small door that led into it, and that door was open. A very brief examination of the tires sufficed for the inspector. 'We have got him, by Jove!' he exclaimed. 'Here is the mark as large as life on the rear left wheel. Now, Mr. Kelvin, I don't think you will be clever enough to wriggle out of this.' "

Raymond West came to a halt.

"Well?" said Joyce. "So far I don't see anything to make a problem about—unless they never found the gold."

"They never found the gold certainly," said Raymond, "and they never got Kelvin either. I expect he was too clever for them, but I don't quite see how he worked it. He was duly arrested—on the evidence of the tire mark. But an extraordinary hitch arose. Just opposite the big doors of the garage was a cottage rented for the summer by a lady artist."

"Oh, these lady artists!" said Joyce, laughing.

"As you say, 'Oh, these lady artists!' This particular one had been ill for some weeks, and, in consequence, had two hospital nurses attending her. The nurse who was on night duty had pulled her arm-chair up to the window, where the blind was up. She declared that the motor lorry could not have left the garage opposite without her seeing it, and she swore that in actual fact it never left the garage that night."

"I don't think that is much of a problem," said Joyce. "The nurse went to sleep, of course. They always do."

"That has—er—been known to happen," said Mr. Petherick, judiciously; "but it seems to me that we are accepting facts without sufficient examination. Before accepting the testimony of the hospital nurse, we should inquire very closely into her bona fides. The alibi coming with such suspicious promptness is inclined to raise doubts in one's mind."

"There is also the lady artist's testimony," said Raymond. "She declared that she was in pain, and awake most of the night, and that she would certainly have heard the lorry, it being an unusual noise, and the night being very quiet after the storm."

"H'm," said the clergyman, "that is certainly an additional fact. Had Kelvin himself any alibi?"

"He declared that he was at home and in bed from ten o'clock onwards, but he could produce no witnesses in support of that statement."

"The nurse went to sleep," said Joyce, "and so did the patient. Ill people always think they have never slept a wink all night."

Raymond West looked inquiringly at Dr. Pender.

"Do you know, I feel sorry for that man Kelvin. It seems to me very much a case of 'Give a dog a bad name.' Kelvin had been in prison. Apart from the tire mark, which certainly seems too remarkable to be coincidence, there doesn't seem to be much against him except his unfortunate record."

"You, Sir Henry?"

Sir Henry shook his head.

"As it happens," he said smiling, "I know something about this case. So, clearly, I mustn't speak."

"Well, go on, Aunt Jane; haven't you got anything to say?"

"In a minute, dear,' said Miss Marple. "I am afraid I

39

have counted wrong. Two purl, three plain, slip one, two purl—yes, that's right. What did you say, dear?"

"What is your opinion?"

"You wouldn't like my opinion, dear. Young people never do, I notice. It is better to say nothing."

"Nonsense, Aunt Jane; out with it."

"Well, dear Raymond," said Miss Marple, laying down her knitting and looking across at her nephew. "I do think you should be more careful how you choose your friends. You are so credulous, dear, so easily gulled. I suppose it is being a writer and having so much imagination. All that story about a Spanish galleon! If you were older and had more experience of life you would have been on your guard at once. A man you had known only a few weeks, too!"

Sir Henry suddenly gave vent to a great roar of laughter and slapped his knee.

"Got you this time, Raymond," he said. "Miss Marple, you are wonderful. Your friend Newman, my boy, has another name—several other names in fact. At the present moment he is not in Cornwall but in Devonshire—Dartmoor, to be exact—a convict in Princetown prison. We didn't catch him over the stolen bullion business, but over the rifling of the strong-room of one of the London banks. Then we looked up his past record and we found a good portion of the gold stolen buried in the garden at Pol House. It was rather a neat idea. All along that Cornish coast there are stories of wrecked galleons full of gold. It accounted for the diver, and it would account later for the gold. But a scapegoat was needed, and Kelvin was ideal for the purpose. Newman played his little comedy very well, and our friend Raymond, with his celebrity as a writer, made an unimpeachable witness."

"But the tire mark?" objected Joyce.

"Oh, I saw that at once, dear, although I know nothing about motors," said Miss Marple. "People change a wheel, you know—I have often seen them doing it—and, of course, they could take a wheel off Kelvin's lorry and take it out through the small door into the alley and put it on to Mr. Newman's lorry and take the lorry out of one gate down to

the beach, fill it up with the gold and bring it up through
the other gate, and then they must have taken the wheel
back and put it back on Mr. Kelvin's lorry while, I suppose,
someone else was tying up Mr. Newman in a ditch. Very
uncomfortable for him and probably longer before he was
found than he expected. I suppose the man who called
himself the gardener attended to that side of the business."

"Why do you say, 'called himself the gardener,' Aunt
Jane?" asked Raymond curiously.

"Well, he can't have been a real gardener, can he?"
said Miss Marple. "Gardeners don't work on Whit Mon-
day. Everybody knows that."

She smiled and folded up her knitting.

"It was really that little fact that put me on the right
scent," she said. She looked across at Raymond.

"When you are a householder, dear, and have a garden
of your own, you will know these little things."

# CHAPTER IV

## THE BLOOD-STAINED PAVEMENT

"IT'S curious," said Joyce Lemprière, "but I hardly like telling you my story. It happened a long time ago—five years ago to be exact—but it's sort of haunted me ever since. The smiling, bright, top part of it—and the hidden gruesomeness underneath. And the queer thing is that the sketch I painted at the time has become tinged with the same atmosphere. When you look at it first it is just a rough sketch of a little steep Cornish street with the sunlight on it. But if you look long enough at it something sinister creeps in. I have never sold it but I never look at it. It lives in the studio in a corner with its face to the wall.

"The name of the place was Rathole. It is a queer little Cornish fishing village, very picturesque—too picturesque perhaps. There is rather too much of the atmosphere of 'Ye Olde Cornish Tea House' about it. It has shops with bobbed-headed girls in smocks doing hand-illuminated mottoes on parchment. It is pretty and it is quaint, but it is very self-consciously so."

"Don't I know," said Raymond West, groaning. "The curse of the charabanc, I suppose. No matter how narrow the lanes leading down to them no picturesque village is safe."

Joyce nodded.

"They are narrow lanes that lead down to Rathole and very steep, like the side of a house. Well, to get on with my story. I had come down to Cornwall for a fortnight, to

42

sketch. There is an old inn in Rathole, The Polharwith
Arms. It was supposed to be the only house left standing
by the Spaniards when they shelled the place in fifteen
hundred and something."

"Not shelled," said Raymond West frowning. "Do try
to be historically accurate, Joyce."

"Well, at all events they landed guns somewhere along
the coast and they fired them and the houses fell down.
Anyway that is not the point. The inn was a wonderful old
place with a kind of porch in front built on four pillars. I
got a very good pitch and was just settling down to work
when a car came creeping and twisting down the hill. Of
course, it *would* stop before the inn—just where it was
most awkward for me. The people got out—a man and a
woman—I didn't notice them particularly. She had a kind
of mauve linen dress on and a mauve hat.

"Presently the man came out again and to my great
thankfulness drove the car down to the quay and left it
there. He strolled back past me towards the inn. Just at
that moment another beastly car came twisting down and
a woman got out of it dressed in the brightest chintz frock I
have ever seen, scarlet poinsettias, I think they were, and
she had on one of these big native straw hats—Cuban,
aren't they?—in very bright scarlet.

"This woman didn't stop in front of the inn but drove
the car farther down the street towards the other one.
Then she got out and the man seeing her gave an aston-
ished shout. 'Carol,' he cried, 'in the name of all that is
wonderful. Fancy meeting you in this out-of-the-way spot.
I haven't seen you for years. Hello, there's Margery—my
wife, you know. You must come and meet her.'

"They went up the street towards the inn side by side,
and I saw the other woman had just come out of the door
and was moving down towards them I had had just a
glimpse of the woman called Carol as she passed by me.
Just enough to see a very white powdered chin and a
flaming scarlet mouth and I wondered—I just wondered—if
Margery would be so very pleased to meet her. I hadn't

seen Margery near to, but in the distance she looked dowdy and extra prim and proper.

"Well, of course, it was not any of my business but you get very queer little glimpses of life sometimes, and you can't help speculating about them. From where they were standing I could just catch fragments of their conversation that floated down to me. They were talking about bathing. The husband, whose name seemed to be Denis, wanted to take a boat and row round the coast. There was a famous cave well worth seeing, so he said, about a mile long. Carol wanted to see the cave too but she suggested walking along the cliffs and seeing it from the land side. She said she hated boats. In the end they fixed it that way. Carol was to go along the cliff path and to meet them at the cave, and Denis and Margery would take a boat and row round.

"Hearing them talk about bathing made me want to bathe too. It was a very hot morning and I wasn't doing particularly good work. Also, I fancied that the afternoon sunlight would be far more attractive in effect. So I packed up my things and went off to a little beach that I knew of—it was quite the opposite direction from the cave, and was rather a discovery of mine. I had a ripping bathe there and I lunched off a tinned tongue and two tomatoes, and I came back in the afternoon full of confidence and enthusiasm to get on with my sketch.

"The whole of Rathole seemed to be asleep. I had been right about the afternoon sunlight, the shadows were far more telling. The Polharwith Arms was the principal note of my sketch. A ray of sunlight came slanting obliquely down and hit the ground in front of it and had rather a curious effect. I gathered that the bathing party had returned safely, because two bathing dresses, a scarlet one and a dark blue one, were hanging from the balcony, drying in the sun.

"Something had gone a bit wrong with one corner of my sketch and I bent over it for some moments doing something to put it right. When I looked up again there was a figure leaning against one of the pillars of the Polharwith Arms, who seemed to have appeared there by magic. He was dressed in seafaring clothes and was, I suppose, a fisherman. But he had a long dark beard, and if I had been looking for a model for a wicked Spanish captain I couldn't have imagined anyone better. I got to work with feverish haste before he should move away, though from his attitude he looked as though he was perfectly prepared to prop up the pillars through all eternity.

"He did move, however, but luckily not until I had got what I wanted. He came over to me and he began to talk. Oh, how that man talked.

" 'Rathole,' he said, 'was a very interesting place.'

"I knew that already but although I said so that didn't save me. I had the whole history of the shelling—I mean the destroying—of the village, and how the landlord of the Polharwith Arms was the last man to be killed. Run through on his own threshold by a Spanish captain's sword. and of how his blood spurted out on the pavement and no one could wash out the stain for a hundred years.

"It all fitted in very well with the languorous drowsy feeling of the afternoon. The man's voice was very suave and yet at the same time there was an undercurrent in it of something rather frightening. He was very obsequious in his manner, yet I felt underneath he was cruel. He made me understand the Inquisition and the terrors of all the things the Spaniards did better than I have ever done before.

"All the time he was talking to me I went on painting, and suddenly I realised that in the excitement of listening to his story I had painted in something that was not there. On that white square of pavement where the sun fell before the door of the Polharwith Arms, I had painted in blood-stains. It seemed extraordinary that the mind could play such tricks with the hand, but as I looked over towards the inn again I got a second shock. My hand had only painted in what my eyes saw—drops of blood on the white pavement.

"I stared for a minute or two. Then I shut my eyes, said to myself, 'Don't be so stupid, there's nothing there.

really,' then I opened them again, but the blood-stains were still there.

"I suddenly felt I couldn't stand it. I interrupted the fisherman's flood of language.

" 'Tell me,' I said, 'my eyesight is not very good. Are those blood-stains on that pavement over there?'

"He looked at me indulgently and kindly.

" 'No blood-stains in these days, lady. What I am telling you about is nearly five hundred years ago.'

" 'Yes,' I said, 'but now—on the pavement'—the words died away in my throat. I *knew*—I knew that he wouldn't see what I was seeing. I got up and with shaking hands began to put my things together. As I did so the young man who had come in the car that morning came out of the inn door. He looked up and down the street perplexedly. On the balcony above his wife came out and collected the bathing things. He walked down towards the car but suddenly swerved and came across the road towards the fisherman.

" 'Tell me, my man,' he said, 'you don't know whether that lady who came in that second car there has got back yet?'

" 'Lady in a dress with flowers all over it? No, sir, I haven't seen her. She went along the cliff towards the cave this morning.'

" 'I know, I know. We all bathed there together, and then she left us to walk home and I have not seen her since. It can't have taken her all this time. The cliffs round here are not dangerous, are they?'

" 'It depends, sir, on the way you go. The best way is to take a man what knows the place with you.'

"He very clearly meant himself and was beginning to enlarge on the theme, but the young man cut him short unceremoniously and ran back towards the inn calling up to his wife on the balcony.

" 'I say, Margery, Carol hasn't come back yet. Odd, isn't it?'

"I didn't hear Margery's reply, but her husband went

on. 'Well, we can't wait any longer. We have got to push on to Penrithar. Are you ready? I will turn the car.'

"He did as he had said, and presently the two of them drove off together. Meanwhile I had deliberately been nerving myself to prove how ridiculous my fancies were. When the car had gone I went over to the inn and examined the pavement closely. Of course there were no blood-stains there. No, all along it had been the result of my distorted imagination. Yet, somehow, it seemed to make the thing more frightening. It was while I was standing there that I heard the fisherman's voice.

"He was looking at me curiously. 'You thought you saw blood-stains here, eh, lady?'

"I nodded.

" 'That is very curious, that is very curious. We have got a superstition here, lady. If anyone sees those blood-stains—'

"He paused.

" 'Well?' I said.

"He went on in his soft voice, Cornish in intonation, but unconsciously smooth and well-bred in its pronunciation, and completely free from Cornish turns of speech.

" 'They do say, lady, that if anyone sees those blood-stains that there will be a death within twenty-four hours.'

"Creepy! It gave me a nasty feeling all down my spine.

"He went on persuasively. 'There is a very interesting tablet in the church, lady, about a death——'

" 'No thanks,' I said decisively, and I turned sharply on my heel and walked up the street towards the cottage where I was lodging. Just as I got there I saw in the distance the woman called Carol coming along the cliff path. She was hurrying. Against the grey of the rocks she looked like some poisonous scarlet flower. Her hat was the colour of blood. . . .

"I shook myself. Really, I had blood on the brain.

"Later I heard the sound of her car. I wondered whether she too was going to Penrithar; but she took the road to the left in the opposite direction. I watched the car crawl up the hill and disappear, and I breathed somehow more easily. Rathole seemed its quiet sleepy self once more."

"If that is all," said Raymond West as Joyce came to a stop, "I will give my verdict at once. Indigestion, spots before the eyes after meals."

"It isn't all," said Joyce. "You have got to hear the sequel. I read it in the paper two days later under the heading of 'Sea Bathing Fatality.' It told how Mrs. Dacre, the wife of Captain Denis Dacre, was unfortunately drowned at Landeer Cove, just a little farther along the coast. She and her husband were staying at the time at the hotel there, and had declared their intention of bathing, but a cold wind sprang up. Captain Dacre had declared it was too cold, so he and some other people in the hotel had gone off to the golf links near by. Mrs. Dacre, however, had said it was not too cold for her and she went off alone down to the cove. As she didn't return her husband became alarmed and in company with his friends went down to the beach. They found her clothes lying beside a rock, but no trace of the unfortunate lady. Her body was not found until nearly a week later when it was washed ashore at a point some distance down the coast. There was a bad blow on her head which had occurred before death, and the theory was that she must have dived into the sea and hit her head on a rock. As far as I could make out her death would have occurred just twenty-four hours after the time I saw the blood-stains."

"I protest," said Sir Henry. "This is not a problem—this is a ghost story. Miss Lemprière is evidently a medium."

Mr. Petherick gave his usual cough.

"One point strikes me—" he said, "that blow on the head. We must not, I think, exclude the possibility of foul play. But I do not see that we have any data to go upon. Miss Lemprière's hallucination, or vision, is interesting, certainly, but I do not see clearly the point on which she wishes us to pronounce."

"Indigestion and coincidence," said Raymond, "and anyway you can't be sure that they were the same people.

48

Besides, the curse, or whatever it was, would only apply to actual inhabitants of Rathole."

"I feel," said Sir Henry, "that the sinister seafaring man has something to do with this tale. But I agree with Mr. Petherick, Miss Lemprière has given us very little data."

Joyce turned to Dr. Pender, who smilingly shook his head.

"It is a most interesting story," he said, "but I am afraid I agree with Sir Henry and Mr. Petherick that there is very little data to go upon."

Joyce then looked curiously at Miss Marple, who smiled back at her.

"I, too, think you are just a little unfair, Joyce dear," she said. "Of course, it is different for me. I mean, we, being women, appreciate the point about clothes. I don't think it is a fair problem to put to a man. It must have meant a lot of rapid changing. What a wicked woman! And a still more wicked man."

Joyce stared at her.

"Aunt Jane," she said. "Miss Marple, I mean, I believe —I do really believe you know the truth."

"Well, dear," said Miss Marple, "it is much easier for me sitting here quietly than it was for you—and being an artist you are so susceptible to atmosphere, aren't you? Sitting here with one's knitting, one just sees the facts. Blood-stains dropped on the pavement from the bathing dress hanging above, and being a red bathing dress, of course, the criminals themselves did not realise it was blood-stained. Poor thing, poor young thing!"

"Excuse me, Miss Marple," said Sir Henry, "but do you know that I am entirely in the dark still. You and Miss Lemprière seem to know what you are talking about, but we mere men are still in utter darkness."

"I will tell you the end of the story now," said Joyce. "It was a year later. I was at a little east coast seaside resort, and I was sketching, when suddenly I had that queer feeling one has of something having happened before. There were two people, a man and a woman, on the

49

pavement in front of me, and they were greeting a third person, a woman dressed in a scarlet poinsettia chintz dress. 'Carol, by all that is wonderful! Fancy meeting you after all these years. You don't know my wife? Joan, this is an old friend of mine, Miss Harding.'

"I recognised the man at once. It was the same Denis I had seen at Rathole. The wife was different—that is, she was a Joan instead of a Margery; but she was the same type, young and rather dowdy and very inconspicuous. I thought for a minute I was going mad. They began to talk of going bathing. I will tell you what I did. I marched straight then and there to the police station. I thought they would probably think I was off my head, but I didn't care. And as it happened everything was quite all right. There was a man from Scotland Yard there, and he had come down just about this very thing. It seems—oh, it's horrible to talk about—that the police had got suspicious of Denis Dacre. That wasn't his real name—he took different names on different occasions. He got to know girls, usually quiet inconspicuous girls without many relatives or friends, he married them and insured their lives for large sums and then—oh, it's horrible! The woman called Carol was his real wife, and they always carried out the same plan. That is really how they came to catch him. The insurance companies became suspicious. He would come to some quiet seaside place with his new wife, then the other woman would turn up and they would all go bathing together. Then the wife would be murdered and Carol would put on her clothes and go back in the boat with him. Then they would leave the place, wherever it was, after inquiring for the supposed Carol and when they got outside the village Carol would hastily change back into her own flamboyant clothes and her vivid make-up and would go back there and drive off in her own car. They would find out which way the current was flowing and the supposed death would take place at the next bathing place along the coast that way. Carol would play the part of the wife and would go down to some lonely beach and would leave the wife's clothes there by a rock and depart in her flowery chintz dress to wait quietly until her husband could rejoin her."

"I suppose when they killed poor Margery some of the blood must have spurted over Carol's bathing suit, and being a red one they didn't notice it, as Miss Marple says. But when they hung it over the balcony it dripped. Ugh!" She gave a shiver. "I can see it still."

"Of course," said Sir Henry. "I remember very well now. Davis was the man's real name. It had quite slipped my memory that one of his many aliases was Dacre. They were an extraordinary, cunning pair. It always seemed so amazing to me that no one spotted the change of identity. I suppose, as Miss Marple says, clothes are more easily identified than faces; but it was a very clever scheme, for although we suspected Davis it was not easy to bring the crime home to him as he always seemed to have an unimpeachable alibi."

"Aunt Jane," said Raymond, looking at her curiously, "how do you do it? You have lived such a peaceful life and yet nothing seems to surprise you."

"I always find one thing very like another in this world," said Miss Marple. "There was Mrs. Green, you know, she buried five children—and every one of them insured. Well, naturally, one began to get suspicious."

She shook her head.

"There is a great deal of wickedness in village life. I hope you dear young people will never realise how very wicked the world is."

# CHAPTER V

# MOTIVE V.
# OPPORTUNITY

M R. Petherick cleared his throat rather more importantly than usual.

"I am afraid my little problem will seem rather tame to you all," he said apologetically, "after the sensational stories we have been hearing. There is no bloodshed in mine, but it seems to me an interesting and rather ingenious little problem, and fortunately I am in the position to know the right answer to it."

"It isn't terribly legal, is it?" asked Joyce Lemprière. "I mean points of law and lots of Barnaby v. Skinner in the year 1881, and things like that."

Mr. Petherick beamed appreciatively at her over his eyeglasses.

"No, no, my dear young lady. You need have no fears on that score. The story I am about to tell is a perfectly simple and straightforward one and can be followed by any layman."

"No legal quibbles, now," said Miss Marple, shaking a knitting needle at him.

"Certainly not," said Mr. Petherick.

"Ah well, I am not so sure, but let's hear the story."

"It concerns a former client of mine. I will call him Mr. Clode—Simon Clode. He was a man of considerable wealth and lived in a large house not very far from here. He had had one son killed in the War and this son had left one child, a little girl. Her mother had died at her birth, and on her father's death she had come to live with her grandfather who at once became passionately attached to her. Little Chris could do anything she liked with her grandfather. I have never seen a man more completely wrapped up in a child, and I cannot describe to you his grief and despair when, at the age of eleven, the child contracted pneumonia and died.

"Poor Simon Clode was inconsolable. A brother of his had recently died in poor circumstances and Simon Clode had generously offered a home to his brother's children—two girls, Grace and Mary, and a boy, George. But though kind and generous to his nephew and nieces, the old man never expended on them any of the love and devotion he had accorded to his little grandchild. Employment was found for George Clode in a bank near by, and Grace married a clever young research chemist of the name of Philip Garrod. Mary, who was a quiet, self-contained girl, lived at home and looked after her uncle. She was, I think, fond of him in her quiet undemonstrative way. And to all appearances things went on very peacefully. I may say that after the death of little Christobel, Simon Clode came to me and instructed me to draw up a new will. By this will, his fortune, a very considerable one, was divided equally between his nephew and nieces, a third share to each.

"Time went on. Chancing to meet George Clode one day I inquired for his uncle, whom I had not seen for some time. To my surprise George's face clouded over. 'I wish you could put some sense into Uncle Simon,' he said ruefully. His honest but not very brilliant countenance looked puzzled and worried. 'This spirit business is getting worse and worse.'

" 'What spirit business?' I asked, very much surprised.

"Then George told me the whole story. How Mr. Clode had gradually got interested in the subject and how on the top of this interest he had chanced to meet an American medium, a Mrs. Eurydice Spragg. This woman, whom George did not hesitate to characterise as an out and out swindler, had gained an immense ascendency over Simon Clode. She was practically always in the house and many séances were held in which the spirit of Christobel manifested itself to the doting grandfather.

"I may say here and now that I do not belong to the ranks of those who cover spiritualism with ridicule and scorn. I am, as I have told you, a believer in evidence. And I think that when we have an impartial mind and weigh the evidence in favour of spiritualism there remains much that cannot be put down to fraud or lightly set aside. Therefore, as I say, I am neither a believer nor an unbeliever. There is certain testimony with which one cannot afford to disagree.

"On the other hand, spiritualism lends itself very easily to fraud and imposture, and from all young George Clode told me about this Mrs. Eurydice Spragg I felt more and more convinced that Simon Clode was in bad hands and that Mrs. Spragg was probably an impostor of the worst type. The old man, shrewd as he was in practical matters, would be easily imposed on where his love for his dead grandchild was concerned.

"Turning things over in my mind I felt more and more uneasy. I was fond of the young Clodes, Mary and George, and I realised that this Mrs. Spragg and her influence over their uncle might lead to trouble in the future.

"At the earliest opportunity I made a pretext for calling on Simon Clode. I found Mrs. Spragg installed as an honoured and friendly guest. As soon as I saw her my worst apprehensions were fulfilled. She was a stout woman of middle-age, dressed in a flamboyant style. Very full of cant phrases about 'Our dear ones who have passed over,' and other things of the kind.

"Her husband was also staying in the house, Mr. Absalom Spragg, a thin lank man with a melancholy expression and extremely furtive eyes. As soon as I could, I got Simon Clode to myself and sounded him tactfully on the subject. He was full of enthusiasm. Eurydice Spragg was wonderful! She had been sent to him directly in answer to prayer! She cared nothing for money, the joy of helping a heart in affliction was enough for her. She had quite a mother's feeling for little Chris. He was beginning to regard her almost as a daughter. Then he went on to give me details—how he had heard his Chris's voice speaking—how she was well and happy with her father and mother. He went on to tell other sentiments expressed by the child, which in my remembrance of little Christobel seemed to me highly unlikely. She laid stress on the fact 'Father and Mother loved dear Mrs. Spragg.'

" 'But, of course,' he broke off, 'you are a scoffer, Petherick.'

" 'No, I am not a scoffer. Very far from it. Some of the men who have written on the subject are men whose testimony I would accept unhesitatingly, and I should accord any medium recommended by them respect and credence. I presume that this Mrs. Spragg is well vouched for?'

"Simon went into ecstasies over Mrs. Spragg. She had been sent to him by Heaven. He had come across her at the watering place where he had spent two months in the summer. A chance meeting, with what a wonderful result!

"I went away very dissatisfied. My worst fears were realised, but I did not see what I could do. After a good deal of thought and deliberation I wrote to Philip Garrod who had, as I mentioned, just married the eldest Clode girl, Grace. I set the case before him—of course, in the most carefully guarded language. I pointed out the danger of such a woman gaining ascendency over the old man's mind. And I suggested that Mr. Clode should be brought into contact if possible with some reputable spiritualistic circles. This, I thought, would not be a difficult matter for Philip Garrod to arrange.

"Garrod was prompt to act. He realised, which I did not, that Simon Clode's health was in a very precarious condition, and as a practical man he had no intention of letting his wife or her sister and brother be despoiled of the inheritance which was so rightly theirs. He came down the following week, bringing with him as a guest no other than the famous Professor Longman. Longman was a scientist of the first order, a man whose association with spiritualism compelled the latter to be treated with respect.

55

Not only a brilliant scientist; he was a man of the utmost uprightness and probity.

"The result of the visit was most unfortunate. Longman, it seemed, had said very little while he was there. Two séances were held—under what conditions I do not know. Longman was noncommittal all the time he was in the house, but after his departure he wrote a letter to Philip Garrod. In it he admitted that he had not been able to detect Mrs. Spragg in fraud, nevertheless his private opinion was that the phenomena were not genuine. Mr. Garrod, he said, was at liberty to show this letter to his uncle if he thought fit, and he suggested that he himself should put Mr. Clode in touch with a medium of perfect integrity.

"Philip Garrod had taken this letter straight to his uncle, but the result was not what he had anticipated. The old man flew into a towering rage. It was all a plot to discredit Mrs. Spragg who was a maligned and injured saint! She had told him already what bitter jealousy there was of her in this country. He pointed out that Longman was forced to say he had not detected fraud. Eurydice Spragg had come to him in the darkest hour of his life, had given him help and comfort, and he was prepared to espouse her cause even if it meant quarrelling with every member of his family. She was more to him than anyone else in the world.

"Philip Garrod was turned out of the house with scant ceremony; but as a result of his rage Clode's own health took a decided turn for the worst. For the last month he had kept his bed pretty continuously, and now there seemed every possibility of his being a bedridden invalid until such time as death should release him. Two days after Philip's departure I received an urgent summons and went hurriedly over. Clode was in bed and looked even to my layman's eye very ill indeed. He was gasping for breath.

" 'This is the end of me,' he said. 'I feel it. Don't argue with me, Petherick. But before I die I am going to do my duty by the one human being who has done more for me than anyone else in the world. I want to make a fresh will.'

" 'Certainly,' I said, 'if you will give me your instructions now I will draft out a will and send it to you.'

" 'That won't do,' he said. 'Why, man, I might not live through the night. I have written out what I want here,' he fumbled under his pillow, 'and you can tell me if it is right.'

"He produced a sheet of paper with a few words roughly scribbled on it in pencil. It was quite simple and clear. He left £5000 to each of his nieces and nephew, and the residue of his vast property outright to Eurydice Spragg 'in gratitude and admiration.'

"I didn't like it, but there it was. There was no question of unsound mind, the old man was as sane as anybody.

"He rang the bell for two of the servants. They came promptly. The housemaid, Emma Gaunt, was a tall middle-aged woman who had been in service there for many years and who had nursed Clode devotedly. With her came the cook, a fresh buxom young woman of thirty. Simon Clode glared at them both from under his bushy eyebrows.

" 'I want you to witness my will. Emma, get me my fountain pen.'

"Emma went over obediently to the desk.

" 'Not that left-hand drawer, girl,' said old Simon irritably. 'Don't you know it is in the right-hand one?'

" 'No, it is here, sir,' said Emma, producing it.

" 'Then you must have put it away wrong last time,' grumbled the old man. 'I can't stand things not being kept in their proper places.'

"Still grumbling he took the pen from her and copied his own rough draft, amended by me, onto a fresh piece of paper. Then he signed his name. Emma Gaunt and the cook, Lucy David, also signed. I folded the will up and put it into a long blue envelope. It was necessarily, you understand, written on an ordinary piece of paper.

"Just as the servants were turning to leave the room Clode lay back on the pillows with a gasp and a distorted face. I bent over him anxiously and Emma Gaunt came quickly back. However, the old man recovered and smiled weakly.

" 'It is all right, Petherick, don't be alarmed. At any rate I shall die easy now having done what I wanted to.'

"Emma Gaunt looked inquiringly at me as if to know whether she could leave the room. I nodded reassuringly and she went out—first stopping to pick up the blue envelope which I had let slip to the ground in my moment of anxiety. She handed it to me and I slipped it into my coat pocket and then she went out.

" 'You are annoyed, Petherick,' said Simon Clode. 'You are prejudiced, like everybody else.'

" 'It is not a question of prejudice,' I said. 'Mrs. Spragg may be all that she claims to be. I should see no objection to you leaving her a small legacy as a memento of gratitude; but I tell you frankly, Clode, that to disinherit your own flesh and blood in favour of a stranger is wrong.'

"With that I turned to depart. I had done what I could and made my protest.

"Mary Clode came out of the drawing-room and met me in the hall.

" 'You will have tea before you go, won't you? Come in here,' and she led me into the drawing-room.

"A fire was burning on the hearth and the room looked cosy and cheerful. She relieved me of my overcoat just as her brother, George, came into the room. He took it from her and laid it across a chair at the far end of the room, then he came back to the fireside where we drank tea. During the meal a question arose about some point concerning the estate. Simon Clode said he didn't want to be bothered with it and had left it to George to decide. George was rather nervous about trusting to his own judgment. At my suggestion, we adjourned to the study after tea and I looked over the papers in question. Mary Clode accompanied us.

"A quarter of an hour later I prepared to take my departure. Remembering that I had left my overcoat in the drawing-room, I went there to fetch it. The only occupant of the room was Mrs. Spragg, who was kneeling by the chair on which the overcoat lay. She seemed to be doing something rather unnecessary to the cretonne cover. She rose with a very red face as we entered.

" 'That cover never did sit right, she complained. 'My! I could make a better fit myself.'

"I took up my overcoat and put it on. As I did so I noticed that the envelope containing the will had fallen out of the pocket and was lying on the floor. I replaced it in my pocket, said good-bye, and took my departure.

"On arrival at my office, I will describe my next actions carefully. I removed my overcoat and took the will from the pocket. I had it in my hand and was standing by the table when my clerk came in. Somebody wished to speak to me on the telephone, and the extension to my desk was out of order. I accordingly accompanied him to the outer office and remained there for about five minutes engaged in conversation over the telephone.

"When I emerged, I found my clerk waiting for me.

" 'Mr. Spragg has called to see you, sir. I showed him into your office.'

"I went there to find Mr. Spragg sitting by the table. He rose and greeted me in a somewhat unctuous manner, then proceeded to a long discursive speech. In the main it seemed to be an uneasy justification of himself and his wife. He was afraid people were saying, etc., etc. His wife had been known from her babyhood upwards for the pureness of her heart and her motives . . . and so on and so on. I was, I am afraid, rather curt with him. In the end I think he realised that his visit was not being a success and left somewhat abruptly. I then remembered that I had left the will lying on the table. I took it, sealed the envelope, and wrote on it and put it away in the safe.

"Now I come to the crux of my story. Two months later Mr. Simon Clode died. I will not go into long-winded discussions, I will just state the bare facts. *When the sealed envelope containing the will was opened it was found to contain a sheet of blank paper.*"

He paused, looking round the circle of interested faces. He smiled himself with a certain enjoyment.

"You appreciate the point, of course? For two months

the sealed envelope had lain in my safe. It could not have been tampered with then. No, the time limit was a very short one. Between the moment the will was signed and my locking it away in the safe. Now who had had the opportunity, and to whose interest would it be to do so?

"I will recapitulate the vital points in a brief summary: The will was signed by Mr. Clode, placed by me in an envelope—so far so good. It was then put by me in my overcoat pocket. That overcoat was taken from me by Mary and handed by her to George, who was in full sight of me whilst handling the coat. During the time that I was in the study Mrs. Eurydice Spragg would have had plenty of time to extract the envelope from the coat pocket and read its contents and, as a matter of fact, finding the envelope on the ground and not in the pocket seemed to point to her having done so. But here we come to a curious point: she had the *opportunity* of substituting the blank paper, but no *motive*. The will was in her favour, and by substituting a blank piece of paper she despoiled herself of the heritage she had been so anxious to gain. The same applies to Mr. Spragg. He, too, had the opportunity. He was left alone with the document in question for some two or three minutes in my office. But again, it was not to his advantage to do so. So we are faced with this curious problem: the two people who had the *opportunity* of substituting a blank piece of paper had no *motive* for doing so, and the two people who had a *motive* had no *opportunity*. By the way, I would not exclude the housemaid, Emma Gaunt, from suspicion. She was devoted to her young master and mistress and detested the Spraggs. She would, I feel sure, have been quite equal to attempting the substitution if she had thought of it. But although she actually handled the envelope when she picked it up from the floor and handed it to me, she certainly had no opportunity of tampering with its contents and she could not have substituted another envelope by some sleight of hand (of which anyway she would not be capable) because the envelope in question was brought into the house by me and no one there would be likely to have a duplicate."

He looked round, beaming on the assembly.

"Now, there is my little problem. I have, I hope, stated it clearly. I should be interested to hear your views."

To everyone's astonishment Miss Marple gave vent to a long and prolonged chuckle. Something seemed to be amusing her immensely.

"What *is* the matter, Aunt Jane? Can't we share the joke?" said Raymond.

"I was thinking of little Tommy Symonds, a naughty little boy, I am afraid, but sometimes very amusing. One of those children with innocent childlike faces who are always up to some mischief or other. I was thinking how last week in Sunday School he said, 'Teacher, do you say yolk of eggs *is* white or yolk of eggs *are* white?' And Miss Durston explained that anyone would say 'yolks of eggs *are* white, or yolk of egg *is* white'—and naughty Tommy said: 'Well, I should say yolk of egg is yellow!' Very naughty of him, of course, and as old as the hills. I knew that one as a child."

"Very funny, my dear Aunt Jane," Raymond said gently, "but surely that has nothing to do with the very interesting story that Mr. Petherick has been telling us."

"Oh yes, it has," said Miss Marple. 'It is a catch! And so is Mr. Petherick's story a catch. So like a lawyer! Ah, my dear old friend!" She shook a reproving head at him.

"I wonder if you really know," said the lawyer with a twinkle.

Miss Marple wrote a few words on a piece of paper, folded it up and passed it across to him.

Mr. Petherick unfolded the paper, read what was written on it and looked across at her appreciatively.

"My dear friend," he said, "is there anything you do not know?"

"I knew that as a child," said Miss Marple. "Played with it too."

"I feel rather out of this," said Sir Henry. "I feel sure that Mr. Petherick has some clever legal legerdemain up his sleeve."

"Not at all," said Mr. Petherick. "Not at all. It is a

perfectly fair straightforward proposition. You must not pay any attention to Miss Marple. She has her own way of looking at things."

"We *should* be able to arrive at the truth," said Raymond West a trifle vexedly. "The facts certainly seem plain enough. Five persons actually touched that envelope. The Spraggs clearly could have meddled with it but equally clearly they did not do so. There remains the other three. Now, when one sees the marvellous ways that conjurers have of doing a thing before one's eyes, it seems to me that that paper could have been extracted and another substituted by George Clode during the time he was carrying the overcoat to the far end of the room."

"Well, *I* think it was the girl," said Joyce. "I think the housemaid ran down and told her what was happening and she got hold of another blue envelope and just substituted the one for the other."

Sir Henry shook his head. "I disagree with you both," he said slowly. "These sort of things are done by conjurers, and they are done on the stage and in novels, but I think they would be impossible to do in real life, especially under the shrewd eyes of a man like my friend Mr. Petherick here. But I have an idea—it is only an idea and nothing more. We know that Professor Longman had just been down for a visit and that he said very little. It is only reasonable to suppose that the Spraggs may have been very anxious as to the result of that visit. If Simon Clode did not take them into his confidence, which is quite probable, they may have viewed his sending for Mr. Petherick from quite another angle. They may have believed that Mr. Clode had already made a will which benefited Eurydice Spragg and that this new one might be made for the express purpose of cutting her out as a result of Professor Longman's revelations, or alternatively, as you lawyers say, Philip Garrod had impressed on his uncle the claims of his own flesh and blood. In that case, suppose Mrs. Spragg prepared to effect a substitution. This she does, but Mr. Petherick coming in at an unfortunate moment she has no time to read the real document and hastily destroys it by fire in case the lawyer should discover his loss. '

Joyce shook her head very decidedly.

"She would never burn it without reading it."

"The solution is rather a weak one," admitted Sir Henry. "I suppose—er—Mr. Petherick did not assist Providence himself."

The suggestion was only a laughing one, but the little lawyer drew himself up in offended dignity.

"A most improper suggestion," he said with some asperity.

"What does Dr. Pender say?" asked Sir Henry.

"I cannot say I have any very clear ideas. I think the substitution must have been effected by either Mrs. Spragg or her husband, possibly for the motive that Sir Henry suggests. If she did not read the will until after Mr. Petherick had departed, she would then be in somewhat of a dilemma, since she could not own up to her action in the matter. Possibly she would place it among Mr. Clode's papers where she thought it would be found after his death. But why it wasn't found I don't know. It *might* be a mere speculation this—that Emma Gaunt came across it—and out of misplaced devotion to her employers—deliberately destroyed it."

"I think Dr. Pender's solution is the best of all," said Joyce. "Is it right, Mr. Petherick?"

The lawyer shook his head.

"I will go on where I left off. I was dumbfounded and quite as much at sea as all of you are. I don't think I should ever have guessed the truth—probably not—but I was enlightened. It was cleverly done too.

"I went and dined with Philip Garrod about a month later, and in the course of our after dinner conversation, he mentioned an interesting case that had recently come to his notice.

" 'I should like to tell you about it, Petherick, in confidence, of course.'

" 'Quite so,' I replied.

" 'A friend of mine who had expectations from one of

his relatives was greatly distressed to find that that relative had thoughts of benefiting a totally unworthy person. My friend, I am afraid, is a trifle unscrupulous in his methods. There was a maid in the house who was greatly devoted to the interests of what I may call the legitimate party. My friend gave her very simple instructions. He gave her a fountain pen, duly filled. She was to place this in a drawer in the writing-table in her master's room, but not the usual drawer where the pen was generally kept. If her master asked her to witness his signature to any document and asked her to bring him his pen, she was to bring him not the right one, but this one which was an exact duplicate of it. That was all she had to do. He gave her no other information. She was a devoted creature and she carried out his instructions faithfully.'

"He broke off and said:

" 'I hope I am not boring you, Petherick.'

" 'Not at all,' I said. 'I am keenly interested.'

"Our eyes met.

" 'My friend is, of course, not known to you,' he said.

" 'Of course not,' I replied.

" 'Then that is all right,' said Philip Garrod.

"He paused, then said smilingly, 'You see the point? The pen was filled with what is commonly known as Evanescent Ink—a solution of starch in water to which a few drops of iodine have been added. This makes a deep blue-black fluid, but the writing disappears entirely in four or five days.' "

Miss Marple chuckled.

"Disappearing ink," she said. "I know it. Many is the time I have played with it as a child."

And she beamed round on them all, pausing to shake a finger once more at Mr. Petherick.

"But all the same it's a catch, Mr. Petherick," she said. "Just like a lawyer."

# CHAPTER VI

# THE THUMB MARK OF ST. PETER

"AND now, Aunt Jane, it is up to you," said Raymond West.

"Yes, Aunt Jane, we are expecting something really spicy," chimed in Joyce Lemprière.

"Now, you are laughing at me, my dears," said Miss Marple placidly. "You think that because I have lived in this out-of-the-way spot all my life I am not likely to have had any very interesting experiences."

"God forbid that I should ever regard village life as peaceful and uneventful," said Raymond with fervour. "Not after the horrible revelations we have heard from you! The cosmopolitan world seems a mild and peaceful place compared with St. Mary Mead."

"Well, my dear," said Miss Marple, "human nature is much the same everywhere, and, of course, one has opportunities of observing it at closer quarters in a village."

"You really are unique, Aunt Jane," cried Joyce. "I hope you don't mind me calling you Aunt Jane?" she added. "I don't know why I do it."

"Don't you, my dear?" said Miss Marple.

She looked up for a moment or two with something quizzical in her glance, which made the blood flame to the girl's cheeks. Raymond West fidgeted and cleared his throat in a somewhat embarrassed manner.

Miss Marple looked at them both and smiled again, and bent her attention once more to her knitting.

"It is true, of course, that I have lived what is called a very uneventful life, but I have had a lot of experiences in solving different little problems that have arisen. Some of them have been really quite ingenious, but it would be no good telling them to you, because they are about such unimportant things that you would not be interested—just things like: Who cut the meshes of Mrs. Jones's string bag? and why Mrs. Sims only wore her new fur coat once. Very interesting things, really, to any student of human nature. No, the only experience that I can remember that would be of interest to you is the one about my poor niece Mabel's husband.

"It is about ten or fifteen years ago now, and happily it is all over and done with, and everyone has forgotten about it. People's memories are very short—a lucky thing, I always think."

Miss Marple paused and murmured to herself:

"I must just count this row. The decreasing is a little awkward. One, two, three, four, five, and then three purl; that is right. Now, what was I saying? Oh, yes, about poor Mabel.

"Mabel was my niece. A nice girl, really a very nice girl, but just a trifle what one might call *silly*. Rather fond of being melodramatic and of saying a great deal more than she meant whenever she was upset. She married a Mr. Denman when she was twenty-two, and I am afraid it was not a very happy marriage. I had hoped very much that the attachment would not come to anything, for Mr. Denman was a man of very violent temper—not the kind of man who would be patient with Mabel's foibles—and I also learned that there was insanity in his family. However, girls were just as obstinate then as they are now, and as they always will be. And Mabel married him.

"I didn't see very much of her after her marriage. She came to stay with me once or twice, and they asked me there several times, but, as a matter of fact, I am not very fond of staying in other people's houses, and I always managed to make some excuse. They had been married ten years when Mr. Denman died suddenly. There were no children, and he left all his money to Mabel. I wrote, of course, and offered to come to Mabel if she wanted me; but she wrote back a very sensible letter, and I gathered that she was not altogether overwhelmed by grief. I thought that was only natural, because I knew they had not been getting on together for some time. It was not until about three months afterwards that I got a most hysterical letter from Mabel, begging me to come to her, and saying that things were going from bad to worse, and she couldn't stand it much longer.

"So, of course," continued Miss Marple, "I put Clara on board wages and sent the plate and the King Charles tankard to the bank, and I went off at once. I found Mabel in a very nervous state. The house, Myrtle Dene, was a fairly large one, very comfortably furnished. There was a cook and a house-parlourmaid as well as a nurse-attendant to look after old Mr. Denman, Mabel's husband's father, who was what is called 'not quite right in the head.' Quite peaceful and well-behaved, but distinctly odd at times. As I say, there was insanity in the family.

"I was really shocked to see the charge in Mabel. She was a mass of nerves, twitching all over, yet I had the greatest difficulty in making her tell me what the trouble was. I got at it, as one always does get at these things, indirectly. I asked her about some friends of hers she was always mentioning in her letters, the Gallaghers. She said, to my surprise, that she hardly ever saw them nowadays. Other friends whom I mentioned elicited the same remark. I spoke to her then of the folly of shutting herself up and brooding, and especially of the silliness of cutting herself adrift from her friends. Then she came bursting out with the truth.

" 'It is not my doing, it is theirs. There is not a soul in the place who will speak to me now. When I go down the High Street they all get out of the way so that they shan't have to meet me or speak to me. I am like a kind of leper. It is awful, and I can't bear it any longer. I shall have to sell the house and go abroad. Yet why should I be driven away from home like this? I have done nothing.' "

"I was more disturbed than I can tell you. I was knitting a comforter for old Mrs. Hay at the time, and in my perturbation I dropped two stitches and never discovered it until long after.

" 'My dear Mabel,' I said, 'you amaze me. But what is the cause of all this?'

"Even as a child Mabel was always difficult. I had the greatest difficulty in getting her to give me a straightforward answer to my question. She would only say vague things about wicked talk and idle people who had nothing better to do than gossip, and people who put ideas into other people's heads.

" 'That is all quite clear to me,' I said. 'There is evidently some story being circulated about you. But what that story is you must know as well as anyone. And you are going to tell me.'

" 'It is so wicked,' moaned Mabel.

" 'Of course it is wicked,' I said briskly. 'There is nothing that you can tell me about people's minds that would astonish or surprise me. Now, Mabel, will you tell me in plain English what people are saying about you?'

"Then it all came out.

"It seemed that Geoffrey Denman's death, being quite sudden and unexpected, gave rise to various rumours. In fact—and in plain English as I had put it to her—people were saying that she had poisoned her husband.

"Now, as I expect you know, there is nothing more cruel than talk, and there is nothing more difficult to combat. When people say things behind your back there is nothing you can refute or deny, and the rumours go on growing and growing, and no one can stop them. I was quite certain of one thing: Mabel was quite incapable of poisoning anyone. And I didn't see why life should be ruined for her and her home made unbearable just because in all probability she had been doing something silly and foolish.

" 'There is no smoke without fire,' I said. 'Now, Mabel, you have got to tell me what started people off on this tack. There must have been something.'

"Mabel was very incoherent, and declared there was nothing—nothing at all, except, of course, that Geoffrey's death had been very sudden. He had seemed quite well at supper that evening, and had taken violently ill in the night. The doctor had been sent for, but the poor man had died a few minutes after the doctor's arrival. Death had been thought to be the result of eating poisoned mushrooms.

" 'Well,' I said, 'I suppose a sudden death of that kind might start tongues wagging, but surely not without some additional facts. Did you have a quarrel with Geoffrey or anything of that kind?'

"She admitted that she had had a quarrel with him on the preceding morning at breakfast time.

" 'And the servants heard it, I suppose?' I asked.

" 'They weren't in the room.'

" 'No, my dear,' I said, 'but they probably were fairly near the door outside.'

"I knew the carrying power of Mabel's high-pitched hysterical voice only too well. Geoffrey Denman, too, was a man given to raising his voice loudly when angry.

" 'What did you quarrel about?' I asked.

" 'Oh, the usual things. It was always the same things over and over again. Some little thing would start us off, and then Geoffrey became impossible and said abominable things, and I told him what I thought of him.'

" 'There had been a lot of quarrelling, then?' I asked.

" 'It wasn't my fault——'

" 'My dear child,' I said, 'it doesn't matter whose fault it was. That is not what we are discussing. In a place like this everybody's private affairs are more or less public property. You and your husband were always quarrelling. You had a particularly bad quarrel one morning, and that night your husband died suddenly and mysteriously. Is that all, or is there anything else?'

" 'I don't know what you mean by anything else,' said Mabel sullenly.

" 'Just what I say, my dear. If you have done anything silly, don't for Heaven's sake keep it back now. I only want to do what I can to help you.'

" 'Nothing and nobody can help,' said Mabel wildly, 'except death.'

" 'Have a little more faith in Providence, dear,' I said. 'Now then, Mabel, I know perfectly well there *is* something else that you are keeping back.'

"I always did know, even when she was a child, when she was not telling me the whole truth. It took a long time, but I got it out at last. She had gone down to the chemist's that morning and had bought some arsenic. She had had, of course, to sign the book for it. Naturally, the chemist had talked.

" 'Who is your doctor?' I asked.

" 'Dr. Rawlinson.'

"I knew him by sight. Mabel had pointed him out to me the other day. To put it in perfectly plain language he was what I would describe as an old dodderer. I have had too much experience of life to believe in the infallibility of doctors. Some of them are clever men and some of them are not, and half the time the best of them don't know what is the matter with you. I have no truck with doctors and their medicines myself.

"I thought things over, and then I put my bonnet on and went to call on Dr. Rawlinson. He was just what I had thought him—a nice old man, kindly, vague, and so short-sighted as to be pitiful, slightly deaf, and, withal, touchy and sensitive to the last degree. He was on his high horse at once when I mentioned Geoffrey Denman's death, talked for a long time about various kinds of fungi, edible and otherwise. He had questioned the cook, and she had admitted that one or two of the mushrooms cooked had been 'a little queer,' but as the shop had sent them she thought they must be all right. The more she thought about them since, the more she was convinced that their appearance was unusual.

" 'She would be,' I said. 'They would start by being quite like mushrooms in appearance, and they would end by being orange with purple spots. There is nothing that class cannot remember if it tries.'

"I gathered that Denman had been past speech when

the doctor got to him. He was incapable of swallowing, and had died within a few minutes. The doctor seemed perfectly satisfied with the certificate he had given. But how much of that was obstinacy and how much of it was genuine belief I could not be sure.

"I went straight home and asked Mabel quite frankly why she had bought arsenic.

" 'You must have had some idea in your mind,' I pointed out.

"Mabel burst into tears. 'I wanted to make away with myself,' she moaned. 'I was too unhappy. I thought I would end it all.'

" 'Have you the arsenic still?' I asked.

" 'No, I threw it away.'

"I sat there turning things over and over in my mind.

" 'What happened when he was taken ill? Did he call you?'

" 'No.' She shook her head. 'He rang the bell violently. He must have rung several times. At last Dorothy, the house-parlourmaid, heard it, and she waked the cook up and they came down. When Dorothy saw him she was frightened. He was rambling and delirious. She left the cook with him and came rushing to me. I got up and went to him. Of course I saw at once he was dreadfully ill. Unfortunately Brewster, who looks after old Mr. Denman, was away for the night, so there was no one who knew what to do. I sent Dorothy off for the doctor, and cook and I stayed with him, but after a few minutes I couldn't bear it any longer; it was too dreadful. I ran away back to my room and locked the door.'

" 'Very selfish and unkind of you,' I said; 'and no doubt that conduct of yours has done nothing to help you since, you may be sure of that. Cook will have repeated it everywhere. Well, well, this is a bad business.'

"Next I spoke to the servants. The cook wanted to tell me about the mushrooms, but I stopped her. I was tired of these mushrooms. Instead, I questioned both of them very closely about their master's condition on that night. They both agreed that he seemed to be in great agony, that he was unable to swallow, and he could only speak in a strangled voice, and when he did speak it was only rambling—nothing sensible.

" 'What did he say when he was rambling?' I asked curiously.

" 'Something about some fish, wasn't it?' turning to the other.

"Dorothy agreed.

" 'A heap of fish,' she said; 'some nonsense like that. I could see at once he wasn't in his right mind, poor gentleman.'

"There didn't seem to be any sense to be made out of that. As a last resource I went up to see Brewster, who was a gaunt, middle-aged woman of about fifty.

" 'It is a pity that I wasn't here that night,' she said. 'Nobody seems to have tried to do anything for him until the doctor came.'

" 'I suppose he was delirious,' I said doubtfully; 'but that is not a symptom of ptomaine poisoning, is it?'

" 'It depends,' said Brewster.

"I asked her how her patient was getting on.

"She shook her head.

" 'He is pretty bad,' she said.

" 'Weak?'

" 'Oh no, he is strong enough physically—all but his eyesight. That is failing badly. He may outlive all of us, but his mind is failing very fast now. I have already told both Mr. and Mrs. Denman that he ought to be in an institution, but Mrs. Denman wouldn't hear of it at any price.'

"I will say for Mabel that she always had a kindly heart.

"Well, there the thing was. I thought it over in every aspect, and at last I decided that there was only one thing to be done. In view of the rumours that were going about, permission must be applied for to exhume the body, and a proper post-mortem must be made and lying tongues quietened once and for all. Mabel, of course, made a fuss, mostly on sentimental grounds—disturbing the dead man in his peaceful grave, etc., etc.—but I was firm.

"I won't make a long story of this part of it. We got the order and they did the autopsy, or whatever they call it, but the result was not so satisfactory as it might have been. There was no trace of arsenic—that was all to the good— but the actual words of the report were *that there was nothing to show by what means deceased had come to his death.*

"So, you see, that didn't lead us out of trouble altogether. People went on talking—about rare poisons impossible to detect, and rubbish of that sort. I had seen the pathologist who had done the post-mortem, and I had asked him several questions, though he tried his best to get out of answering most of them; but I got out of him that he considered it highly unlikely that the poisoned mushrooms were the cause of death. An idea was simmering in my mind, and I asked him what poison, if any, could have been employed to obtain that result. He made a long explanation to me, most of which, I must admit, I did not follow, but it amounted to this: That death might have been due to some strong vegetable alkaloid.

"The idea I had was this: Supposing the taint of insanity was in Geoffrey Denman's blood also, might he not have made away with himself? He had, at one period of his life, studied medicine, and he would have a good knowledge of poisons and their effects.

"I didn't think it sounded very likely, but it was the only thing I could think of. And I was nearly at my wits' end, I can tell you. Now, I dare say you modern young people will laugh, but when I am in really bad trouble I always say a little prayer to myself—anywhere, when I am walking along the street, or at a bazaar. And I always get an answer. It may be some trifling thing, apparently quite unconnected with the subject, but there it is. I had that text pinned over my bed when I was a little girl: *Ask and you shall receive.* On the morning that I am telling you about, I was walking along the High Street, and I was praying hard. I shut my eyes, and when I opened them, what do you think was the first thing that I saw?"

Five faces with varying degrees of interest were turned

73

to Miss Marple. It may be safely assumed, however, that no one would have guessed the answer to the question right.

"I saw," said Miss Marple impressively, *"the window of the fishmonger's shop.* There was only one thing in it, *a fresh haddock."*

She looked round triumphantly.

"Oh, my God!" said Raymond West. "An answer to prayer—a fresh haddock!"

"Yes, Raymond," said Miss Marple severely, "and there is no need to be profane about it. The hand of God is everywhere. The first thing I saw were the black spots— the marks of St. Peter's thumb. That is the legend, you know. St. Peter's thumb. And that brought things home to me. I needed faith, the ever-true faith of St. Peter. I connected the two things together, faith—and fish."

Sir Henry blew his nose rather hurriedly. Joyce bit her lip.

"Now what did that bring to my mind? Of course, both the cook and the house-parlourmaid mentioned fish as being one of the things spoken of by the dying man. I was convinced, absolutely convinced, that there was some solution of the mystery to be found in these words. I went home determined to get to the bottom of the matter."

She paused.

"Has it ever occurred to you," the old lady went on, "how much we go by what is called, I believe, the context? There is a place on Dartmoor called Grey Wethers. If you were talking to a farmer there and mentioned Grey Wethers, he would probably conclude that you were speaking of these stone circles, yet it is possible that you might be speaking of the atmosphere; and in the same way, if you were meaning the stone circles, an outsider, hearing a fragment of the conversation, might think you meant the weather. So when we repeat a conversation, we don't, as a rule, repeat the actual words; we put in some other words that seem to us to mean exactly the same thing.

"I saw both the cook and Dorothy separately. I asked the cook if she was quite sure that her master had really mentioned a heap of fish. She said she was quite sure.

" 'Were these his exact words,' I asked, 'or did he mention some particular kind of fish?'

" 'That's it,' said the cook; 'it was some particular kind of fish, but I can't remember what now. A heap of—now what was it? Not any of the fish you send to table. Would it be a perch now—or pike? No. It didn't begin with a P.'

"Dorothy also recalled that her master had mentioned some special kind of fish. 'Some outlandish kind of fish it was,' she said.

" 'A pile of—now what was it?

" 'Did he say heap or pile?' I asked.

" 'I think he said pile. But there, I really can't be sure—it's so hard to remember the actual words, isn't it, Miss, especially when they don't seem to make sense. But now I come to think of it, I am pretty sure that it was a pile, and the fish began with C; but it wasn't a cod, or a crayfish.'

"The next part is where I am really proud of myself," said Miss Marple, "because, of course, I don't know anything about drugs—nasty, dangerous things I call them. I have got an old recipe of my grandmother's for tansy tea that is worth any amount of your drugs. But I knew that there were several medical volumes in the house, and in one of them there was an index of drugs. You see, my idea was that Geoffrey had taken some particular poison, and was trying to say the name of it.

"Well, I looked down the list of H s, beginning He Nothing there that sounded likely; then I began on the P's, and almost at once I came to—what do you think?"

She looked round, postponing her moment of triumph.

"Pilocarpine. Can't you understand a man who could hardly speak trying to drag that word out? What would that sound like to a cook who had never heard the word? Wouldn't it convey the impression 'pile of carp'?"

"By Jove!" said Sir Henry.

"I should never have hit upon that," said Dr. Pender.

"Most interesting," said Mr. Petherick. "Really most interesting."

"I turned quickly to the page indicated in the index. I read about pilocarpine and its effect on the eyes and other things that didn't seem to have any bearing on the case, but at last I came to a most significant phrase: *Has been tried with success as an antidote for atropine poisoning.*

"I can't tell you the light that dawned upon me then. I never had thought it likely that Geoffrey Denman would commit suicide. No, this new solution was not only possible, but I was absolutely sure it was the correct one, because all the pieces fitted in logically."

"I am not going to try to guess," said Raymond. "Go on, Aunt Jane, and tell us what was so startlingly clear to you."

"I don't know anything about medicine, of course," said Miss Marple, "but I did happen to know this, that when my eyesight was failing, the doctor ordered me drops with atropine sulphate in them. I went straight upstairs to old Mr. Denman's room. I didn't beat about the bush.

" 'Mr. Denman,' I said, 'I know everything. Why did you poison your son?'

"He looked at me for a minute or two—rather a handsome old man he was, in his way—and then he burst out laughing. It was one of the most vicious laughs I have ever heard. I can assure you it made my flesh creep. I had only heard anything like it once before, when poor Mrs. Jones went off her head.

" 'Yes,' he said, 'I got even with Geoffrey. I was too clever for Geoffrey. He was going to put me away, was he? Have me shut up in an asylum? I heard them talking about it. Mabel is a good girl—Mabel stuck up for me, but I knew she wouldn't be able to stand up against Geoffrey. In the end he would have his own way; he always did. But I settled him—I settled my kind, loving son! Ha, ha! I crept down in the night. It was quite easy. Brewster was away. My dear son was asleep; he had a glass of water by the side of his bed; he always woke up in the middle of the night and drank it off. I poured it away—ha, ha!—and I emptied the bottle of eye-drops into the glass. He would wake up and swill it down before he knew what it was. There was only a tablespoon of it—quite enough, quite enough. And so he did! They came to me in the morning and broke it to me very gently. They were afraid it would upset me. Ha! Ha! Ha! Ha! Ha!'

"Well," said Miss Marple, "that is the end of the story. Of course, the poor old man was put in an asylum. He wasn't really responsible for what he had done, and the truth was known, and everyone was sorry for Mabel and could not do enough to make up to her for the unjust suspicions they had had. But if it hadn't been for Geoffrey realising what the stuff was he had swallowed and trying to get everybody to get hold of the antidote without delay, it might never have been found out. I believe there are very definite symptoms with atropine—dilated pupils of the eyes, and all that; but, of course, as I have said, Dr. Rawlinson was very short-sighted, poor old man. And in the same medical book which I went on reading—and some of it was *most* interesting—it gave the symptoms of ptomaine poisoning and atropine, and they are not unlike. But I can assure you I have never seen a pile of fresh haddock without thinking of the thumb mark of St. Peter."

There was a very long pause.

"My dear friend," said Mr. Petherick. "My very dear friend, you really are amazing."

"I shall recommend Scotland Yard to come to you for advice," said Sir Henry.

"Well, at all events, Aunt Jane," said Raymond, "there is one thing that you don't know."

"Oh, yes, I do, dear," said Miss Marple. "It happened just before dinner, didn't it? When you took Joyce out to admire the sunset. It is a very favourite place, that. There by the jasmine hedge. That is where the milkman asked Annie if he could put up the banns."

"Dash it all, Aunt Jane," said Raymond. "don't spoil all the romance. Joyce and I aren't like the milkman and Annie."

"That is where you make a mistake, dear," said Miss Marple. "Everybody is very much alike, really. But fortunately, perhaps, they don't realise it."

# CHAPTER VII

# THE BLUE GERANIUM

"WHEN I was down here last year—" said Sir Henry Clithering, and stopped.

His hostess, Mrs. Bantry, looked at him curiously.

The Ex-Commissioner of Scotland Yard was staying with old friends of his, Colonel and Mrs. Bantry, who lived near St. Mary Mead.

Mrs. Bantry, pen in hand, had just asked his advice as to who should be invited to make a sixth guest at dinner that evening.

"Yes?" said Mrs. Bantry encouragingly. "When you were here last year?"

"Tell me," said Sir Henry, "do you know a Miss Marple?"

Mrs. Bantry was surprised. It was the last thing she had expected.

"Know Miss Marple? Who doesn't! The typical old maid of fiction. Quite a dear, but hopelessly behind the times. Do you mean you would like me to ask *her* to dinner?"

"You are surprised?"

"A little, I must confess. I should hardly have thought you—but perhaps there's an explanation?"

"The explanation is simple enough. When I was down here last year we got into the habit of discussing unsolved mysteries—there were five or six of us—Raymond West, the novelist, started it. We each supplied a story to which we knew the answer, but nobody else did. It was supposed to be an exercise in the deductive faculties—to see who could get nearest the truth."

"Well?"

"Like in the old story—we hardly realised that Miss Marple was playing; but we were very polite about it— didn't want to hurt the old dear's feelings. And now comes the cream of the jest. The old lady outdid us every time!"

"What?"

"I assure you—straight to the truth like a homing pigeon."

"But how extraordinary! Why, dear old Miss Marple has hardly ever been out of St. Mary Mead."

"Ah! But according to her, that has given her unlimited opportunities of observing human nature—under the microscope as it were."

"I suppose there's something in that," conceded Mrs. Bantry. "One would at least know the petty side of people. But I don't think we have any really exciting criminals in our midst. I think we must try her with Arthur's ghost story after dinner. I'd be thankful if she'd find a solution to that."

"I didn't know that Arthur believed in ghosts?"

"Oh! he doesn't. That's what worries him so. And it happened to a friend of his, George Pritchard—a most prosaic person. It's really rather tragic for poor George. Either this extraordinary story is true—or else——'

"Or else what?"

Mrs. Bantry did not answer. After a minute or two she said irrelevantly:

"You know, I like George—everyone does. One can't believe that he—but people do do such extraordinary things."

Sir Henry nodded. He knew, better than Mrs. Bantry, the extraordinary things that people did.

So it came about that that evening Mrs. Bantry looked around her dinner table (shivering a little as she did so, because the dining-room, like most English dining-rooms, was extremely cold) and fixed her gaze on the very upright old lady sitting on her husband's right. Miss Marple wore black lace mittens; an old lace fichu was draped round her shoulders and another piece of lace surmounted her white hair. She was talking animatedly to the elderly doctor, Dr. Lloyd, about the Workhouse and the suspected shortcomings of the District Nurse.

Mrs. Bantry marvelled anew. She even wondered whether Sir Henry had been making an elaborate joke—but there seemed no point in that. Incredible that what he had said could be really true.

Her glance went on and rested affectionately on her red-faced broad-shouldered husband as he sat talking horses to Jane Helier, the beautiful and popular actress. Jane, more beautiful (if that were possible) off the stage than on, opened enormous blue eyes and murmured at discreet intervals: "Really?" "Oh fancy!" "How extraordinary!" She knew nothing whatever about horses and cared less.

"Arthur," said Mrs. Bantry, "you're boring poor Jane to distraction. Leave horses alone and tell her your ghost story instead. You know . . . George Pritchard."

"Eh, Dolly? Oh! but I don't know——"

"Sir Henry wants to hear it too. I was telling him something about it this morning. It would be interesting to hear what everyone has to say about it."

"Oh, do!" said Jane. "I love ghost stories."

"Well—" Colonel Bantry hesitated. "I've never believed much in the supernatural. But this——

"I don't think any of you know George Pritchard. He's one of the best. His wife—well, she's dead now, poor woman. I'll just say this much: she didn't give George any too easy a time when she was alive. She was one of those semi-invalids—I believe she had really something wrong with her, but whatever it was she played it for all it was worth. She was capricious, exacting, unreasonable. She complained from morning to night. George was expected to wait on her hand and foot, and everything he did was always wrong and he got cursed for it. Most men, I'm fully convinced, would have hit her over the head with a hatchet long ago. Eh, Dolly, isn't that so?"

"She was a dreadful woman," said Mrs. Bantry with conviction. "If George Pritchard had brained her with a

80

hatchet, and there had been any woman on the jury, he would have been triumphantly acquitted."

"I don't quite know how this business started. George was rather vague about it. I gather Mrs. Pritchard had always had a weakness for fortune-tellers, palmists, clairvoyants—anything of that sort. George didn't mind. If she found amusement in it well and good. But he refused to go into rhapsodies himself, and that was another grievance.

"A succession of hospital nurses was always passing through the house, Mrs. Pritchard usually becoming dissatisfied with them after a few weeks. One young nurse had been very keen on this fortune-telling stunt, and for a time Mrs. Pritchard had been very fond of her. Then she suddenly fell out with her and insisted on her going. She had back another nurse who had been with her previously— an older woman, experienced and tactful in dealing with a neurotic patient. Nurse Copling, according to George, was a very good sort—a sensible woman to talk to. She put up with Mrs. Pritchard's tantrums and nerve-storms with complete indifference.

"Mrs. Pritchard always lunched upstairs, and it was usual at lunch time for George and the nurse to come to some arrangement for the afternoon. Strictly speaking, the nurse went off from two to four, but 'to oblige' as the phrase goes, she would sometimes take her time off after tea if George wanted to be free for the afternoon. On this occasion, she mentioned that she was going to see a sister at Golders Green and might be a little late returning. George's face fell, for he had arranged to play a round of golf. Nurse Copling, however, reassured him.

" 'We'll neither of us be missed, Mr. Pritchard.' A twinkle came into her eye. 'Mrs. Pritchard's going to have more exciting company than ours.'

" 'Who's that?'

" 'Wait a minute,' Nurse Copling's eyes twinkled more than ever. 'Let me get it right. *Zarida, Psychic Reader of the Future.*'

" 'Oh Lord!' groaned George. 'That's a new one, isn't it?'

" 'Quite new. I believe my predecessor, Nurse Carstairs, sent her along. Mrs. Pritchard hasn't seen her yet. She made me write, fixing an appointment for this afternoon.'

" 'Well, at any rate, I shall get my golf,' said George, and he went off with the kindliest feelings towards Zarida, the Reader of the Future.

"On his return to the house, he found Mrs. Pritchard in a state of great agitation. She was, as usual, lying on her invalid couch, and she had a bottle of smelling-salts in her hand which she sniffed at frequent intervals.

" 'George,' she exclaimed. 'What did I tell you about this house? The moment I came into it, I *felt* there was something wrong! Didn't I tell you so at the time?'

"Repressing his desire to reply, 'You always do,' George said, 'No, can't say I remember it.'

" 'You never do remember anything that has to do with me. Men are all extraordinarily callous—but I really believe that you are even more insensitive than most.'

" 'Oh, come now, Mary dear, that's not fair.'

" 'Well, as I was telling you, this woman *knew* at once! She—she actually blenched—if you know what I mean—as she came in at that door, and she said: "There is evil here—evil and danger. I feel it." ' "

"Very unwisely George laughed.

" 'Well, you have had your money's worth this afternoon.'

"His wife closed her eyes and took a long sniff from her smelling-bottle.

" 'How you hate me! You would jeer and laugh if I were dying.'

"George protested and after a minute or two she went on.

" 'You may laugh, but I shall tell you the whole thing. This house is definitely dangerous to me—the woman said so.'

"George's formerly kind feeling towards Zarida underwent a change. He knew his wife was perfectly capable of insisting on moving to a new house if the caprice got hold of her.

" 'What else did she say?' he asked.

" 'She couldn't tell me very much. She was so upset. One thing she did say. I had some violets in a glass. She pointed at them and cried out.

" 'Take those away. No blue flowers—never have blue flowers. *Blue flowers are fatal to you—remember that.*'

" 'And you know,' added Mrs. Pitchard, 'I always have told you that blue as a colour is repellent to me. I feel a natural instinctive sort of warning against it.'

"George was much too wise to remark that he had never heard her say so before. Instead he asked what the mysterious Zarida was like. Mrs. Pritchard entered with gusto upon a description.

" 'Black hair in coiled knobs over her ears—her eyes were half closed—great black rims round them—she had a black veil over her mouth and chin—she spoke in a kind of singing voice with a marked foreign accent—Spanish, I think——'

" 'In fact all the usual stock-in-trade,' said George cheerfully.

"His wife immediately closed her eyes.

" 'I feel extremely ill,' she said. 'Ring for nurse. Unkindness upsets me, as you know only too well.'

"It was two days later that Nurse Copling came to George with a grave face.

" 'Will you come to Mrs. Pritchard, please. She has had a letter which upsets her greatly.'

"He found his wife with the letter in her hand. She held it out to him.

" 'Read it,' she said.

"George read it. It was on heavily scented paper, and the writing was big and black.

" '*I have seen the Future. Be warned before it is too late. Beware of the Full moon. The Blue Primrose means Warning; the Blue Hollyhock means Danger; the Blue Geranium means Death. . . .*'

"Just about to burst out laughing, George caught Nurse Copling's eye. She made a quick warning gesture. He said rather awkwardly, 'The woman's probably trying to frighten you, Mary. Anyway there aren't such things as blue prim-roses and blue geraniums.'

"But Mrs. Pritchard began to cry and say her days were numbered. Nurse Copling came out with George upon the landing.

" 'Of all the silly tomfoolery,' he burst out.

" 'I suppose it is.'

"Something in the nurse's tone struck him, and he stared at her in amazement.

" 'Surely, nurse, you don't believe——'

" 'No, no, Mr. Pritchard. I don't believe in reading the future—that's nonsense. What puzzles me is the *meaning* of this. Fortune-tellers are usually out for what they can get. But this woman seems to be frightening Mrs. Pritchard with no advantage to herself. I can't see the point. There's another thing——'

" 'Yes?'

" 'Mrs. Pritchard says that something about Zarida was faintly familiar to her.'

" 'Well?'

" 'Well, I don't like it, Mr. Pritchard, that's all.'

" 'I didn't know you were so superstitious, nurse.'

" 'I'm not superstitious; but I know when a thing is fishy.'

"It was about four days after this that the first incident happened. To explain it to you, I shall have to describe Mrs. Pritchard's room——"

"You'd better let me do that," interrupted Mrs. Bantry. "It was prepared with one of these new wallpapers where you apply clumps of flowers to make a kind of herbaceous border. The effect is almost like being in a garden—though, of course, the flowers are all wrong. I mean they simply couldn't be in bloom all at the same time——"

"Don't let a passion for horticultural accuracy run away with you, Dolly," said her husband. "We all know you're an enthusiastic gardener."

"Well, it *is* absurd," protested Mrs. Bantry. "To have

bluebells and daffodils and lupins and hollyhocks and Michaelmas daisies all grouped together."

"Most unscientific," said Sir Henry. "But to proceed with the story."

"Well, among these massed flowers were primroses, clumps of yellow and pink primroses and—oh go on, Arthur, this is your story——"

Colonel Bantry took up the tale.

"Mrs. Pritchard rang her bell violently one morning. The household came running—thought she was in extremis; not at all. She was violently excited and pointing at the wallpaper; and there sure enough was *one blue primrose* in the midst of the others. . . ."

"Oh!" said Miss Helier, "how creepy!"

"The question was: Hadn't the blue primrose always been there? That was George's suggestion and the nurse's. But Mrs. Pritchard wouldn't have it at any price. She had never noticed it till that very morning and the night before had been full moon. She was very upset about it."

"I met George Pritchard that same day and he told me about it," said Mrs. Bantry. "I went to see Mrs. Pritchard and did my best to ridicule the whole thing; but without success. I came away really concerned, and I remember I met Jean Instow and told her about it. Jean is a queer girl. She said, 'So she's really upset about it?' I told her that I thought the woman was perfectly capable of dying of fright— she was really abnormally superstitious.

"I remember Jean rather startled me with what she said next. She said, 'Well, that might be all for the best, mightn't it?' And she said it so coolly, in so matter-of-fact a tone that I was really—well, shocked. Of course I know it's done nowadays—to be brutal and outspoken; but I never get used to it. Jean smiled at me rather oddly and said, 'You don't like my saying that—but it's true. What use is Mrs. Pritchard's life to her? None at all; and it's hell for George Pritchard. To have his wife frightened out of existence would be the best thing that could happen to him.' I said, 'George is most awfully good to her always.' And she said, 'Yes, he deserves a reward, poor dear. He's a very

attractive person, George Pritchard. The last nurse thought
so—the pretty one—what was her name? Carstairs. That
was the cause of the row between her and Mrs. P.'

"Now I didn't like hearing Jean say that. Of course one
had *wondered*——"

Mrs. Bantry paused significantly.

"Yes, dear," said Miss Marple placidly. "One always
does. Is Miss Instow a pretty girl? I suppose she plays
golf?"

"Yes. She's good at all games. And she's nice looking,
attractive-looking, very fair with a healthy skin, and nice
steady blue eyes. Of course we always have felt that she
and George Pritchard—I mean if things had been different—
they are so well suited to one another."

"And they were friends?" asked Miss Marple.

"Oh yes. Great friends."

"Do you think, Dolly," said Colonel Bantry plaintively,
"that I might be allowed to go on with my story?"

"Arthur," said Mrs. Bantry resignedly, "wants to get
back to his ghosts."

"I had the rest of the story from George himself,"
went on the colonel. "There's no doubt that Mrs. Pritchard
got the wind up badly towards the end of the next month.
She marked off on a calendar the day when the moon
would be full, and on that night she had both the nurse and
then George into her room and made them study the wallpaper carefully. There were pink hollyhocks and red ones,
but there were no blue amongst them. Then when George
left the room she locked the door——"

"And in the morning there was a large blue hollyhock," said Miss Helier joyfully.

"Quite right," said Colonel Bantry. "Or at any rate,
nearly right. One flower of a hollyhock just above her head
had turned blue. It staggered George; and of course the
more it staggered him the more he refused to take the thing
seriously. He insisted that the whole thing was some kind
of practical joke. He ignored the evidence of the locked
door and the fact that Mrs. Pritchard discovered the change
before anyone—even Nurse Copling—was admitted.

"It staggered George; and it made him unreasonable. His wife wanted to leave the house, and he wouldn't let her. He was inclined to believe in the supernatural for the first time, but he wasn't going to admit it. He usually gave in to his wife, but this time he wouldn't. Mary was not to make a fool of herself, he said. The whole thing was the most infernal nonsense.

"And so the next month sped away. Mrs. Pritchard made less protest than one would have imagined. I think she was superstitious enough to believe that she couldn't escape her fate. She repeated again and again: 'The blue primrose—warning. The blue hollyhock—danger. The blue geranium—*death*.' And she would lie looking at the clump of pinky-red geraniums nearest her bed.

"The whole business was pretty nervy. Even the nurse caught the infection. She came to George two days before full moon and begged him to take Mrs. Pritchard away. George was angry.

" 'If all the flowers on that damned wall turned into blue devils it couldn't kill anyone!' he shouted.

" 'It might. Shock has killed people before now.'

" 'Nonsense,' said George.

"George has always been a shade pig-headed. You can't drive him. I believe he had a secret idea that his wife worked the changes herself and that it was all some morbid hysterical plan of hers.

"Well, the fatal night came. Mrs. Pritchard locked her door as usual. She was very calm—in almost an exalted state of mind. The nurse was worried by her state—and wanted to give her a stimulant, an injection of strychnine, but Mrs. Pritchard refused. In a way, I believe, she was enjoying herself. George said she was."

"I think that's quite possible," said Mrs. Bantry. "There must have been a strange sort of glamour about the whole thing."

"There was no violent ringing of a bell the next morning. Mrs. Pritchard usually woke about eight. When, at eight-thirty, there was no sign from her, nurse rapped loudly on the door. Getting no reply, she fetched George, and insisted on the door being broken open. They did so with the help of a chisel.

"One look at the still figure on the bed was enough for Nurse Copling. She sent George to telephone for the doctor, but it was too late. Mrs. Pritchard, he said, must have been dead at least eight hours. Her smelling salts lay by her hand on the bed, *and on the wall beside her one of the pinky-red geraniums was a bright deep blue.*"

"Horrible," said Miss Helier with a shiver.

Sir Henry was frowning.

"No additional details?"

Colonel Bantry shook his head, but Mrs. Bantry spoke quickly.

"The gas."

"What about the gas?" asked Sir Henry.

"When the doctor arrived there was a slight smell of gas, and sure enough he found the gas ring in the fireplace very slightly turned on; but so little that it couldn't have mattered."

"Did Mr. Pritchard and the nurse not notice it when they first went in?"

"The nurse said she did notice a slight smell. George said he didn't notice gas, but something made him feel very queer and overcome; but he put that down to shock— and probably it was. At any rate there was no question of gas poisoning. The smell was scarcely noticeable."

"And that's the end of the story?"

"No, it isn't. One way and another, there was a lot of talk. The servants, you see, had overheard things—had heard, for instance, Mrs. Pritchard telling her husband that he hated her and would jeer if she were dying. And also more recent remarks. She said one day, apropos of his refusing to leave the house: 'Very well, when I am dead, I hope everyone will realise that you have killed me.' And as ill luck would have it, he had been mixing some weed killer for the garden paths the very day before. One of the younger servants had seen him and had afterwards seen him taking up a glass of hot milk to his wife.

"The talk spread and grew. The doctor had given a

certificate—I don't know exactly in what terms—shock, syncope, heart failure, probably some medical term meaning nothing much. However the poor lady had not been a month in her grave before an exhumation order was applied for and granted."

"And the result of the autopsy was nil, I remember," said Sir Henry gravely. "A case, for once, of smoke without fire."

"The whole thing is really very curious," said Mrs. Bantry. "That fortune-teller, for instance—Zarida. At the address where she was supposed to be, no one had ever heard of any such person!"

"She appeared once—out of the blue," said her husband, "and then utterly vanished. Out of the *blue*—that's rather good!"

"And what is more," continued Mrs. Bantry, "little Nurse Carstairs, who was supposed to have recommended her, had never even heard of her.'

They looked at each other.

"It's a mysterious story," said Dr Lloyd. "One can make guesses; but to guess——"

He shook his head.

"Has Mr. Pritchard married Miss Instow?" asked Miss Marple in her gentle voice.

"Now why do you ask that?" inquired Sir Henry.

Miss Marple opened gentle blue eyes.

"It seems to me so important," she said. "Have they married?"

Colonel Bantry shook his head.

"We—well, we expected something of the kind—but it's eighteen months now. I don't believe they even see much of each other."

"That is important," said Miss Marple. "Very important."

"Then you think the same as I do," said Mrs. Bantry. "You think——"

"Now, Dolly," said her husband. "It's unjustifiable—what you're going to say. You can't go about accusing people without a shadow of proof."

"Don't be so—so manly, Arthur. Men are always afraid to say *anything*. Anyway, this is all between ourselves. It's just a wild fantastic idea of mine that possibly—only *possibly*—Jean Instow disguised herself as a fortune-teller. Mind you, she may have done it for a joke. I don't for a minute think that she meant any harm; but if she did do it, and if Mrs. Pritchard was foolish enough to die of fright—well, that's what Miss Marple meant, wasn't it?"

"No, dear, not quite," said Miss Marple. "You see if I were going to kill anyone—which, of course, I wouldn't dream of doing for a minute, because it would be very wicked, and besides I don't like killing—not even wasps, though I know it has to be, and I'm sure the gardener does it as humanely as possible. Let me see, what was I saying?"

"If you wished to kill anyone," prompted Sir Henry.

"Oh yes. Well, if I did, I shouldn't be at all satisfied to trust to *fright*. I know one reads of people dying of it, but it seems a very uncertain sort of thing, and the most nervous people are far more brave than one really thinks they are. I should like something definite and certain, and make a thoroughly good plan about it."

"Miss Marple," said Sir Henry, "you frighten me. I hope you will never wish to remove me. Your plans would be too good."

Miss Marple looked at him reproachfully.

"I thought I had made it clear that I would never contemplate such wickedness," she said. "No, I was trying to put myself in the place of—er—a certain person."

"Do you mean George Pritchard?" asked Colonel Bantry. "I'll never believe it of George—though, mind you, even the nurse believes it. I went and saw her about a month afterwards, at the time of the exhumation. She didn't know how it was done—in fact, she wouldn't say anything at all—but it was clear enough that she believed George to be in some way responsible for his wife's death. She was convinced of it."

"Well," said Dr. Lloyd, "perhaps she wasn't so far wrong. And mind you, a nurse often *knows*. She can't say— she's got no proof—but she *knows*."

Sir Henry leant forward.

"Come now, Miss Marple," he said persuasively. "You're lost in a daydream. Won't you tell us all about it?"

Miss Marple started and turned pink.

"I beg your pardon," she said. "I was just thinking about our District Nurse. A most difficult problem."

"More difficult than the problem of a blue geranium?"

"It really depends on the primroses," said Miss Marple. "I mean, Mrs. Bantry said they were yellow and pink. If it was a pink primrose that turned blue, of course, that fits in perfectly. But if it happened to be a yellow one——"

"It was a pink one," said Mrs. Bantry.

She stared. They all stared at Miss Marple.

"Then that seems to settle it," said Miss Marple. She shook her head regretfully. "And the wasp season and everything. And of course the gas."

"It reminds you, I suppose, of countless village tragedies?" said Sir Henry.

"Not tragedies," said Miss Marple. "And certainly nothing criminal. But it does remind me a little of the trouble we are having with the District Nurse. After all, nurses are human beings, and what with having to be so correct in their behaviour and wearing those uncomfortable collars and being so thrown with the family—well, can you wonder that things sometimes happen?"

A glimmer of light broke upon Sir Henry.

"You mean Nurse Carstairs?"

"Oh no. Not Nurse Carstairs. Nurse Copling. You see, she had been there before, and very much thrown with Mr. Pritchard, who you say is an attractive man. I daresay she thought, poor thing—well, we needn't go into that. I don't suppose she knew about Miss Instow, and of course afterwards, when she found out, it turned her against him and she tried to do all the harm she could. Of course the letter really gave her away, didn't it?"

"What letter?"

"Well, she wrote to the fortune-teller at Mrs. Pritchard's request, and the fortune-teller came, apparently in answer to the letter. But later it was discovered that there

91

never had been such a person at that address. So that shows that Nurse Copling was in it. She only pretended to write—so what could be more likely than that *she* was the fortune-teller herself?"

"I never saw the point about the letter," said Sir Henry. "That's a most important point, of course."

"Rather a bold step to take," said Miss Marple, "because Mrs. Pritchard might have recognised her in spite of the disguise—though of course if she had, the nurse could have pretended it was a joke."

"What did you mean," said Sir Henry, "when you said that if you were a certain person you would not have trusted to fright?"

"One couldn't be *sure* that way," said Miss Marple. "No, I think that the warnings and the blue flowers were, if I may use a military term," she laughed self-consciously— "just *camouflage.*"

"And the real thing?"

"I know," said Miss Marple apologetically, "that I've got wasps on the brain. Poor things, destroyed in their thousands—and usually on such a beautiful summer's day. But I remember thinking, when I saw the gardener shaking up the cyanide of potassium in a bottle with water, how like smelling-salts it looked. And if it were put in a smelling-salt bottle and substituted for the real one—well, the poor lady was in the habit of using her smelling-salts. Indeed you said they were found by her hand. Then, of course, while Mr. Pritchard went to telephone to the doctor, the nurse would change it for the real bottle, and she'd just turn on the gas a little bit to mask any smell of almonds and in case anyone felt queer, and I always have heard that cyanide leaves no trace if you wait long enough. But, of course I may be wrong, and it may have been something entirely different in the bottle; but that doesn't really matter, does it?"

Miss Marple paused, a little out of breath.

Jane Helier leant forward and said, "But the blue geranium, and the other flowers?"

"Nurses always have litmus paper, don't they?" said

Miss Marple, "for—well, for testing. Not a very pleasant subject. We won't dwell on it. I have done a little nursing myself." She grew delicately pink. "Blue turns red with acids, and red turns blue with alkalies. So easy to paste some red litmus over a red flower—near the bed, of course. And then, when the poor lady used her smelling-salts, the strong ammonia fumes would turn it blue. Really most ingenious. Of course, the geranium wasn't blue when they first broke into the room—nobody noticed it till afterwards. When nurse changed the bottle, she held the Sal Ammoniac against the wallpaper for a minute, I expect."

"You might have been there, Miss Marple," said Sir Henry.

"What worries me," said Miss Marple, "is poor Mr. Pritchard and that nice girl, Miss Instow. Probably both suspecting each other and keeping apart—and life so very short."

She shook her head.

"You needn't worry," said Sir Henry. "As a matter of fact I have something up my sleeve. A nurse has been arrested on a charge of murdering an elderly patient who had left her a legacy. It was done with cyanide of potassium substituted for smelling-salts. Nurse Copling trying the same trick again. Miss Instow and Mr. Pritchard need have no doubts as to the truth."

"Now isn't that nice?" cried Miss Marple. "I don't mean about the new murder, of course. That's very sad, and shows how much wickedness there is in the world, and that if once you give way—which reminds me I *must* finish my little conversation with Dr. Lloyd about the village nurse."

# Chapter VIII

## The Companion

"Now, Dr. Lloyd," said Miss Helier. "Don't you know any creepy stories?"

She smiled at him—the smile that nightly bewitched the theatre-going public. Jane Helier was sometimes called the most beautiful woman in England, and jealous members of her own profession were in the habit of saying to each other: "Of course Jane's not an *artist*. She can't *act*—if you know what I mean. It's those eyes!"

And those "eyes" were at this minute fixed appealingly on the grizzled elderly bachelor doctor who, for the last five years, had ministered to the ailments of the village of St. Mary Mead.

With an unconscious gesture, the doctor pulled down his waistcoat (inclined of late to be uncomfortably tight) and racked his brains hastily, so as not to disappoint the lovely creature who addressed him so confidently.

"I feel," said Jane dreamily, "that I would like to wallow in crime this evening."

"Splendid," said Colonel Bantry, her host. "Splendid, splendid." And he laughed a loud hearty military laugh. "Eh, Dolly?"

His wife, hastily recalled to the exigencies of social life (she had been planning her spring border) agreed enthusiastically.

"Of course, it's splendid," she said heartily but vaguely. "I always thought so."

"Did you, my dear?" said old Miss Marple, and her eyes twinkled a little.

"We don't get much in the creepy line—and still less in the criminal line—in St. Mary Mead, you know, Miss Helier," said Dr. Lloyd.

"You surprise me," said Sir Henry Clithering. The ex-Commissioner of Scotland Yard turned to Miss Marple. "I always understood from our friend here that St. Mary Mead is a positive hot-bed of crime and vice."

"Oh, Sir Henry!" protested Miss Marple, a spot of colour coming into her cheeks. "I'm sure I never said anything of the kind. The only thing I ever said was that human nature is much the same in a village as anywhere else, only one has opportunities and leisure for seeing it at closer quarters."

"But *you* haven't always lived here," said Jane Helier, still addressing the doctor. "You've been in all sorts of queer places all over the world—places where things *happen!*"

"That is so, of course," said Dr. Lloyd, still thinking desperately. "Yes, of course . . . Yes . . . Ah! I have it!"

He sank back with a sigh of relief.

"It is some years ago now—I had almost forgotten. But the facts were really very strange—very strange indeed. And the final coincidence which put the clue into my hand was strange also."

Miss Helier drew her chair a little nearer to him, applied some lipstick and waited expectantly. The others also turned interested faces towards him.

"I don't know whether any of you know the Canary Islands," began the doctor.

"They must be wonderful," said Jane Helier. "They're in the South Seas, aren't they? Or is it the Mediterranean?"

"I've called in there on my way to South Africa," said the Colonel. "The Peak of Teneriffe is a fine sight with the setting sun on it."

"The incident I am describing happened in the island of Grand Canary, not Teneriffe. It is a good many years ago now. I had had a breakdown in health and was forced to give up my practice in England to go abroad. I practiced in Las Palmas, which is the principal town of Grand Canary. In many ways I enjoyed the life out there very much. The climate was mild and sunny, there was excellent surf bathing (and I am an enthusiastic bather) and the sea life of the port attracted me. Ships from all over the world put in at Las Palmas. I used to walk along the mole every morning far more interested than any member of the fair sex could be in a street of hat shops.

"As I say, ships from all over the world put in at Las Palmas. Sometimes they stay a few hours, sometimes a day or two. In the principal hotel there, the Metropole, you will see people of all races and nationalities—birds of passage. Even the people going to Teneriffe usually come here and stay a few days before crossing to the other island.

"My story begins there, in the Metropole Hotel, one Thursday evening in January. There was a dance going on and I and a friend had been sitting at a small table watching the scene. There were a fair sprinkling of English and other nationalities, but the majority of the dancers were Spanish; and when the orchestra struck up a tango, only half a dozen couples of the latter nationality took the floor. They all danced well and we looked on and admired. One woman in particular excited our lively admiration. Tall, beautiful and sinuous, she moved with the grace of a half-tamed leopardess. There was something dangerous about her. I said as much to my friend and he agreed.

" 'Women like that,' he said, 'are bound to have a history. Life will not pass them by.'

" 'Beauty is perhaps a dangerous possession,' I said.

" 'It's not only beauty,' he insisted. 'There is something else. Look at her again. Things are bound to happen to that woman, or because of her. As I said, life will not pass her by. Strange and exciting events will surround her. You've only got to look at her to know it.'

"He paused and then added with a smile:

" 'Just as you've only got to look at those two women over there, and know that nothing out of the way could ever happen to either of them! They are made for a safe and uneventful existence.'

"I followed his eyes. The two women he referred to were travellers who had just arrived—a Holland Lloyd boat had put into port that evening, and the passengers were just beginning to arrive.

"As I looked at them I saw at once what my friend meant. They were two English ladies—the thoroughly nice travelling English that you do find abroad. Their ages, I should say, were round about forty. One was fair and a little—just a little—too plump; the other was dark and a little—again just a little—inclined to scragginess. They were what is called well-preserved, quietly and inconspicuously dressed in well-cut tweeds, and innocent of any kind of make-up. They had that air of quiet assurance which is the birthright of well-bred Englishwomen. There was nothing remarkable about either of them. They were like thousands of their sisters. They would doubtless see what they wished to see, assisted by Baedeker, and be blind to everything else. They would use the English library and attend the English church in any place they happened to be, and it was quite likely that one or both of them sketched a little. And as my friend said, nothing exciting or remarkable would ever happen to either of them, though they might quite likely travel half over the world. I looked from them back to our sinuous Spanish woman with her half-closed smouldering eyes and I smiled."

"Poor things," said Jane Helier with a sigh. "But I do think it's so silly of people not to make the most of themselves. That woman in Bond Street—Valentine—is really wonderful. Audrey Denman goes to her and have you seen her in 'The Downward Step'? As the school-girl in the first act she's really marvellous. And yet Audrey is fifty if she's a day. As a matter of fact I happen to know she's really nearer sixty."

"Go on," said Mrs. Bantry to Dr. Lloyd. "I love stories about sinuous Spanish dancers. It makes me forget how old and fat I am."

"I'm sorry," said Dr. Lloyd apologetically. "But you

97

see, as a matter of fact, this story isn't about the Spanish woman."

"It isn't?"

"No. As it happens my friend and I were wrong. Nothing in the least exciting happened to the Spanish beauty. She married a clerk in a shipping office, and by the time I left the island she had had five children and was getting very fat."

"Just like that girl of Israel Peters," commented Miss Marple. "The one who went on the stage and had such good legs that they made her principal boy in the pantomime. Everyone said she'd come to no good, but she married a commercial traveller and settled down splendidly."

"The village parallel," murmured Sir Henry softly.

"No," went on the doctor. "My story is about the two English ladies."

"Something happened to them?" breathed Miss Helier.

"Something happened to them—and the very next day, too."

"Yes?" said Mrs. Bantry encouragingly.

"Just for curiosity, as I went out that evening, I glanced at the hotel register. I found the names easily enough. Miss Mary Barton and Miss Amy Durrant of Little Paddocks, Caughton Weir, Bucks. I little thought then how soon I was to encounter the owners of those names again—and under what tragic circumstances.

"The following day I had arranged to go for a picnic with some friends. We were to motor across the island, taking our lunch, to a place called (as far as I remember—it is so long ago) Las Nieves, a well-sheltered bay where we could bathe if we felt inclined. This programme we duly carried out, except that we were somewhat late in starting, so that we stopped on the way and picnicked, going on to Las Nieves afterwards for a bathe before tea.

"As we approached the beach, we were at once aware of a tremendous commotion. The whole population of the small village seemed to be gathered on the shore. As soon as they saw us they rushed towards the car and began explaining excitedly. My Spanish not being very good, it took me a few minutes to understand, but at last I got it.

"Two of the mad English ladies had gone in to bathe, and one had swum out too far and got into difficulties. The other had gone after her and had tried to bring her in, but her strength in turn had failed and she too would have drowned had not a man rowed out in a boat and brought in rescuer and rescued—the latter beyond help.

"As soon as I got the hang of things I pushed the crowd aside and hurried down the beach. I did not at first recognise the two women. The plump figure in the black stockinette costume and the tight green rubber bathing cap awoke no chord of recognition as she looked up anxiously. She was kneeling beside the body of her friend, making somewhat amateurish attempts at artificial respiration. When I told her that I was a doctor she gave a sigh of relief, and I ordered her off at once to one of the cottages for a rub down and dry clothing. One of the ladies in my party went with her. I myself worked unavailingly on the body of the drowned woman in vain. Life was only too clearly extinct, and in the end I had reluctantly to give in.

"I rejoined the others in the small fisherman's cottage and there I had to break the sad news. The survivor was attired now in her own clothes, and I immediately recognised her as one of the two arrivals of the night before. She received the sad news fairly calmly, and it was evidently the horror of the whole thing that struck her more than any great personal feeling.

" 'Poor Amy,' she said. 'Poor, poor Amy. She had been looking forward to the bathing here so much. And she was a good swimmer too. I can't understand it. What do you think it can have been, doctor?'

" 'Possibly cramp. Will you tell me exactly what happened?'

" 'We had both been swimming about for some time—twenty minutes, I should say. Then I thought I would go in, but Amy said she was going to swim out once more. She did so, and suddenly I heard her call and realised she was crying for help. I swam out as fast as I could. She was still afloat when I got to her, but she clutched at me wildly and we both went under. If it hadn't been for that man coming out with his boat I should have been drowned too.'

" 'That has happened fairly often,' I said. 'To save anyone from drowning is not an easy affair.'

" 'It seems so awful,' continued Miss Barton. 'We only arrived yesterday, and were so delighting in the sunshine and our little holiday. And now this—this terrible tragedy occurs.'

"I asked her then for particulars about the dead woman, explaining that I would do everything I could for her, but that the Spanish authorities would require full information. This she gave me readily enough.

"The dead woman, Miss Amy Durrant, was her companion and had come to her about five months previously. They had got on very well together, but Miss Durrant had spoken very little about her people. She had been left an orphan at an early age and had been brought up by an uncle and had earned her own living since she was twenty-one.

"And so that was that," went on the doctor. He paused and said again, but this time with a certain finality in his voice, "And so that was that."

"I don't understand," said Jane Helier. "Is that all? I mean, it's very tragic, I suppose, but it isn't—well, it isn't what I call *creepy*."

"I think there's more to follow," said Sir Henry.

"Yes," said Dr. Lloyd, "there's more to follow. You see, right at the time there was one queer thing. Of course I asked questions of the fishermen, etc., as to what they'd seen. They were eye-witnesses. And one woman had rather a funny story. I didn't pay any attention to it at the time, but it came back to me afterwards. She insisted, you see, that Miss Durrant wasn't in difficulties when she called out. The other swam out to her and, according to this woman, deliberately held Miss Durrant's head under water. I didn't, as I say, pay much attention. It was such a fantastic story, and these things look so differently from the shore. Miss Barton might have tried to make her friend

100

lose consciousness, realising that the latter's panic-stricken clutching would drown them both. You see, according to the Spanish woman's story, it looked as though—well, as though Miss Barton was deliberately trying to drown her companion.

"As I say, I paid very little attention to this story at the time. It came back to me later. Our great difficulty was to find out anything about this woman, Amy Durrant. She didn't seem to have any relations. Miss Barton and I went through her things together. We found one address and wrote there, but it proved to be simply a room she had taken in which to keep some of her things. The landlady knew nothing, had only seen her when she took the room. Miss Durrant had remarked at the time that she always liked to have one place she could call her own to which she could return at any moment. There were one or two nice pieces of old furniture and some bound numbers of Academy pictures, and a trunk full of pieces of material bought at sales, but no personal belongings. She had mentioned to the landlady that her father and mother had died in India when she was a child and that she had been brought up by an uncle who was a clergyman, but she did not say if he was her father's or her mother's brother, so the name was no guide.

"It wasn't exactly mysterious, it was just unsatisfactory. There must be many lonely women, proud and reticent, in just that position. There were a couple of photographs amongst her belongings in Las Palmas—rather old and faded and they had been cut to fit the frames they were in, so that there was no photographer's name upon them, and there was an old daguerreotype which might have been her mother or more probably her grandmother.

"Miss Barton had had two references with her. One she had forgotten, the other name she recollected after an effort. It proved to be that of a lady who was now abroad, having gone to Australia. She was written to. Her answer, of course, was a long time in coming, and I may say that when it did arrive there was no particular help to be gained from it. She said Miss Durrant had been with her as companion and had been most efficient and that she was a very charming woman, but that she knew nothing of her private affairs or relations.

"So there it was—as I say, nothing unusual, really. It was just the two things together that aroused my uneasiness. This Amy Durrant of whom no one knew anything, and the Spanish woman's queer story. Yes, and I'll add a third thing: When I was first bending over the body and Miss Barton was walking away towards the huts, she looked back. Looked back with an expression on her face that I can only describe as one of poignant anxiety—a kind of anguished uncertainty that imprinted itself on my brain.

"It didn't strike me as anything unusual at the time. I put it down to her terrible distress over her friend. But, you see, later I realised that they weren't on those terms. There was no devoted attachment between them, no terrible grief. Miss Barton was fond of Amy Durrant and shocked by her death—that was all.

"But, then, why that terrible poignant anxiety? That was the question that kept coming back to me. I had not been mistaken in that look. And almost against my will, an answer began to shape itself in my mind. Supposing the Spanish woman's story were true; supposing that Mary Barton willfully and in cold blood tried to drown Amy Durrant. She succeeds in holding her under water whilst pretending to be saving her. She is rescued by a boat. They are on a lonely beach far from anywhere. And then I appear—the last thing she expects. A doctor! And an English doctor! She knows well enough that people who have been under water far longer than Amy Durrant have been revived by artificial respiration. But she has to play her part—to go off leaving me alone with her victim. And as she turns for one last look, a terrible poignant anxiety shows in her face. Will Amy Durrant come back to life *and tell what she knows?*"

"Oh!" said Jane Helier. "I'm thrilled now."

"Viewed in that aspect the whole business seemed more sinister, and the personality of Amy Durrant became more mysterious. Who was Amy Durrant? Why should she, an insignificant paid companion, be murdered by her employer? What story lay behind that fatal bathing expedition? She had entered Mary Barton's employment only a few months before. Mary Barton had brought her abroad, and the very day after they landed the tragedy had occurred. And they were both nice commonplace refined Englishwomen! The whole thing was fantastic, and I told myself so. I had been letting my imagination run away with me."

"You didn't do anything, then?" asked Miss Helier.

"My dear young lady, what could I do? There was no evidence. The majority of the eye-witnesses told the same story as Miss Barton. I had built up my own suspicions out of a fleeting expression which I might quite possibly have imagined. The only thing I could and did do was to see that the widest inquiries were made for the relations of Amy Durrant. The next time I was in England I even went and saw the landlady of her room, with the results I have told you."

"But you felt there was something wrong," said Miss Marple.

Dr. Lloyd nodded.

"Half the time I was ashamed of myself for thinking so. Who was I to go suspecting this nice, pleasant-mannered English lady of a foul and cold-blooded crime? I did my best to be as cordial as possible to her during the short time she stayed on the island. I helped her with the Spanish authorities. I did everything I could do as an Englishman to help a compatriot in a foreign country; and yet I am convinced that she knew I suspected and disliked her."

"How long did she stay out here?" asked Miss Marple.

"I think it was about a fortnight. Miss Durrant was buried there, and it must have been about ten days later when she took a boat back to England. The shock had upset her so much that she felt she couldn't spend the winter there as she had planned. That's what she said."

"Did it seem to have upset her?" asked Miss Marple.

The doctor hesitated.

"Well, I don't know that it affected her appearance at all," he said cautiously.

"She didn't, for instance, grow fatter?" asked Miss Marple.

"Do you know—it's a curious thing your saying that. Now I come to think back, I believe you're right. She—yes, she did seem, if anything, to be putting on weight."

"How horrible," said Jane Helier with a shudder. "It's like—it's like fattening on your victim's blood."

"And yet, in another way, I may be doing her an injustice," went on Dr. Lloyd. "She certainly said something before she left, which pointed in an entirely different direction. There may be, I think there are, consciences which work very slowly—which take some time to awaken to the enormity of the deed committed.

"It was the evening before her departure from the Canaries. She had asked me to go and see her, and had thanked me very warmly for all I had done to help her. I, of course, made light of the matter, said I had only done what was natural under the circumstances, and so on. There was a pause after that, and then she suddenly asked me a question.

" 'Do you think,' she asked, 'that one is ever justified in taking the law into one's own hands?'

"I replied that that was rather a difficult question, but that on the whole, I thought not. The law was the law, and we had to abide by it.

" 'Even when it is powerless?'

" 'I don't quite understand.'

" 'It's difficult to explain; but one might do something that is considered definitely wrong—that is considered a crime, even, for a very good and sufficient reason.'

"I replied dryly that possibly several criminals had thought that in their time, and she shrank back.

" 'But that's horrible,' she murmured. 'Horrible.'

"And then with a change of tone she asked me to give her something to make her sleep. She had not been able to sleep properly since—she hesitated—since that terrible shock.

" 'You're sure it is that? There is nothing worrying you? Nothing on your mind?'

" 'On my mind? What should be on my mind?'

"She spoke fiercely and suspiciously

" 'Worry is a cause of sleeplessness sometimes,' I said lightly.

"She seemed to brood for a moment.

" 'Do you mean worrying over the future, or worrying over the past, which can't be altered?'

" 'Either.'

" 'Only it wouldn't be any good worrying over the past. You couldn't bring back—Oh! what's the use! One mustn't think. One must not think.'

"I prescribed her a mild sleeping draught and made my adieu. As I went away I wondered not a little over the words she had spoken. 'You couldn't bring back——' What? Or *who*?

"I think that last interview prepared me in a way for what was to come. I didn't expect it, of course, but when it happened, I wasn't surprised. Because, you see, Mary Barton struck me all along as a conscientious woman—not a weak sinner, but a woman with convictions, who would act up to them, and who would not relent as long as she still believed in them. I fancied that in that last conversation we had she was beginning to doubt her own convictions. I know her words suggested to me that she was feeling the first faint beginnings of that terrible soul-searcher—remorse.

"The thing happened in Cornwall, in a small watering-place, rather deserted at that season of the year. It must have been—let me see—late March. I read about it in the papers. A lady had been staying at a small hotel there—a Miss Barton. She had been very odd and peculiar in her manner. That had been noticed by all. At night she would walk up and down her room, muttering to herself, and not allowing the people on either side of her to sleep. She had called on the vicar one day and had told him that she had a communication of the gravest importance to make to him. She had, she said, committed a crime. Then, instead of proceeding, she had stood up abruptly and said she would

105

call another day. The vicar put her down as being slightly unbalanced, and did not take her self-accusation seriously.

"The very next morning she was found to be missing from her room. A note was left addressed to the coroner. It ran as follows:

> *"I tried to speak to the vicar yesterday, to confess all, but was not allowed. She would not let me. I can make amends only one way—a life for a life; and my life must go the same way as hers did. I, too, must drown in the deep sea. I believed I was justified. I see now that that was not so. If I desire Amy's forgiveness I must go to her. Let no one be blamed for my death—Mary Barton.*

"Her clothes were found lying on the beach in a secluded cove near by, and it seemed clear that she had undressed there and swum resolutely out to sea where the current was known to be dangerous, sweeping one down the coast.

"The body was not discovered, but after a time leave was given to presume death. She was a rich woman, her estate being proved at a hundred thousand pounds. Since she died intestate it all went to her next of kin—a family of cousins in Australia. The papers made discreet references to the tragedy in the Canary Islands, putting forward the theory that the death of Miss Durrant had unhinged her friend's brain. At the inquest the usual verdict of *Suicide whilst temporarily insane* was returned.

"And so the curtain falls on the tragedy of Amy Durrant and Mary Barton."

There was a long pause and then Jane Helier gave a great gasp.

"Oh, but you mustn't stop there—just in the most interesting part. Go on."

"But you see, Miss Helier, this isn't a serial story. This is real life; and real life stops just where it chooses."

"But I don't want it to," said Jane. "I want to know."

"This is where we use our brains, Miss Helier," explained Sir Henry. "Why did Mary Barton kill her companion? That's the problem Dr. Lloyd has set us."

"Oh, well," said Miss Helier, "she might have killed her for lots of reasons. I mean—oh, I don't know. She might have got on her nerves, or else she got jealous, although Dr. Lloyd doesn't mention any men, but still on the boat out—well, you know what everyone says about boats and sea voyages."

Miss Helier paused, slightly out of breath, and it was borne in upon her audience that the outside of Jane's charming head was distinctly superior to the inside.

"I would like to have a lot of guesses," said Mrs. Bantry. "But I suppose I must confine myself to one. Well, I think that Miss Barton's father made all his money out of ruining Amy Durrant's father, so Amy determined to have her revenge. Oh, no, that's the wrong way round. How tiresome! Why does the rich employer kill the humble companion? I've got it. Miss Barton had a young brother who shot himself for love of Amy Durrant. Miss Barton waits her time. Amy comes down in the world. Miss B. engages her as companion and takes her to the Canaries and accomplishes her revenge. How's that?"

"Excellent," said Sir Henry. "Only we don't know that Miss Barton ever had a young brother."

"We deduce that," said Mrs. Bantry. "Unless she had a young brother there's no motive. So she must have had a young brother. Do you see, Watson?"

"That's all very fine, Dolly," said her husband. "But it's only a guess."

"Of course it is," said Mrs. Bantry. "That's all we can do—guess. We haven't got any clues. Go on, dear, have a guess yourself."

"Upon my word, I don't know what to say. But I think there's something in Miss Helier's suggestion that they fell out about a man. Look here, Dolly, it was probably some high church parson. They both embroidered him a cope or something, and he wore the Durrant woman's first. Depend upon it, it was something like that. Look how she went off to a parson at the end. These women all lose their heads over a good-looking clergyman. You hear of it over and over again."

"I think I must try and make my explanation a little more subtle," said Sir Henry, "though I admit it's only a guess. I suggest that Miss Barton was always mentally unhinged. There are more cases like that than you would imagine. Her mania grew stronger and she began to believe it her duty to rid the world of certain persons—possibly what is termed unfortunate females. Nothing much is known about Miss Durrant's past. So very possibly she *had* a past—an 'unfortunate' one. Miss Barton learns of this and decides on extermination. Later, the righteousness of her act begins to trouble her and she is overcome by remorse. Her end shows her to be completely unhinged. Now, do say you agree with me, Miss Marple."

"I'm afraid I don't, Sir Henry," said Miss Marple, smiling apologetically. "I think her end shows her to have been a very clever and resourceful woman."

Jane Helier interrupted with a little scream.

"Oh! I've been so stupid. May I guess again? Of course it must have been that. Blackmail! The companion woman was blackmailing her. Only I don't see why Miss Marple says it was clever of her to kill herself. I can't see that at all."

"Ah!" said Sir Henry. "You see, Miss Marple knew a case just like it in St. Mary Mead."

"You always laugh at me, Sir Henry," said Miss Marple reproachfully. "I must confess it does remind me, just a little, of old Mrs. Trout. She drew the old age pension, you know, for three old women who were dead, in different parishes."

"It sounds like a most complicated and resourceful crime," said Sir Henry. "But it doesn't seem to me to throw any light upon our present problem."

"Of course not," said Miss Marple. "It wouldn't—to you. But some of the families were very poor, and the old age pension was a great boon to the children. I know it's difficult for anyone outside to understand. But what I really meant was that the whole thing hinged upon one old woman being so like any other old woman."

"Eh?" said Sir Henry, mystified.

"I always explain things so badly. What I mean is that when Dr. Lloyd described the two ladies first, he didn't know which was which, and I don't suppose anyone else in the hotel did. They would have, of course, after a day or so, but the very next day one of the two was drowned, and if the one who was left said she was Miss Barton, I don't suppose it would ever occur to anyone that she mightn't be."

"You think—Oh! I see," said Sir Henry slowly.

"It's the only natural way of thinking of it. Dear Mrs. Bantry began that way just now. Why *should* the rich employer kill the humble companion? It's so much more likely to be the other way about. I mean—that's the way things happen."

"Is it?" said Sir Henry. "You shock me."

"But of course," went on Miss Marple, "she would have to wear Miss Barton's clothes, and they would probably be a little tight on her, so that her general appearance would look as though she had got a little fatter. That's why I asked that question. A gentleman would be sure to think it was the lady who had got fatter, and not the clothes that had got smaller—though that isn't quite the right way of putting it."

"But if Amy Durrant killed Miss Barton, what did she gain by it?" asked Mrs. Bantry. "She couldn't keep up the deception for ever."

"She only kept it up for another month or so," pointed out Miss Marple. "And during that time I expect she travelled, keeping away from anyone who might know her. That's what I meant by saying that one lady of a certain age looks so like another. I don't suppose the different photograph on her passport was ever noticed—you know what passports are. And then in March she went down to this Cornish place and began to act queerly and draw attention to herself so that when people found her clothes on the beach and read her last letter they shouldn't think of the common-sense conclusion."

"Which was?" asked Sir Henry.

"*No body*," said Miss Marple firmly. "That's the thing that would stare you in the face, if there weren't such a lot of red herrings to draw you off the trail—including the suggestion of foul play and remorse. *No body*. That was the real significant fact."

"Do you mean—" said Mrs. Bantry, "do you mean that there wasn't any remorse? That there wasn't—that she didn't drown herself?"

"Not she!" said Miss Marple. "It's just Mrs. Trout over again. Mrs. Trout was very good at red herrings, but she met her match in me. And I can see through your remorse-driven Miss Barton. Drown herself? Went off to Australia, if I'm any good at guessing."

"You are, Miss Marple," said Dr. Lloyd. "Undoubtedly you are. Now it again took me quite by surprise. Why, you could have knocked me down with a feather that day in Melbourne."

"Was that what you spoke of as a final coincidence?"

Dr. Lloyd nodded.

"Yes, it was rather rough luck on Miss Barton—or Miss Amy Durrant—whatever you like to call her. I became a ship's doctor for a while, and landing in Melbourne, the first person I saw as I walked down the street was the lady I thought had been drowned in Cornwall. She saw the game was up as far as I was concerned, and she did the bold thing—took me into her confidence. A curious woman, completely lacking, I suppose, in some moral sense. She was the eldest of a family of nine, all wretchedly poor. They had applied once for help to their rich cousin in England and been repulsed, Miss Barton having quarrelled with their father. Money was wanted desperately, for the three youngest children were delicate and wanted expensive medical treatment. Amy Barton then and there seems to have decided on her plan of cold-blooded murder. She set out for England, working her passage over as a children's nurse. She obtained the situation of companion to Miss Barton, calling herself Amy Durrant. She engaged a room and put some furniture into it so as to create more of a personality for herself. The drowning plan was a sudden inspiration. She had been waiting for some opportunity to present itself. Then she staged the final scene of the drama and returned to Australia, and in due time she and her brothers and sisters inherited Miss Barton's money as next of kin."

"A very bold and perfect crime," said Sir Henry. "Almost *the* perfect crime. If it had been Miss Barton who had died in the Canaries, suspicion might attach to Amy Durrant and her connection with the Barton family might have been discovered; but the change of identity and the double crime, as you may call it, effectually did away with that. Yes, almost the perfect crime."

"What happened to her?" asked Mrs. Bantry. "What did you do in the matter, Dr. Lloyd?"

"I was in a very curious position, Mrs. Bantry. Of evidence, as the law understands it, I still had very little. Also, there were certain signs, plain to me as a medical man, that though strong and vigorous in appearance, the lady was not long for this world. I went home with her and saw the rest of the family—a charming family, devoted to their eldest sister and without an idea in their heads that she might prove to have committed a crime. Why bring sorrow on them when I could prove nothing. The lady's admission to me was unheard by anyone else. I let Nature take its course. Miss Amy Barton died six months after my meeting with her. I have often wondered if she was cheerful and unrepentant up to the last."

"Surely not," said Mrs. Bantry.

"I expect so," said Miss Marple. "Mrs. Trout was."

Jane Helier gave herself a little shake.

"Well," she said. "It's very, very thrilling. I don't quite understand now who drowned which. And how does this Mrs. Trout come into it?"

"She doesn't, my dear," said Miss Marple. "She was only a person—not a very nice person—in the village."

"Oh!" said Jane. "In the village. But nothing ever happens in a village, does it?" She sighed. "I'm sure I shouldn't have any brains at all if I lived in a village."

# CHAPTER IX

# THE FOUR SUSPECTS

THE conversation hovered round undiscovered and unpunished crimes. Everyone in turn vouchsafed their opinion: Colonel Bantry, his plump amiable wife, Jane Helier, Dr. Lloyd, and even old Miss Marple. The one person who did not speak was the one best fitted in most people's opinion to do so. Sir Henry Clithering, ex-Commissioner of Scotland Yard, sat silent, twisting his moustache—or rather stroking it—and half smiling, as though at some inward thought that amused him.

"Sir Henry," said Mrs. Bantry at last. "If you don't say something I shall scream. Are there a lot of crimes that go unpunished, or are there not?"

"You're thinking of newspaper headlines, Mrs. Bantry. SCOTLAND YARD AT FAULT AGAIN. And a list of unsolved mysteries to follow."

"Which really, I suppose, form a very small percentage of the whole?" said Dr. Lloyd.

"Yes; that is so. The hundreds of crimes that are solved and the perpetrators punished are seldom heralded and sung. But that isn't quite the point at issue, is it? When you talk of *undiscovered* crimes and *unsolved* crimes, you are talking of two different things. In the first category come all the crimes that Scotland Yard never hears about, the crimes that no one even knows have been committed."

"But I suppose there aren't very many of those?" said Mrs. Bantry.

113

"Aren't there?"

"Sir Henry! You don't mean there *are?*"

"I should think," said Miss Marple thoughtfully, "that there must be a very large number."

The charming old lady, with her old-world unruffled air, made her statement in a tone of the utmost placidity.

"My dear Miss Marple," said Colonel Bantry.

"Of course," said Miss Marple, "a lot of people are stupid. And stupid people get found out, whatever they do. But there are quite a number of people who aren't stupid, and one shudders to think of what they might accomplish unless they had very strongly rooted principles."

"Yes," said Sir Henry, "there are a lot of people who aren't stupid. How often does some crime come to light simply by reason of a bit of unmitigated bungling, and each time one asks oneself the question: If this hadn't been bungled, would anyone ever have known?"

"But that's very serious, Clithering," said Colonel Bantry. "Very serious, indeed."

"Is it?"

"What do you mean! Is it! Of course it's serious."

"You say crime goes unpunished; but does it? Unpunished by the law perhaps; but cause and effect work outside the law. To say that every crime brings its own punishment is by way of being a platitude, and yet in my opinion nothing can be truer."

"Perhaps, perhaps," said Colonel Bantry. "But that doesn't alter the seriousness—the—er—seriousness——" He paused, rather at a loss.

Sir Henry Clithering smiled.

"Ninety-nine people out of a hundred are doubtless of your way of thinking," he said. "But you know, it isn't really guilt that is important—it's innocence. That's the thing that nobody will realise."

"I don't understand," said Jane Helier.

"I do," said Miss Marple. "When Mrs. Trent found half a crown missing from her bag, the person it affected most was the daily woman, Mrs. Arthur. Of course the Trents thought it was her, but being kindly people and knowing she had a large family and a husband who drinks, well—they naturally didn't want to go to extremes. But they felt differently towards her, and they didn t leave her in charge of the house when they went away, which made a great difference to her; and other people began to get a feeling about her too. And then it suddenly came out that it was the governess. Mrs. Trent saw her through a door reflected in a mirror. The purest chance—though I prefer to call it Providence. And that, I think, is what Sir Henry means. Most people would be only interested in who took the money, and it turned out to be the most unlikely person— just like in detective stories! But the real person it was life and death to was poor Mrs. Arthur, who had done nothing. That's what you mean, isn't it, Sir Henry?"

"Yes, Miss Marple, you've hit off my meaning exactly. Your charwoman person was lucky in the instance you relate. Her innocence was shown. But some people may go through a lifetime crushed by the weight of a suspicion that is really unjustified."

"Are you thinking of some particular instance, Sir Henry?" asked Mrs. Bantry shrewdly.

"As a matter of fact, Mrs. Bantry, I am. A very curious case. A case where we believe murder to have been com- mitted, but with no possible chance of ever proving it."

"Poison, I suppose," breathed Jane. "Something un- traceable."

Dr. Lloyd moved restlessly and Sir Henry shook his head.

"No, dear lady. *Not* the secret arrow poison of the South American Indians! I wish it *were* something of that kind. We have to deal with something much more prosaic—so prosaic, in fact, that there is no hope of bringing the deed home to its perpetrator. An old gentleman who fell down- stairs and broke his neck; one of those regrettable acci- dents which happen every day."

"But what happened really?"

"Who can say?" Sir Henry shrugged his shoulders. "A push from behind? A piece of cotton or string tied across the top of the stairs and carefully removed afterwards? That we shall never know."

"But you do think that it—well, wasn't an accident? Now why?" asked the doctor.

"That's rather a long story, but—well, yes, we're pretty sure. As I said there's no chance of being able to bring the deed home to anyone—the evidence would be too flimsy. But there's the other aspect of the case—the one I was speaking about. You see, there were four people who might have done the trick. One's guilty; *but the other three are innocent.* And unless the truth is found out, those three are going to remain under the terrible shadow of doubt."

"I think," said Mrs. Bantry, "that you'd better tell us your long story."

"I needn't make it so very long after all," said Sir Henry. "I can at any rate condense the beginning. That deals with a German secret society—the *Schwartze Hand*—something after the lines of the Camorra or what is most people's idea of the Camorra. A scheme of blackmail and terrorisation. The thing started quite suddenly after the War, and spread to an amazing extent. Numberless people were victimised by it. The authorities were not successful in coping with it, for its secrets were jealously guarded, and it was almost impossible to find anyone who could be induced to betray them.

"Nothing much was ever known about it in England, but in Germany it was having a most paralysing effect. It was finally broken up and dispersed through the efforts of one man, a Dr. Rosen, who had at one time been very prominent in Secret Service work. He became a member, penetrated its inmost circle, and was, as I say, instrumental in bringing about its downfall.

"But he was, in consequence, a marked man, and it was deemed wise that he should leave Germany—at any rate for a time. He came to England, and we had letters about him from the police in Berlin. He came and had a personal interview with me. His point of view was both dispassionate and resigned. He had no doubts of what the future held for him.

" 'They will get me, Sir Henry,' he said. 'Not a doubt of it.' He was a big man with a fine head, and a very deep voice, with only a slight guttural intonation to tell of his nationality. 'That is a foregone conclusion. It does not matter. I am prepared. I faced the risk when I undertook this business. I have done what I set out to do. The organisation can never be gotten together again. But there are many members of it at liberty, and they will take the only revenge they can—my life. It is simply a question of time; but I am anxious that that time should be as long as possible. You see, I am collecting and editing some very interesting material—the result of my life's work. I should like, if possible, to be able to complete my task.'

"He spoke very simply, with a certain grandeur which I could not but admire. I told him we would take all precautions, but he waved my words aside.

" 'Some day, sooner or later, they will get me,' he repeated. 'When that day comes, do not distress yourself. You will, I have no doubt, have done all that is possible.'

"He then proceeded to outline his plans which were simple enough. He proposed to take a small cottage in the country where he could live quietly and go on with his work. In the end he selected a village in Somerset—King's Gnaton, which was seven miles from a railway station, and singularly untouched by civilisation. He bought a very charming cottage, had various improvements and alterations made, and settled down there most contentedly. His household consisted of his niece, Greta, a secretary, an old German servant who had served him faithfully for nearly forty years, and an outside handy-man and gardener who was a native of King's Gnaton."

"The four suspects," said Dr. Lloyd softly.

"Exactly. The four suspects. There is not much more to tell. Life went on peacefully at King's Gnaton for five months and then the blow fell. Dr. Rosen fell down the stairs one morning and was found dead about half an hour later. At the time the accident must have taken place, Gertrud was in her kitchen with the door closed and heard nothing—so *she* says. Fräulein Greta was in the garden

117

planting some bulbs—again, so *she* says. The gardener, Dobbs, was in the small potting-shed having his elevenses—so *he* says; and the secretary was out for a walk, and once more there is only his word for it. No one had an alibi—no one can corroborate anyone else's story. But one thing *is* certain. No one from outside could have done it, for a stranger in the little village of King's Gnaton would be noticed without fail. Both the back and the front doors were locked, each member of the household having their own key. So you see it narrows down to those four. And yet each one seems to be above suspicion. Greta, his own brother's child. Gertrud, with forty years of faithful service. Dobbs, who has never been out of King's Gnaton. And Charles Templeton, the secretary——"

"Yes," said Colonel Bantry, "what about him? He seems the suspicious person to my mind. What do you know about him?"

"It is what I knew about him that put him completely out of court—at any rate at the time," said Sir Henry gravely. "You see, Charles Templeton was one of my own men."

"Oh!" said Colonel Bantry, considerably taken aback.

"Yes. I wanted to have someone on the spot, and at the same time I didn't want to cause talk in the village. Rosen really needed a secretary. I put Templeton on the job. He's a gentleman, he speaks German fluently, and he's altogether a very able fellow."

"But, then, which do you suspect?" asked Mrs. Bantry in a bewildered tone. "They all seem so—well, impossible."

"Yes, so it appears. But you can look at the thing from another angle. Fräulein Greta was his niece and a very lovely girl, but the War has shown us time and again that brother can turn against sister, or father against son and so on, and the loveliest and gentlest of young girls did some of the most amazing things. The same thing applies to Gertrud, and who knows what other forces might be at work in her case. A quarrel, perhaps, with her master, a growing resentment all the more lasting because of the long faithful years behind her. Elderly women of that class can be amazingly bitter sometimes. And Dobbs? Was he right outside it because he had no connection with the family? Money will do much. In some way Dobbs might have been approached and bought.

"For one thing seems certain: Some message or some order must have come from outside. Otherwise why five months' immunity? No, the agents of the society must have been at work. Not yet sure of Rosen's perfidy, they delayed till the betrayal had been traced to him beyond any possible doubt. And then, all doubts set aside, they must have sent their message to the spy within the gates— the message that said, 'Kill.' "

"How nasty!" said Jane Helier, and shuddered.

"But how did the message come? That was the point I tried to elucidate—the one hope of solving my problem. One of those four people must have been approached or communicated with in some way. There would be no delay—I knew that—as soon as the command came, it would be carried out. That was a peculiarity of the *Schwartze Hand.*

"I went into the question, went into it in a way that will probably strike you as being ridiculously meticulous. Who had come to the cottage that morning? I eliminated nobody. Here is the list."

He took an envelope from his pocket and selected a paper from its contents.

"*The butcher,* bringing some neck of mutton. Investigated and found correct.

"*The grocer's assistant,* bringing a packet of corn flour, two pounds of sugar, a pound of butter, and a pound of coffee. Also investigated and found correct.

"*The postman,* bringing two circulars for Fräulein Rosen, a local letter for Gertrud, three letters for Dr. Rosen, one with a foreign stamp, and two letters for Mr. Templeton, one also with a foreign stamp."

Sir Henry paused and then took a sheaf of documents from the envelope.

"It may interest you to see these for yourself. They were handed me by the various people concerned, or collected from the wastepaper basket. I need hardly say they've been tested by experts for invisible ink, etc. No excitement of that kind is possible."

Everyone crowded round to look. The catalogues were respectively from a nurseryman and from a prominent London fur establishment. The two bills addressed to Dr. Rosen were a local one for seeds for the garden and one from a London stationery firm. The latter addressed to him ran as follows:

"MY DEAR ROSEN—Just back from Dr. Helmuth Spath's I saw Edgar Jackson the other day. He and Amos Perry have just come back from Tsingtau. In all Honesty I can't say I envy them the trip. Let me have news of you soon. As I said before: Beware of a certain person. You know who I mean, though you don't agree.—Yours,

"GEORGINA."

"Mr. Templeton's mail consisted of this bill, which as you see, is an account rendered from his tailor, and a letter from a friend in Germany," went on Sir Henry. The latter, unfortunately, he tore up whilst out on his walk. Finally we have the letter received by Gertrud."

DEAR MRS. SWARTZ,—We're hoping as how you be able to come the social on friday evening. the vicar says has he hopes you will—one and all being welcome. The resipy for the ham was very good, and I thanks you for it. Hoping as this finds you well and that we shall see you friday i remain

"Yours faithfully,
"EMMA GREENE."

Dr. Lloyd smiled a little over this and so did Mrs. Bantry.

"I think the last letter can be put out of court," said Dr. Lloyd.

"I thought the same," said Sir Henry; "but I took the

precaution of verifying that there was a Mrs. Greene and a Church Social. One can't be too careful you know."

"That's what our friend Miss Marple always says," said Dr. Lloyd, smiling. "You're lost in a day-dream, Miss Marple. What are you thinking out?"

Miss Marple gave a start.

"So stupid of me," she said. "I was just wondering why the word Honesty in Dr. Rosen's letter was spelt with a capital H."

Mrs. Bantry picked it up.

"So it is," she said. "*Oh!*"

"Yes, dear," said Miss Marple. "I thought you'd notice!"

"There's a definite warning in that letter," said Colonel Bantry. "That's the first thing caught my attention. I notice more than you'd think. Yes, a definite warning—against whom?"

"There's rather a curious point about that letter," said Sir Henry. "According to Templeton, Dr. Rosen opened the letter at breakfast and tossed it across to him saying he didn't know who the fellow was from Adam."

"But it wasn't a fellow," said Jane Helier. "It was signed 'Georgina.' "

"It's difficult to say which it is," said Dr. Lloyd. "It might be Georgey; but it certainly looks more like Georgina. Only it strikes me that the writing is a man's."

"You know, that's interesting," said Colonel Bantry. "His tossing it across the table like that and pretending he knew nothing about it. Wanted to watch somebody's face. Whose face—the girl's? or the man's?"

"Or even the cook's?" suggested Mrs. Bantry. "She might have been in the room bringing in the breakfast. But what I don't see is . . . it's most peculiar——"

She frowned over the letter. Miss Marple drew closer to her. Miss Marple's finger went out and touched the sheet of paper. They murmured together.

"But why did the secretary tear up the other letter?" asked Jane Helier suddenly. "It seems—oh I don't know—it seems queer. Why should he have letters from Germany? Although, of course, if he's above suspicion, as you say——"

"But Sir Henry didn't say that," said Miss Marple, quickly looking up from her murmured conference with Mrs. Bantry. "He said *four* suspects. So that shows that he includes Mr. Templeton. I'm right, am I not, Sir Henry?"

"Yes, Miss Marple. I have learned one thing through bitter experience. Never say to yourself that *anyone* is above suspicion. I gave you reasons just now why three of these people might after all be guilty, unlikely as it seemed. I did not at that time apply the same process to Charles Templeton. But I came to it at last through pursuing the rule I have just mentioned. And I was forced to recognise this: That every army and every navy and every police force has a certain number of traitors within its ranks, much as we hate to admit the idea. And I examined dispassionately the case against Charles Templeton.

"I asked myself very much the same questions as Miss Helier has just asked. Why should he, alone of all the house, not be able to produce the letter he had received—a letter, moreover, with a German stamp on it. Why should he have letters from Germany?

"The last question was an innocent one, and I actually put it to him. His reply came simply enough. His mother's sister was married to a German. The letter had been from a German girl cousin. So I learned something I did not know before—that Charles Templeton had relations with people in Germany. And that put him definitely on the list of suspects—very much so. He is my own man—a lad I have always liked and trusted; but in common justice and fairness I must admit that he heads that list.

"But there it is—I do not know! I do not *know*. . . . And in all probability I never shall know. It is not a question of punishing a murderer. It is a question that to me seems a hundred times more important. It is the blighting, perhaps, of an honourable man's whole career . . . because of suspicion—a suspicion that I dare not disregard."

Miss Marple coughed and said gently:

"Then, Sir Henry, if I understand you rightly, it is this young Mr. Templeton only who is so much on your mind?"

"Yes, in a sense. It should, in theory, be the same for

all four, but that is not actually the case. Dobbs, for instance—suspicion may attach to him in my mind, but it will not actually affect his career. Nobody in the village has ever had any idea that old Dr. Rosen's death was anything but an accident. Gertrud is slightly more affected. It must make, for instance, a difference in Fräulein Rosen's attitude toward her. But that possibly is not of great importance to her.

"As for Greta Rosen—well, here we come to the crux of the matter. Greta is a very pretty girl and Charles Templeton is a good-looking young man, and for five months they were thrown together with no oueer distractions. The inevitable happened. They fell in love with each other—even if they did not come to the point of admitting the fact in words.

"And then the catastrophe happens. It is three months ago now and a day or two after I returned, Greta Rosen came to see me. She had sold the cottage and was returning to Germany, having finally settled up her uncle's affairs. She came to me personally, although she knew I had retired, because it was really about a personal matter she wanted to see me. She beat about the bush a little, but at last it all came out. What did I think? That letter with the German stamp—she had worried about it and worried about it—the one Charles had torn up. Was it all right? Surely it *must* be all right. Of course she believed his story, but—oh! if she only *knew!* If she knew—for certain.

"You see? The same feeling: the wish to trust—but the horrible lurking suspicion, thrust resolutely to the back of the mind, but persisting nevertheless. I spoke to her with absolute frankness, and asked her to do the same. I asked her whether she had been on the point of caring for Charles, and he for her.

" 'I think so,' she said. 'Oh, yes, I know it was so. We were so happy. Every day passed so contentedly. We knew—we both knew. There was no hurry—there was all the time in the world. Some day he would tell me he loved me, and I should tell him that I too—Ah! But you can guess! And now it is all changed. A black cloud has come between us—we are constrained, when we meet we do not know what to say. It is, perhaps, the same with him as with me. . . . We are each saying to ourselves, "If I were *sure!*" That is why, Sir Henry, I beg of you to say to me, "You may be sure, whoever killed your uncle, it was not Charles Templeton!" Say it to me! Oh, say it to me! I beg—I beg!'

"And, damn it all," cried Sir Henry, bringing down his fist with a bang on the table, "I couldn't say it to her. They'll drift farther and farther apart, those two—with suspicion like a ghost between them—a ghost that can't be laid."

He leant back in his chair, his face looked tired and grey. He shook his head once or twice despondently.

"And there's nothing more can be done, unless—" He sat up straight again and a tiny whimsical smile crossed his face—"unless Miss Marple can help us. Can't you, Miss Marple? I've a feeling that letter might be in your line, you know. The one about the Church Social. Doesn't it remind you of something or someone that makes everything perfectly plain? Can't you do something to help two helpless young people who want to be happy?"

Behind the whimsicality there was something earnest in his appeal. He had come to think very highly of the mental powers of this frail old-fashioned maiden lady. He looked across at her with something very like hope in his eyes.

Miss Marple coughed and smoothed her lace.

"It does remind me a little of Annie Poultny," she admitted. "Of course the letter is perfectly plain—both to Mrs. Bantry and myself. I don't mean the Church Social letter, but the other one. You living so much in London and not being a gardener, Sir Henry, would not have been likely to notice."

"Eh?" said Sir Henry. "Notice what?"

Mrs. Bantry reached out a hand and selected a catalogue. She opened it and read aloud with gusto:

"Dr. Helmuth Spath. Pure lilac, a wonderfully fine flower, carried on exceptionally long and stiff stem. Splendid for cutting and garden decoration. A novelty of striking beauty.

"Edgar Jackson. Beautifully shaped chrysanthemum-like flower of a distinct brick-red colour.

"Amos Perry. Brilliant red, highly decorative.

"Tsingtau. Brilliant orange-red, showy garden plant and lasting cut flower.

"Honesty——"

"With a capital H, you remember," mumured Miss Marple.

"Honesty. Rose and white shades, enormous perfect-shaped flower."

Mrs. Bantry flung down the catalogue, and said with immense explosive force:

"*Dahlias!*"

"And their initial letters spell 'DEATH,' " explained Miss Marple.

"But the letter came to Dr. Rosen himself," objected Sir Henry.

"That was the clever part of it," said Miss Marple. "That and the warning in it. What would he do, getting a letter from someone he didn't know, full of names he didn't know. Why, of course, toss it over to his secretary."

"Then, after all——"

"*Oh, no!*" said Miss Marple. "*Not* the secretary. Why, that's what makes it so perfectly clear that it *wasn't* him. He'd never have let that letter be found if so. And equally he'd never have destroyed a letter to himself with a German stamp on it. Really, his innocence is—if you'll allow me to use the word—just *shining.*"

"Then who——"

"Well, it seems almost certain—as certain as anything can be in this world. There was another person at the breakfast table, and she would—quite naturally under the circumstances—put out her hand for the letter and read it. And that would be that. You remember that she got a gardening catalogue by the same post——"

"Greta Rosen," said Sir Henry, slowly. "Then her visit to me——"

"Gentlemen never see through these things," said Miss Marple. "And I'm afraid they often think we old women are—well, cats, to see things the way we do. But there it is. One does know a great deal about one's own sex, unfortunately. I've no doubt there was a barrier between them. The young man felt a sudden inexplicable repulsion. He suspected, purely through instinct, and couldn't hide the suspicion. And I really think that the girl's visit to you was just pure *spite*. She was safe enough really; but she just went out of her way to fix your suspicions definitely on poor Mr. Templeton. You weren't nearly so sure about him until after her visit."

"I'm sure it was nothing that she said—" began Sir Henry.

"Gentlemen," said Miss Marple calmly, "never see through these things."

"And that girl—" He stopped. "She commits a cold-blooded murder and gets off Scot free!"

"Oh! no, Sir Henry," said Miss Marple. "Not Scot free. Neither you nor I believe that. Remember what you said not long ago. No. Greta Rosen will not escape punishment. To begin with, she must be in with a very queer set of people—blackmailers and terrorists—associates who will do her no good, and will probably bring her to a miserable end. As you say, one mustn't waste thoughts on the guilty— it's the innocent who matter. Mr. Templeton, who I daresay will marry that German cousin, his tearing up her letter looks—well, it looks *suspicious*—using the word in quite a different sense from the one we've been using all the evening. A little as though he were afraid of the other girl noticing or asking to see it? Yes, I think there must have been some little romance there. And then there's Dobbs—though, as you say, I daresay it won't much matter to him. His elevenses are probably all he thinks about. And then there's that poor old Gertrud—the one who reminded me of Annie Poultny. Poor Annie Poultny. Fifty years faithful service and suspected of making away with Miss Lamb's will, though nothing could be proved. Almost broke the poor creature's faithful heart; and then after she was dead it came to light in the secret drawer of the tea caddy where old Miss Lamb had put it herself for safety. But too late then for poor Annie.

"That's what worries me so about that poor old German woman. When one is old, one becomes embittered very easily. I felt much more sorry for her than for Mr. Templeton, who is young and good-looking and evidently a favourite with the ladies. You will write to her, won't you, Sir Henry, and just tell her that her innocence is established beyond doubt? Her dear old master dead and she no doubt brooding and feeling herself suspected of ... Oh! It won't bear thinking about!"

"I will write, Miss Marple," said Sir Henry. He looked at her curiously. "You know, I shall never quite understand you. Your outlook is always a different one from what I expect."

"My outlook, I am afraid, is a very petty one," said Miss Marple humbly. "I hardly ever go out of St. Mary Mead."

"And yet you have solved what may be called an International mystery," said Sir Henry. "For you *have* solved it. I am convinced of that."

Miss Marple blushed, then bridled a little.

"I was, I think, well educated for the standard of my day. My sister and I had a German governess—a Fräulein. A very sentimental creature. She taught us the language of flowers—a forgotten study nowadays, but most charming. A yellow tulip, for instance, means Hopeless Love, whilst a China Aster means I die of Jealousy at your feet. That letter was signed Georgina, which I seem to remember is Dahlia in German, and that of course made the whole thing perfectly clear. I wish I could remember the meaning of Dahlia, but alas, that eludes me. My memory is not what it was."

"At any rate it didn't mean DEATH."

"No, indeed. Horrible, is it not? There are very sad things in the world."

"There are," said Mrs. Bantry with a sigh. "It's lucky one has flowers and one's friends."

"She puts us last, you observe," said Dr. Lloyd.

"A man used to send me purple orchids every night to the theatre," said Jane dreamily.

" 'I await your favours,'—that's what that means," said Miss Marple brightly.

Sir Henry gave a peculiar sort of cough and turned his head away.

Miss Marple gave a sudden exclamation.

"I've remembered. Dahlias mean 'Treachery and Misrepresentation.' "

"Wonderful," said Sir Henry. "Absolutely wonderful."

And he sighed.

# CHAPTER X

# A CHRISTMAS TRAGEDY

"I have a complaint to make," said Sir Henry Clithering.

His eyes twinkled gently as he looked round at the assembled company. Colonel Bantry, his legs stretched out, was frowning at the mantelpiece as though it were a delinquent soldier on parade, his wife was surreptitiously glancing at a catalogue of bulbs which had come by the late post, Dr. Lloyd was gazing with frank admiration at Jane Helier, and that beautiful young actress herself was thoughtfully regarding her pink polished nails. Only that elderly, spinster lady, Miss Marple, was sitting bolt upright, and her faded blue eyes met Sir Henry's with an answering twinkle.

"A complaint?" she murmured.

"A very serious complaint. We are a company of six, three representatives of each sex, and I protest on behalf of the down-trodden males. We have had three stories told tonight—and told by the three men! I protest that the ladies have not done their fair share."

"Oh!" said Mrs. Bantry with indignation. "I'm sure we have. We've listened with the most intelligent appreciation. We've displayed the true womanly attitude—not wishing to thrust ourselves into the limelight!"

"It's an excellent excuse," said Sir Henry; "but it won't do. And there's a very good precedent in the Arabian Nights! So, forward, Scheherazade!"

"Meaning me?" said Mrs. Bantry. "But I don't know

anything to tell. I've never been surrounded by blood or mystery."

"I don't absolutely insist upon blood," said Sir Henry. "But I'm sure one of you three ladies has got a pet mystery. Come now, Miss Marple—the 'Curious Coincidence of the Charwoman' or the 'Mystery of the Mothers' Meeting.' Don't disappoint me in St. Mary Mead."

Miss Marple shook her head.

"Nothing that would interest you, Sir Henry. We have our little mysteries, of course—there was that gill of picked shrimps that disappeared so incomprehensibly; but that wouldn't interest you because it all turned out to be so trivial, though throwing a considerable light on human nature."

"You have taught me to dote on human nature," said Sir Henry solemnly.

"What about you, Miss Helier?" asked Colonel Bantry. "You must have had some interesting experiences."

"Yes, indeed," said Dr. Lloyd.

"Me?" said Jane. "You mean—you want me to tell you something that happened to me?"

"Or to one of your friends," amended Sir Henry.

"Oh!" said Jane vaguely. "I don't think anything has ever happened to me—I mean not that kind of thing. Flowers, of course, and queer messages—but that's just men, isn't it? I don't think"—she paused and appeared lost in thought.

"I see we shall have to have that epic of the shrimps," said Sir Henry. "Now then, Miss Marple."

"You're so fond of your joke, Sir Henry. The shrimps are only nonsense; but now I come to think of it, I *do* remember one incident—at least not exactly an incident, something very much more serious—a tragedy. And I was, in a way, mixed up in it; and for what I did, I have never had any regrets—no, no regrets at all. But it didn't happen in St. Mary Mead."

"That disappoints me," said Sir Henry. "But I will endeavour to bear up. I knew we should not rely upon you in vain."

He settled himself in the attitude of a listener. Miss Marple grew slightly pink.

"I hope I shall be able to tell it properly," she said anxiously. "I fear I am very inclined to become *rambling*. One wanders from the point—altogether without knowing that one is doing so. And it is so hard to remember each fact in its proper order. You must all bear with me if I tell my story badly. It happened a very long time ago now.

"As I say it was not connected with St. Mary Mead. As a matter of fact, it had to do with a Hydro——"

"Do you mean a seaplane?" asked Jane with wide eyes.

"You wouldn't know, dear," said Mrs. Bantry, and explained. Her husband added his quota:

"Beastly places—absolutely beastly! Got to get up early and drink filthy-tasting water. Lot of old women sitting about. Ill-natured tittle tattle. God, when I think——"

"Now, Arthur," said Mrs. Bantry placidly. "You know it did you all the good in the world.'

"Lot of old women sitting round talking scandal," grunted Colonel Bantry.

"That, I am afraid, is true," said Miss Marple. "I myself——"

"My dear Miss Marple,' cried the colonel, horrified. "I didn't mean for one moment——"

With pink cheeks and a little gesture of the hand, Miss Marple stopped him.

"But it is *true*, Colonel Bantry. Only I should just like to say this. Let me recollect my thoughts. Yes. Talking scandal, as you say—well, it *is* done a good deal. And people are very down on it—especially young people. My nephew, who writes books—and very clever ones, I believe—has said some most *scathing* things about taking people's characters away without any kind of proof—and how wicked it is, and all that. But what I say is that none of these young people ever stop to *think*. They really don't examine the facts. Surely the whole crux of the matter is this: *How often is tittle tattle,* as you call it, *true!* And I think if, as I say, they really examined the facts they would find that it

131

was true nine times out of ten! That's really just what makes people so annoyed about it."

"The inspired guess," said Sir Henry.

"No, not that, not that at all! It's really a matter of practice and experience. An Egyptologist, so I've heard, if you show him one of those curious little beetles, can tell you by the look and the feel of the thing what date B.C. it is, or if it's a Birmingham imitation. And he can't always give a definite rule for doing so. He just *knows*. His life has been spent handling such things.

"And that's what I'm trying to say (very badly, I know). What my nephew calls 'superfluous women' have a lot of time on their hands, and their chief interest is usually *people*. And so, you see, they get to be what one might call *experts*. Now young people nowadays—they talk very freely about things that weren't mentioned in my young days, but on the other hand their minds are terribly innocent. They believe in everyone and everything. And if one tries to warn them, ever so gently, they tell one that one has a Victorian mind—and that, they say, is like a *sink*."

"After all," said Sir Henry, "what is wrong with a *sink?*"

"Exactly," said Miss Marple eagerly. "It's the most necessary thing in any house; but, of course, not romantic. Now I must confess that I have my *feelings*, like everyone else, and I have sometimes been cruelly hurt by unthinking remarks. I know gentlemen are not interested in domestic matters, but I must just mention my maid Ethel—a very good-looking girl and obliging in every way. Now I realised as soon as I saw her that she was the same type as Annie Webb and poor Mrs. Bruitt's girl. If the opportunity arose *mine and thine* would mean nothing to her. So I let her go at the month and I gave her a written reference saying she was honest and sober, but privately I warned old Mrs. Edwards against taking her; and my nephew, Raymond, was exceedingly angry and said he had never heard of anything so wicked—yes, *wicked*. Well, she went to Lady Ashton, whom I felt no obligation to warn—and what happened? All the lace cut off her underclothes and two diamond brooches taken—and the girl departed in the middle of the night and never heard of since!"

Miss Marple paused, drew a long breath, and then went on.

"You'll be saying this has nothing to do with what went on at Keston Spa Hydro—but it has in a way. It explains why I felt no doubt in my mind the first moment I saw the Sanders together that he meant to do away with her."

"Eh?" said Sir Henry, leaning forward.

Miss Marple turned a placid face to him.

"As I say, Sir Henry, I felt no doubt in my own mind. Mr. Sanders was a big, good-looking, florid-faced man, very hearty in his manner and popular with all. And nobody could have been pleasanter to his wife than he was. But I knew! He meant to make away with her."

"My dear Miss Marple——"

"Yes, I know. That's what my nephew, Raymond West, would say. He'd tell me I hadn't a shadow of proof. But I remember Walter Hones, who kept the Green Man. Walking home with his wife one night she fell into the river—and *he* collected the insurance money! And one or two other people that are walking about Scot free to this day—one indeed in our own class of life. Went to Switzerland for a summer holiday climbing with his wife. I warned her not to go—the poor dear didn't get angry with me as she might have done—she only laughed. It seemed to her funny that a queer old thing like me should say such things about her Harry. Well, well, there was an accident—and Harry is married to another woman now. But what could I *do*? I *knew*, but there was no proof."

"Oh! Miss Marple," cried Mrs. Bantry. "You don't really mean——"

"My dear, these things are very common—very common indeed. And gentlemen are especially tempted, being so much the stronger. So easy if a thing looks like an accident. As I say, I knew at once with the Sanders. It was on a tram. It was full inside and I had had to go on top. We all three got up to get off and Mr. Sanders lost his balance and fell right against his wife, sending her headfirst down the stairs. Fortunately the conductor was a very strong young man and caught her."

"But surely that must have been an accident."

"Of course it was an accident—nothing could have looked more accidental. But Mr. Sanders had been in the Merchant Service, so he told me, and a man who can keep his balance on a nasty tilting boat doesn't lose it on top of a tram if an old woman like me doesn't. Don't tell me!"

"At any rate we can take it that you made up your mind, Miss Marple," said Sir Henry. "Made it up then and there."

The old lady nodded.

"I was sure enough, and another incident in crossing the street not long afterwards made me surer still. Now I ask you, what could I do, Sir Henry? Here was a nice contented happy little married woman shortly going to be murdered."

"My dear lady, you take my breath away."

"That's because, like most people nowadays, you won't face facts. You prefer to think such a thing couldn't be. But it was so, and I knew it. But one is so sadly handicapped! I couldn't, for instance, go to the police. And to warn the young woman would, I could see, be useless. She was devoted to the man. I just made it my business to find out as much as I could about them. One has a lot of opportunities, doing one's needlework round the fire. Mrs. Sanders (Gladys, her name was) was only too willling to talk. It seems they had not been married very long. Her husband had some property that was coming to him, but for the moment they were very badly off. In fact, they were living on her little income. One has heard that tale before. She bemoaned the fact that she could not touch the capital. It seems that somebody had had some sense somewhere! But the money was hers to will away—I found that out. And she and her husband had made wills in favour of each other directly after their marriage. Very touching. Of course, when Jack's affairs came right—that was the burden all day long, and in the meantime they were very hard up indeed—actually had a room on the top floor, all among the servants—and so dangerous in case of fire, though, as it happened, there was a fire escape just outside their window. I inquired carefully if there was a balcony—dangerous things, balconies. One push—you know!

"I made her promise not to go out on the balcony; I said I'd had a dream. That impressed her—one can do a lot with superstition sometimes. She was a fair girl, rather washed-out complexion, and an untidy roll of hair on her neck. Very credulous. She repeated what I had said to her husband, and I noticed him looking at me in a curious way once or twice. He wasn't credulous; and he knew I'd been on that tram.

"But I was very worried—terribly worried—because I couldn't see how to circumvent him. I could prevent anything happening at the Hydro, just by saying a few words to show him I suspected. But that only meant his putting off his plan till later. No, I began to believe that the only policy was a bold one—somehow or other to lay a trap for him. If I could induce him to attempt her life in a way of my own choosing—well, then he would be unmasked, and she would be forced to face the truth however much of a shock it was to her."

"You take my breath away," said Dr. Lloyd. "What conceivable plan could you adopt?"

"I'd have found one—never fear," said Miss Marple. "But the man was too clever for me. He didn't wait. He thought I might suspect, and so he struck before I could be sure. He knew I would suspect an accident. So he made it murder."

A little gasp went round the circle. Miss Marple nodded and set her lips grimly together.

"I'm afraid I've put that rather abruptly. I must try and tell you exactly what occurred. I've always felt very bitterly about it—it seems to me that I ought, somehow, to have prevented it. But doubtless Providence knew best. I did what I could at all events.

"There was what I can only describe as a curiously eerie feeling in the air. There seemed to be something weighing on us all. A feeling of misfortune. To begin with, there was George, the hall porter. Had been there for years and knew everybody. Bronchitis and pneumonia, and passed away on the fourth day. Terribly sad. A real blow to everybody. And four days before Christmas too. And then one of the housemaids—such a nice girl—a septic finger, actually died in twenty-four hours.

"I was in the drawing-room with Miss Trollope and old Mrs. Carpenter, and Mrs. Carpenter was being positively ghoulish—relishing it all, you know.

" 'Mark my words,' she said. *'This isn't the end.* You know the saying? *Never two without three.* I've proved it true time and again. There'll be another death. Not a doubt of it. And we shan't have long to wait. *Never two without three.'*

"As she said the last words, nodding her head and clicking her knitting needles, I just chanced to look up and there was Mr. Sanders standing in the doorway. Just for a minute he was off guard, and I saw the look in his face as plain as plain. I shall believe till my dying day that it was that ghoulish Mrs. Carpenter's words that put the whole thing into his head. I saw his mind working.

"He came forward into the room smiling in his genial way.

" 'Any Christmas shopping I can do for you ladies?' he asked. 'I'm going down to Keston presently.'

"He stayed a minute or two, laughing and talking, and then went out. As I tell you I was troubled, and I said straight away:

" 'Where's Mrs. Sanders? Does anyone know?'

"Mrs. Trollope said she'd gone out to some friends of hers, the Mortimers, to play bridge, and that eased my mind for the moment. But I was still very worried and most uncertain as to what to do. About half an hour later I went up to my room. I met Dr. Coles, my doctor, there, coming down the stairs as I was going up, and as I happened to want to consult him about my rheumatism, I took him into my room with me then and there. He mentioned to me then (in confidence, he said) about the death of the poor girl Mary. The manager didn't want the news to get about, he said, so would I keep it to myself. Of course I didn't tell him that we'd all been discussing nothing else for the last hour—ever since the poor girl breathed her last. These things are always known at once, and a man of his experience should know that well enough; but Dr. Coles always was a simple unsuspicious fellow who believed what he wanted to believe and that's just what alarmed me a minute later. He said as he was leaving that Sanders had asked him to have a look at his wife. It seemed she'd been seedy of late—indigestion, etc.

*"Now that very self-same day Gladys Sanders had said to me that she'd got a wonderful digestion and was thankful for it.*

"You see? All my suspicions of that man came back a hundredfold. He was preparing the way—for what? Dr. Coles left before I could make up my mind whether to speak to him or not—though really if I had spoken I shouldn't have known what to say. As I came out of my room, the man himself—Sanders—came down the stairs from the floor above. He was dressed to go out and he asked me again if he could do anything for me in town. It was all I could do to be civil to the man! I went straight into the lounge and ordered tea. It was just on half-past five, I remember.

"Now I'm very anxious to put clearly what happened next. I was still in the lounge at a quarter to seven when Mr. Sanders came in. There were two gentlemen with him and all three of them were inclined to be a little on the lively side. Mr. Sanders left his two friends and came right over to where I was sitting with Miss Trollope. He explained that he wanted our advice about a Christmas present he was giving his wife. It was an evening bag

" 'And you see, ladies,' he said. 'I'm only a rough sailor-man. What do I know about such things? I've had three sent to me on approval and I want an expert opinion on them.'

"We said, of course, that we would be delighted to help him, and he asked if we'd mind coming upstairs, as his wife might come in any minute if he brought the things down. So we went up with him. I shall never forget what happened next—I can feel my little fingers tingling now.

"Mr. Sanders opened the door of the bedroom and switched on the light. I don't know which of us saw it first. . . .

"*Mrs. Sanders was lying on the floor, face downwards—dead.*

"I got to her first. I knelt down and took her hand and felt for the pulse, but it was useless, the arm itself was cold and stiff. Just by her head was a stocking filled with sand—the weapon she had been struck down with. Miss Trollope, silly creature, was moaning and moaning by the door and holding her head. Sanders gave a great cry of 'My wife, my wife,' and rushed to her. I stopped him touching her. You see, I was sure at the moment that he had done it, and there might have been something that he wanted to take away or hide.

" 'Nothing must be touched,' I said. 'Pull yourself together, Mr. Sanders. Miss Trollope, please go down and fetch the manager.'

"I stayed there, kneeling by the body. I wasn't going to leave Sanders alone with it. And yet I was forced to admit that if the man was acting, he was acting marvelously. He looked dazed and bewildered and scared out of his wits.

"The manager was with us in no time. He made a quick inspection of the room, then turned us all out and locked the door, the key of which he took. Then he went off and telephoned to the police. It seemed a positive age before they came (we learnt afterwards that the line was out of order). The manager had to send a messenger to the police station, and the Hydro is right out of the town, up on the edge of the moor; and Mrs. Carpenter tried us all very severely. She was so pleased at her prophecy of "Never two without three" coming true so quickly. Sanders, I hear, wandered out into the grounds, clutching his head and groaning and displaying every sign of grief.

"However, the police came at last. They went upstairs with the manager and Mr. Sanders. Later they sent down for me. I went up. The inspector was there, sitting at a table writing. He was an intelligent-looking man and I liked him.

" 'Miss Jane Marple?' he said.

" 'Yes.'

" 'I understand, Madam, that you were present when the body of the deceased was found?'

"I said I was and I described exactly what had occurred. I think it was a relief to the poor man to find someone who could answer his questions coherently, having previously had to deal with Sanders and Emily Trollope, who, I gather, was completely demoralised—she would be, the silly creature! I remember my dear mother teaching me that a gentlewoman should always be able to control herself in public, however much she may give way in private."

"An admirable maxim," said Sir Henry gravely.

"When I had finished the inspector said:

" 'Thank you, Madam. Now I'm afraid I must ask you just to look at the body once more. Is that exactly the position in which it was lying when you entered the room? It hasn't been moved in any way?'

"I explained that I had prevented Mr. Sanders from doing so, and the inspector nodded approval.

" 'The gentleman seems terribly upset,' he remarked.

" 'He seems so—yes,' I replied.

"I don't think I put any special emphasis on the 'seems,' but the inspector looked at me rather keenly.

" 'So we can take it that the body is exactly as it was when found?' he said.

" 'Except for the hat, yes,' I replied.

"The inspector looked up sharply.

" 'What do you mean—the hat?'

"I explained that the hat had been on poor Gladys' head, whereas now it was lying beside her. I thought, of course, that the police had done this. The inspector, however, denied it emphatically. Nothing had, as yet, been moved or touched. He stood looking down at that poor prone figure with a puzzled frown. Gladys was dressed in her outdoor clothes—a big dark-red tweed coat with a grey fur collar. The hat, a cheap affair of red felt, lay just by her head.

"The inspector stood for some minutes in silence, frowning to himself. Then an idea struck him.

" 'Can you, by any chance, remember, Madam, whether there were earrings in the ears, or whether the deceased habitually wore earrings?'

"Now fortunately I am in the habit of observing closely. I remembered that there had been a glint of pearls just below the hat brim, though I had paid no particular notice to it at the time. I was able to answer his first question in the affirmative.

" 'Then that settles it. The lady's jewel case was rifled— not that she had anything much of value, I understand— and the rings were taken from her fingers. The murderer must have forgotten the earrings, and come back for them after the murder was discovered. A cool customer! Or perhaps'— He stared round the room and said slowly, 'He may have been concealed here in this room—all the time.'

"But I negatived that idea. I myself, I explained, had looked under the bed. And the manager had opened the doors of the wardrobe. There was nowhere else where a man could hide. It is true the hat cupboard was locked in the middle of the wardrobe, but as that was only a shallow affair with shelves, no one could have been concealed there.

"The inspector nodded his head slowly whilst I explained all this.

" 'I'll take your word for it, Madam,' he said. 'In that case, as I said before, he must have come back. A very cool customer.'

" 'But the manager locked the door and took the key!'

" 'That's nothing. The balcony and the fire escape— that's the way the thief came. Why, as likely as not, you actually disturbed him at work. He slips out of the window, and when you've all gone, back he comes and goes on with his business.'

" 'You are sure,' I said, 'that there *was* a thief?'

"He said dryly:

" 'Well, it looks like it, doesn't it?'

"But something in his tone satisfied me. I felt that he wouldn't take Mr. Sanders in the rôle of the bereaved widower too seriously.

"You see, I admit it frankly, I was absolutely under the opinion of what I believe our neighbours, the French call the *idée fixe*. I knew that that man, Sanders, intended his wife to die. What I didn't allow for was that strange and fantastic thing, coincidence. My views about Mr. Sanders were—I was sure of it—absolutely right and *true*. The man was a scoundrel. But although his hypocritical assumptions of grief didn't deceive me for a minute, I do remember feeling at the time that his *surprise* and *bewilderment* were marvellously well done. They seemed absolutely *natural*—if you know what I mean. I must admit that after my conversation with the inspector, a curious feeling of doubt crept over me. Because if Sanders had done this dreadful thing, I couldn't imagine any conceivable reason why he should creep back by means of the fire escape and take the earrings from his wife's ears. It wouldn't have been a *sensible* thing to do, and Sanders was such a very sensible man—that's just why I always felt he was so dangerous."

Miss Marple looked round at her audience.

"You see, perhaps, what I am coming to? It is, so often, the unexpected that happens in this world. I was so *sure*, and that, I think, was what blinded me. The result came as a shock to me. *For it was proved, beyond any possible doubt, that Mr. Sanders could not possibly have committed the crime. . . ."*

A surprised gasp came from Mrs. Bantry. Miss Marple turned to her.

"I know, my dear, that isn't what you expected when I began this story. It wasn't what I expected. But facts are facts, and if one is proved to be wrong, one must just be humble about it and start again. That Mr. Sanders was a murderer at heart I knew—and nothing ever occurred to upset that firm conviction of mine.

"And now, I expect you would like to hear the actual facts themselves. Mrs. Sanders, as you know, spent the afternoon playing bridge with some friends, the Mortimers. She left them at about a quarter past six. From her friends' house to the Hydro was about a quarter of an hour's walk—less if one hurried. She must have come in then, about six-thirty. No one saw her come in, so she must have entered by the side door and hurried straight up to her room. There she changed (the fawn coat and skirt she wore to the bridge party were hanging up in the cupboard) and was evidently preparing to go out again, when the blow fell. Quite possibly, they say, she never even knew who struck her. The sandbag, I understand, is a very efficient weapon. That looks as though the attackers were concealed in the room, possibly in one of the big wardrobe cupboards—the one she didn't open.

"Now as to the movements of Mr. Sanders. He went out, as I have said, at about five-thirty—or a little after. He did some shopping at a couple of shops and at about six o'clock he entered the Grand Spa Hotel where he encountered two friends—the same with whom he returned to the Hydro later. They played billiards and, I gather, had a good many whiskies and sodas together. These two men (Hitchcock and Spender, their names were) were actually with him the whole time from six o'clock onwards. They walked back to the Hydro with him and he only left them to come across to me and Miss Trollope. That, as I told you, was about a quarter to seven—at which time his wife must have been already dead.

"I must tell you that I talked myself to these two friends of his. I did not like them. They were neither pleasant nor gentlemanly men, but I was quite certain of one thing, that they were speaking the absolute truth when they said that Sanders had been the whole time in their company.

"There was just one other little point that came up. It seems that while bridge was going on Mrs. Sanders was called to the telephone. A Mr. Littleworth wanted to speak to her. She seemed both excited and pleased about something—and incidentally made one or two bad mistakes. She left rather earlier than they had expected her to do.

"Mr. Sanders was asked whether he knew the name of Littleworth as being one of his wife's friends, but he declared he had never heard of anyone of that name. And to me that seems borne out by his wife's attitude—she too, did not seem to know the name of Littleworth. Nevertheless she came back from the telephone smiling and blushing, so it looks as though whoever it was did not give his real name, and that in itself has a suspicious aspect, does it not?

"Anyway, that is the problem that was left. The burglar story, which seems unlikely—or the alternative theory that Mrs. Sanders was preparing to go out and meet somebody. Did that somebody come to her room by means of the fire escape? Was there a quarrel? Or did he treacherously attack her?"

Miss Marple stopped.

"Well?" said Sir Henry. 'What is the answer?"

"I wondered if any of you could guess."

"I'm never good at guessing," said Mrs. Bantry. "It seems a pity that Sanders had such a wonderful alibi; but if it satisfied you it must have been all right."

Jane Helier moved her beautiful head and asked a question.

"Why," she said, "was the hat cupboard locked?"

"How very clever of you, my dear," said Miss Marple, beaming. "That's just what I wondered myself, though the explanation was quite simple. In it were a pair of embroidered slippers and some pocket handkerchiefs that the poor girl was embroidering for her husband for Christmas. That's why she locked the cupboard. The key was found in her handbag."

"Oh!" said Jane. "Then it isn't very interesting after all."

"Oh! but it is," said Miss Marple. "It's just the one really interesting thing—the thing that made all the murderer's plans go wrong."

Everyone stared at the old lady.

"I didn't see it myself for two days," said Miss Marple. "I puzzled and puzzled—and then suddenly there it was, all clear. I went to the inspector and asked him to try something and he did."

"What did you ask him to try?"

"*I asked him to fit that hat on the poor girl's head*—and of course he couldn't. It wouldn't go on. *It wasn't her hat, you see.*"

Mrs. Bantry stared.

"But it was on her head to begin with?"

"Not on *her* head——"

Miss Marple stopped a moment to let her words sink in, and then went on.

"We took it for granted that it was poor Gladys's body there; but we never looked at the face. She was face downwards, remember, and the hat hid everything."

"But she *was* killed?"

"Yes, later. At the moment that we were telephoning to the police, Gladys Sanders was alive and well."

"You mean it was someone pretending to be her? But surely when you touched her——"

"It was a dead body, right enough," said Miss Marple gravely.

"But, dash it all," said Colonel Bantry, "you can't get hold of dead bodies right and left. What did they do with the—the first corpse afterwards?"

"He put it back," said Miss Marple. "It was a wicked idea—but a very clever one. It was our talk in the drawing-room that put it into his head. The body of poor Mary, the housemaid—why not use it? Remember, the Sanders' room was up amongst the servants' quarters. Mary's room was two doors off. The undertakers wouldn't come till after dark—he counted on that. He carried the body along the balcony (it was dark at five), dressed it in one of his wife's dresses and her big red coat. And then he found the hat cupboard locked! There was only one thing to be done, he fetched one of the poor girl's own hats. No one would notice. He put the sandbag down beside her. Then he went off to establish his alibi.

"He telephoned to his wife—calling himself Mr. Little-worth. I don't know what he said to her—she was a credu-

144

lous girl, as I said just now. But he got her to leave the bridge party early and not to go back to the Hydro, and arranged with her to meet him in the grounds of the Hydro near the fire escape at seven o'clock. He probably told her he had some surprise for her.

"He returns to the Hydro with his friends and arranges that Miss Trollope and I shall discover the crime with him. He even pretends to turn the body over—and I stop him! Then the police are sent for, and he staggers out into the grounds.

"Nobody asked him for an alibi *after* the crime. He meets his wife, takes her up the fire escape, they enter their room. Perhaps he has already told her some story about the body. She stoops over it, and he picks up his sandbag and strikes. . . . Oh, dear! it makes me sick to think of, even now! Then quickly he strips off her coat and skirt, hangs them up, and dresses her in the clothes from the other body.

*"But the hat won't go on.* Mary's head is shingled. Gladys Sanders, as I say, had a great bun of hair. He is forced to leave it beside the body and hope no one will notice. Then he carries poor Mary's body back to her own room and arranges it decorously once more."

"It seems incredible." said Dr. Lloyd. "The risks he took. The police might have arrived too soon."

"You remember the line was out of order," said Miss Marple. "That was a piece of *his* work. He couldn't afford to have the police on the spot too soon. When they did come, they spent some time in the manager's office before going up to the bedroom. That was the weakest point—the chance that someone might notice the difference between a body that had been dead two hours and one that had been dead just over half an hour; but he counted on the fact that the people who first discovered the crime would have no expert knowledge."

Dr. Lloyd nodded.

"The crime would be supposed to have been committed about a quarter to seven or thereabouts, I suppose," he said. "It was actually committed at seven or a few minutes after. When the police surgeon examined the body it would be about half-past seven at earliest. He couldn't possibly tell."

"I am the person who should have known," said Miss Marple. "I felt the poor girl's hand and it was icy cold. Yet a short time later the inspector spoke as though the murder must have been committed just before we arrived—and I saw nothing!"

"I think you saw a good deal, Miss Marple," said Sir Henry. "The case was before my time. I don't even remember hearing of it. What happened?"

"Sanders was hanged," said Miss Marple crisply. "And a good job too. I have never regretted my part in bringing that man to justice. I've no patience with modern humanitarian scruples about capital punishments."

Her stern face softened.

"But I have often reproached myself bitterly with failing to save the life of that poor girl. But who would have listened to an old woman jumping to conclusions? Well, well—who knows? Perhaps it was better for her to die while life was still happy than it would have been for her to live on, unhappy and disillusioned, in a world that would have seemed suddenly horrible. She loved that scoundrel and trusted him. She never found him out."

"Well, then," said Jane Helier, "she was all right. Quite all right. I wish——" She stopped.

Miss Marple looked at the famous, the beautiful, the successful Jane Helier and nodded her head gently.

"I see, my dear," she said very gently. "I see."

# CHAPTER XI

# THE HERB OF DEATH

"Now then, Mrs. B.," said Sir Henry Clithering encouragingly.

Mrs. Bantry, his hostess, looked at him in cold reproof.

"I've told you before that I will *not* be called Mrs. B. It's not dignified."

"Scheherazade, then."

"And even less am I Sche—what's her name! I never can tell a story properly, ask Arthur if you don't believe me."

"You're quite good at the facts, Dolly," said Colonel Bantry, "but poor at the embroidery."

"That's just it," said Mrs. Bantry. She flapped the bulb catalogue she was holding on the table in front of her. "I've been listening to you all and I don't know how you do it. 'He said, she said, you wondered, they thought, everyone implied'—well, I just couldn't, and here it is! And besides I don't know anything to tell a story about."

"We can't believe that, Mrs. Bantry," said Dr. Lloyd. He shook his grey head in mocking disbelief.

Old Miss Marple said in her gentle voice: "Surely, dear——"

Mrs. Bantry continued obstinately to shake her head.

"You don't know how banal my life is. What with the servants and the difficulties of getting scullery maids, and just going to town for clothes, and dentists, and Ascot (which Arthur hates) and then the garden——"

"Ah!" said Dr. Lloyd. "The garden. We all know where your heart lies, Mrs. Bantry."

"It must be nice to have a garden," said Jane Helier, the beautiful young actress. "That is, if you hadn't got to dig, or to get your hands messed up. I'm ever so fond of flowers."

"The garden," said Sir Henry. "Can't we take that as a starting point? Come, Mrs. B. The poisoned bulb, the deadly daffodils, the herb of death!"

"Now it's odd your saying that," said Mrs. Bantry. "You've just reminded me. Arthur, do you remember that business at Clodderham Court? You know. Old Sir Ambrose Bercy. Do you remember what a courtly charming old man we thought him?"

"Why, of course. Yes, that *was* a strange business. Go ahead, Dolly."

"You'd better tell it, dear."

"Nonsense. Go ahead. Must paddle your own canoe. I did my bit just now."

Mrs. Bantry drew a deep breath. She clasped her hands and her face registered complete mental anguish. She spoke rapidly and fluently.

"Well, there's really not much to tell. The Herb of Death—that's what put it into my head, though in my own mind I call it *sage and onions.*"

"Sage and onions?" asked Dr. Lloyd.

Mrs. Bantry nodded.

"That was how it happened, you see," she explained. "We were staying, Arthur and I, with Sir Ambrose Bercy at Clodderham Court, and one day, by mistake (though very stupidly, I've always thought) a lot of foxglove leaves were picked with the sage. The ducks for dinner that night were stuffed with it and everyone was very ill, and one poor girl—Sir Ambrose's ward—died of it."

She stopped.

"Dear, dear," said Miss Marple, "how very tragic."

"Wasn't it?"

"Well," said Sir Henry, "what next?"

"There isn't any next," said Mrs. Bantry, "that's all."

Everyone gasped. Though warned beforehand, they had
not expected quite such brevity as this.

"But, my dear lady," remonstrated Sir Henry, "it can't
be all. What you have related is a tragic occurrence, but not
in any sense of the word a problem."

"Well, of course there's some more," said Mrs. Bantry.
"But if I were to tell you it, you'd know what it was."

She looked defiantly round the assembly and said plaintively:

"I told you I couldn't dress things up and make it
sound properly like a story ought to do."

"Ah ha!" said Sir Henry. He sat up in his chair and
adjusted an eyeglass. "Really, you know, Scheherazade,
this is most refreshing. Our ingenuity is challenged. I'm
not so sure you haven't done it on purpose—to stimulate
our curiosity. A few brisk rounds of 'Twenty Questions' is
indicated, I think. Miss Marple, will you begin?"

"I'd like to know something about the cook," said Miss
Marple. "She must have been a very stupid woman, or else
very inexperienced."

"She was just very stupid," said Mrs. Bantry. "She
cried a great deal afterwards and said the leaves had been
picked and brought in to her as sage, and how was she to
know?"

"Not one who thought for herself," said Miss Marple.
"Probably an elderly woman and, I daresay, a very
good cook?"

"Oh! excellent," said Mrs. Bantry.

"Your turn, Miss Helier," said Sir Henry.

"Oh! You mean—to ask a question?" There was a
pause while Jane pondered. Finally she said helplessly,
"Really—I don't know what to ask."

Her beautiful eyes looked appealingly at Sir Henry.

"Why not Dramatis Personae, Miss Helier?" he suggested smiling.

Jane still looked puzzled.

"Characters in order of their appearance," said Sir
Henry gently.

"Oh, yes," said Jane. "That's a good idea."

Mrs. Bantry began briskly to tick people off on her fingers.

"Sir Ambrose—Sylvia Keene (that's the girl who died)—a friend of hers who was staying there, Maud Wye, one of those dark ugly girls who manage to make an effect somehow—I never know how they do it. Then there was a Mr. Curle who had come down to discuss books with Sir Ambrose—you know, rare books—queer old things in Latin—all musty parchment. There was Jerry Lorimer—he was a kind of next door neighbour. His place, Fairlies, joined Sir Ambrose's estate. And there was Mrs. Carpenter, one of those middle-aged pussies who always seem to manage to dig themselves in comfortably somewhere. She was by way of being *dame de compagnie* to Sylvia, I suppose."

"If it is my turn," said Sir Henry, "and I suppose it is, as I'm sitting next to Miss Helier, I want a good deal. I want a short verbal portrait, please, Mrs. Bantry, of all the foregoing."

"Oh!" Mrs. Bantry hesitated.

"Sir Ambrose now," continued Sir Henry. "Start with him. What was he like?"

"Oh, he was a very distinguished-looking old man—and not so very old really—not more than sixty, I suppose. But he was very delicate—he had a weak heart, could never go upstairs—had had to have a lift put in, and so that made him seem older than he was. Very charming manners—*courtly*—that's the word that describes him best. You never saw him ruffled or upset. He had beautiful white hair and a particularly charming voice."

"Good," said Sir Henry. "I see Sir Ambrose. Now the girl Sylvia—what did you say her name was?"

"Sylvia Keene. She was pretty—really *very* pretty. Fair-haired, you know, and a lovely skin. Not, perhaps, very clever. In fact, rather stupid."

"Oh! come, Dolly," protested her husband.

"Arthur, of course, wouldn't think so," said Mrs. Bantry drily. "But she *was* stupid—she really never said anything worth listening to."

"One of the most graceful creatures I ever saw," said

Colonel Bantry warmly. "See her playing tennis—charming, simply charming. And she was full of fun—most amusing little thing. And such a pretty way with her. I bet the young fellows all thought so."

"That's just where you're wrong," said Mrs. Bantry. "Youth, as such, has no charms for young men nowadays. It's only old duffers like you, Arthur, who sit maundering on about young girls."

"Being young's no good," said Jane. "You've got to have S.A."

"What," said Miss Marple, "is S.A.?"

"Sex appeal," said Jane.

"Ah! yes," said Miss Marple. "What in my day they used to call 'having the come hither in your eye.' "

"Not a bad description." said Sir Henry. "The *dame de compagnie*, you described, I think, as a pussy, Mrs. Bantry?"

"I didn't mean a *cat*, you know," said Mrs. Bantry. "It's quite different. Just a big soft white purry person. Always very sweet. That's what Adelaide Carpenter was like."

"What sort of aged woman?"

"Oh, I should say fortyish. She'd been there some time—ever since Sylvia was eleven, I believe. A very tactful person. One of those widows left in unfortunate circumstances, with plenty of aristocratic relations, but no ready cash. I didn't like her myself—but then I never do like people with very white long hands. And I don't like pussies."

"Mr. Curle?"

"Oh! one of those elderly stooping men. There are so many of them about, you'd hardly know one from the other. He showed enthusiasm when talking about his musty books, but not at any other time. I don't think Sir Ambrose knew him very well."

"And Jerry next door?"

"A really charming boy. He was engaged to Sylvia. That's what made it so sad."

"Now I wonder—" began Miss Marple, and then stopped.

"What?"

"Nothing, dear."

Sir Henry looked at the old lady curiously. Then he said thoughtfully:

"So this young couple were engaged. Had they been engaged long?"

"About a year. Sir Ambrose had opposed the engagement on the plea that Sylvia was too young. But after a year's engagement he had given in and the marriage was to have taken place quite soon."

"Ah! Had the young lady any property?"

"Next to nothing—a bare hundred or two a year."

"No rat in that hole, Clithering," said Colonel Bantry, and laughed.

"It's the doctor's turn to ask a question," said Sir Henry. "I stand down."

"My curiosity is mainly professional," said Dr. Lloyd. "I should like to know what medical evidence was given at the inquest—that is, if our hostess remembers, or, indeed, if she knows."

"I know roughly," said Mrs. Bantry. "It was poisoning by digitalin—is that right?"

Dr. Lloyd nodded.

"The active principle of the foxglove—digitalis—acts on the heart. Indeed, it is a very valuable drug in some forms of heart trouble. A very curious case altogether. I would never have believed that eating a preparation of foxglove leaves could possibly result fatally. These ideas of eating poisonous leaves and berries are very much exaggerated. Very few people realise that the vital principle, or alkaloid, has to be extracted with much care and preparation."

"Mrs. MacArthur sent some special bulbs round to Mrs. Toomie the other day," said Miss Marple. "And Mrs. Toomie's cook mistook them for onions, and all the Toomies were very ill indeed."

"But they didn't die of it," said Dr. Lloyd.

"No. They didn't die of it," admitted Miss Marple.

"A girl I knew died of ptomaine poisoning," said Jane Helier.

"We must get on with investigating the crime," said Sir Henry.

"Crime?" said Jane, startled. "I thought it was an accident."

"If it were an accident," said Sir Henry gently, 'I do not think Mrs. Bantry would have told us this story. No, as I read it, this was an accident only in appearance—behind it is something more sinister. I remember a case—various guests in a house party were chatting after dinner. The walls were adorned with all kinds of old-fashioned weapons. Entirely as a joke one of the party seized an ancient horse pistol and pointed it at another man, pretending to fire it. The pistol was loaded and went off, killing the man. We had to ascertain, in that case, first, who had secretly prepared and loaded that pistol, and secondly who had so led and directed the conversation that that final bit of horseplay resulted—for the man who had fired the pistol was entirely innocent!

"It seems to me we have much the same problem here. Those digitalin leaves were deliberately mixed with the sage, knowing what the result would be. Since we exonerate the cook—we do exonerate the cook, don't we?—the question arises: Who picked the leaves and delivered them to the kitchen?"

"That's easily answered," said Mrs. Bantry. "At least the last part of it is. It was Sylvia herself who took the leaves to the kitchen. It was part of her daily job to gather things like salad or herbs, bunches of young carrots—all the sort of things that gardeners never pick right. They hate giving you anything young and tender—they wait for them to be fine specimens. Sylvia and Mrs. Carpenter used to see to a lot of these things themselves. And there was foxglove actually growing all amongst the sage in one corner, so the mistake was quite natural."

"But did Sylvia actually pick them herself?"

"That, nobody ever knew. It was assumed so."

"Assumptions," said Sir Henry, "are dangerous things."

"But I do know that Mrs. Carpenter didn't pick them," said Mrs. Bantry. "Because, as it happened, she was walking with me on the terrace that morning. We went out there after breakfast. It was unusually nice and warm for early spring. Sylvia went alone down into the garden, but later I saw her walking arm-in-arm with Maud Wye."

"So they were great friends, were they?" asked Miss Marple.

"Yes," said Mrs. Bantry. She seemed as though about to say something, but did not do so.

"Had she been staying there long?" asked Miss Marple.

"About a fortnight," said Mrs. Bantry.

There was a note of trouble in her voice.

"You didn't like Miss Wye?" suggested Sir Henry.

"I did. That's just it. I did."

The trouble in her voice had grown to distress.

"You're keeping something back, Mrs. Bantry," said Sir Henry accusingly.

"I wondered just now," said Miss Marple, "but I didn't like to go on."

"When did you wonder?"

"When you said that the young people were engaged. You said that that was what made it so sad. But, if you know what I mean, your voice didn't sound right when you said it—not convincing, you know."

"What a dreadful person you are," said Mrs. Bantry. "You always seem to *know*. Yes, I was thinking of something. But I don't really know whether I ought to say it or not."

"You must say it," said Sir Henry. "Whatever your scruples, it mustn't be kept back."

"Well, it was just this," said Mrs. Bantry. "One evening—in fact the very evening before the tragedy—I happened to go out on the terrace before dinner. The window in the drawing-room was open. And as it chanced I saw Jerry Lorimer and Maud Wye. He was—well—kissing her. Of course I didn't know whether it was just a sort of chance affair, or whether—well, I mean one can't *tell*. I

154

knew Sir Ambrose never had really liked Jerry Lorimer—so perhaps he knew he was that kind of young man. But one thing I *am* sure of: that girl, Maud Wye, was *really fond* of him. You'd only to see her looking at him when she was off guard. And I think, too, they were really better suited than he and Sylvia were."

"I am going to ask a question quickly before Miss Marple can," said Sir Henry. "I want to know whether, after the tragedy, Jerry Lorimer married Maud Wye?"

"Yes," said Mrs. Bantry. "He did. Six months afterwards."

"Oh! Scheherazade, Scheherazade,' said Sir Henry. "To think of the way you told us this story at first! Bare bones indeed—and to think of the amount of flesh we're finding on them now."

"Don't speak so ghoulishly," said Mrs. Bantry. "And don't use the word flesh. Vegetarians always do. They say, 'I never eat flesh' in a way that puts you right off your nice little beefsteak. Mr. Curle was a vegetarian. He used to eat some peculiar stuff that looked like bran for breakfast. Those elderly stooping men with beards are often faddy. They have patent kinds of underwear, too."

"What on earth, Dolly," said her husband, "do you know about Mr. Curle's underwear?"

"Nothing," said Mrs. Bantry with dignity. "I was just making a guess."

"I'll amend my former statement," said Sir Henry. "I'll say instead that the Dramatis Personae in your problem are very interesting. I'm beginning to see them all—eh, Miss Marple?"

"Human nature is always interesting, Sir Henry. And it's curious to see how certain types always tend to act in exactly the same way."

"Two women and a man," said Sir Henry. "The old eternal human triangle. Is that the base of our problem here? I rather fancy it is."

Dr. Lloyd cleared his throat.

"I've been thinking," he said rather diffidently. "Do you say, Mrs. Bantry, that you yourself were ill?"

"Was I not! So was Arthur! So was everyone!"

"That's just it—everyone," said the doctor. "You see what I mean? In Sir Henry's story which he told us just now, one man shot another—he didn't have to shoot the whole room full."

"I don't understand," said Jane. "Who shot who?"

"I'm saying that whoever planned this thing went about it very curiously, either with a blind belief in chance, or else with an absolutely reckless disregard for human life. I can hardly believe there is a man capable of deliberately poisoning eight people with the object of removing one amongst them."

"I see your point," said Sir Henry, thoughtfully. "I confess I ought to have thought of that."

"And mightn't he have poisoned himself too?" asked Jane.

"Was anyone absent from dinner that night?" asked Miss Marple.

Mrs. Bantry shook her head.

"Everyone was there."

"Except Mr. Lorimer, I suppose, my dear. He wasn't staying in the house, was he?"

"No; but he was dining there that evening," said Mrs. Bantry.

"Oh!" said Miss Marple in a changed voice. "That makes all the difference in the world."

She frowned vexedly to herself.

"I've been very stupid," she murmured. "Very stupid indeed."

"I confess your point worries me, Lloyd," said Sir Henry.

"How ensure that the girl, and the girl only, should get a fatal dose?"

"You can't," said the doctor. "That brings me to the point I'm going to make. *Supposing the girl was not the intended victim after all?*"

"What?"

"In all cases of food poisoning, the result is very uncertain. Several people share a dish. What happens? One or two are slightly ill, two more, say, are seriously indisposed, one dies. That's the way of it—there's no certainty anywhere. But there are cases where another factor might enter in. Digitalin is a drug that acts directly on the heart—as I've told you it's prescribed in certain cases. *Now, there was one person in that house who suffered from a heart complaint.* Suppose he was the victim selected? What would not be fatal to the rest *would* be fatal to him—or so the murderer might reasonably suppose. That the thing turned out differently is only proof of what I was saying just now—the uncertainty and unreliability of the effect of drugs on human beings."

"Sir Ambrose," said Sir Henry, "you think *he* was the person aimed at? Yes, yes—and the girl's death was a mistake."

"Who got his money after he was dead?" asked Jane.

"A very sound question, Miss Helier. One of the first we always ask in my late profession," said Sir Henry.

"Sir Ambrose had a son," said Mrs Bantry slowly. "He had quarrelled with him many years previously. The boy was wild, I believe. Still, it was not in Sir Ambrose's power to disinherit him—Clodderham Court was entailed. Martin Bercy succeeded to the title and estate. There was, however, a good deal of other property that Sir Ambrose could leave as he chose, and that he left to his ward Sylvia. I know this because Sir Ambrose died less than a year after the events I am telling you of, and he had not troubled to make a new will after Sylvia's death. I think the money went to the Crown—or perhaps it was to his son as next of kin—I don't really remember."

"So it was only to the interest of a son who wasn't there and the girl who died herself to make away with him," said Sir Henry thoughtfully "That doesn't seem very promising."

"Didn't the other woman get anything?" asked Jane. "The one Mrs. Bantry calls the Pussy woman."

"She wasn't mentioned in the will," said Mrs. Bantry.

"Miss Marple, you're not listening," said Sir Henry. "You're somewhere far away."

157

"I was thinking of old Mr. Badger, the chemist," said Miss Marple. "He had a very young housekeeper—young enough to be not only his daughter, but his grand-daughter. Not a word to anyone, and his family, a lot of nephews and nieces, full of expectations. And when he died, would you believe it, he'd been secretly married to her for two years? Of course Mr. Badger was a chemist, and a very rude, common old man as well, and Sir Ambrose Bercy was a very courtly gentleman, so Mrs. Bantry says, but for all that human nature is much the same everywhere."

There was a pause. Sir Henry looked very hard at Miss Marple who looked back at him with gently quizzical blue eyes. Jane Helier broke the silence.

"Was this Mrs. Carpenter good-looking?" she asked.

"Yes, in a very quiet way. Nothing startling."

"She had a very sympathetic voice," said Colonel Bantry.

"Purring—that's what I call it," said Mrs. Bantry. "Purring!"

"You'll be called a cat yourself one of these days, Dolly."

"I like being a cat in my home circle," said Mrs. Bantry. "I don't much like women anyway, and you know it. I like men and flowers."

"Excellent taste," said Sir Henry. "Especially in putting men first."

"That was tact," said Mrs. Bantry. "Well, now, what about my little problem? I've been quite fair, I think. Arthur, don't you think I've been fair?"

"Yes, my dear. I don't think there'll be any inquiry into the running by the stewards of the Jockey Club."

"First boy," said Mrs. Bantry, pointing a finger at Sir Henry.

"I'm going to be long winded. Because, you see, I haven't really got any feeling of certainty about the matter. First, Sir Ambrose. Well, he wouldn't take such an original method of committing suicide—and on the other hand he certainly had nothing to gain by the death of his ward. Exit Sir Ambrose. Mr. Curle. No motive for death of girl. If Sir Ambrose was intended victim, he might possibly have purloined a rare manuscript or two that no one else would miss. Very thin, and most unlikely. So I think, that in spite of Mrs. Bantry's suspicions as to his 'underclothing,' Mr. Curle is cleared. Miss Wye. Motive for death of Sir Ambrose—none. Motive for death of Sylvia pretty strong. She wanted Sylvia's young man, and wanted him rather badly—from Mrs. Bantry's account. She was with Sylvia that morning in the garden so had opportunity to pick leaves. No, we can't dismiss Miss Wye so easily. Young Lorimer. He's got a motive in either case. If he gets rid of his sweetheart, he can marry the other girl. Still it seems a bit drastic to kill her—what's a broken engagement these days? If Sir Ambrose dies, he will marry a rich girl instead of a poor one. That might be important or not—depends on his financial position. If I find that his estate was heavily mortgaged and that Mrs. Bantry has deliberately withheld that fact from us, I shall claim a foul. Now Mrs. Carpenter. You know, I have suspicions of Mrs. Carpenter. Those white hands, for one thing, and her excellent alibi at the time the herbs were picked—I always distrust alibis. And I've got another reason for suspecting her which I shall keep to myself. Still, on the whole, if I've got to plump, I shall plump for Miss Maud Wye, because there's more evidence against her than anyone else."

"Next boy," said Mrs. Bantry, and pointed at Dr. Lloyd.

"I think you're wrong, Clithering, in sticking to the theory that the girl's death was meant. I am convinced that the murderer intended to do away with Sir Ambrose. I don't think that young Lorimer had the necessary knowledge. I am inclined to believe that Mrs. Carpenter was the guilty party. She had been a long time with the family, knew all about the state of Sir Ambrose's health, and could easily arrange for this girl Sylvia (who, you said yourself, was rather stupid) to pick the right leaves. Motive, I confess, I don't see; but I hazard the guess that Sir Ambrose had at one time made a will in which she was mentioned. That's the best I can do."

Mrs. Bantry's pointing finger went on to Jane Helier.

"I don't know what to say," said Jane, "except this:

Why shouldn't the girl herself have done it? She took the leaves into the kitchen after all. And you say Sir Ambrose had been sticking out against her marriage. If he died, she'd get the money and be able to marry at once. She'd know just as much about Sir Ambrose's health as Mrs. Carpenter would."

Mrs. Bantry's finger came slowly round to Miss Marple. "Now then, School Marm," she said.

"Sir Henry has put it all very clearly—very clearly indeed," said Miss Marple. "And Dr. Lloyd was so right in what he said. Between them they seem to have made things so very clear. Only I don't think Dr. Lloyd quite realised one aspect of what he said. You see, not being Sir Ambrose's medical adviser, he couldn't know just what kind of heart trouble Sir Ambrose had, could he?"

"I don't quite see what you mean, Miss Marple," said Dr. Lloyd.

"You're assuming—aren't you?—that Sir Ambrose had the kind of heart that digitalin would affect adversely? But there's nothing to prove that that's so. It might be just the other way about."

"The other way about?"

"Yes, you did say that it was often prescribed for heart trouble?"

"Even then, Miss Marple, I don't see what that leads to?"

"Well, it would mean that he would have digitalin in his possession quite naturally—without having to account for it. What I am trying to say (I always express myself so badly) is this: Supposing you wanted to poison anyone with a fatal dose of digitalin. Wouldn't the simplest and the easiest way be to arrange for everyone to be poisoned— actually by digitalin leaves? It wouldn't be fatal in anyone else's case, of course, but no one would be surprised at one victim because, as Dr. Lloyd said, these things are so uncertain. No one would be likely to ask whether the girl had actually had a fatal dose of infusion of digitalis or something of that kind. He might have put it in a cocktail, or in her coffee or even made her drink it quite simply as a tonic."

"You mean Sir Ambrose poisoned his ward, the charming girl whom he loved?"

"That's just it," said Miss Marple. "Like Mr. Badger and his young housekeeper. Don't tell me it's absurd for a man of sixty to fall in love with a girl of twenty. It happens every day—and I daresay with an old autocrat like Sir Ambrose, it might take him queerly. These things become a madness sometimes. He couldn't bear the thought of her getting married—did his best to oppose it—and failed. His mad jealousy became so great that he preferred killing her to letting her go to young Lorimer. He must have thought of it some time beforehand, because that foxglove seed would have to be sown among the sage. He'd pick it himself when the time came, and send her into the kitchen with it. It's horrible to think of, but I suppose we must take as merciful a view of it as we can. Gentlemen of that age are sometimes very peculiar indeed where young girls are concerned. Our last organist—but there, I mustn't talk scandal."

"Mrs. Bantry," said Sir Henry. "Is this so?"

Mrs. Bantry nodded.

"Yes. I'd no idea of it—never dreamed of the thing being anything but an accident. Then, after Sir Ambrose's death, I got a letter. He had left directions to send it to me. He told me the truth in it. I don't know why—but he and I always got on very well together."

In the momentary silence, she seemed to feel an unspoken criticism and went on hastily:

"You think I'm betraying a confidence—but that isn't so. I've changed all the names. He wasn't really called Sir Ambrose Bercy. Didn't you see how Arthur stared stupidly when I said that name to him? He didn't understand at first. I've changed everything. It's like they say in magazines and in the beginning of books: 'All the characters in this story are purely fictitious.' You'll never know who they really are."

# CHAPTER XII

# THE AFFAIR AT THE BUNGALOW

"I'VE thought of something," said Jane Helier.

Her beautiful face was lit up with the confident smile of a child expecting approbation. It was a smile such as moved audiences nightly in London, and which had made the fortunes of photographers.

"It happened," she went on carefully, "to a friend of mine."

Everyone made encouraging but slightly hypocritical noises. Colonel Bantry, Mrs. Bantry, Sir Henry Clithering, Dr. Lloyd and old Miss Marple were one and all convinced that Jane's "friend" was Jane herself. She would have been quite incapable of remembering or taking an interest in anything affecting anyone else.

"My friend," went on Jane, "(I won't mention her name) was an actress—a very well-known actress."

No one expressed surprise. Sir Henry Clithering thought to himself: "Now I wonder how many sentences it will be before she forgets to keep up the fiction, and says 'I' instead of 'She'?"

"My friend was on tour in the provinces—this was a year or two ago. I suppose I'd better not give the name of the place. It was a riverside town not very far from London. I'll call it——"

She paused, her brows perplexed in thought. The invention of even a simple name appeared to be too much for her. Sir Henry came to the rescue.

162

"Shall we call it Riverbury?" he suggested gravely.

"Oh, yes, that would do splendidly. Riverbury, I'll remember that. Well, as I say, this—my friend—was at Riverbury with her company, and a very curious thing happened."

She puckered her brows again.

"It's very difficult," she said plaintively, "to say just what you want. One gets things mixed up and tells the wrong thing first."

"You're doing it beautifully," said Dr. Lloyd encouragingly. "Go on."

"Well, this curious thing happened. My friend was sent for to the police station. And she went. It seemed there had been a burglary at a riverside bungalow and they'd arrested a young man, and he told a very odd story. And so they sent for her.

"She'd never been to a police station before, but they were very nice to her—very nice indeed."

"They would be, I'm sure," said Sir Henry.

"The Sergeant—I think it was a Sergeant—or it may have been an Inspector—gave her a chair and explained things, and of course I saw at once that it was some mistake——"

"Aha," thought Sir Henry. "I! Here we are. I thought as much."

"My friend said so," continued Jane, serenely unconscious of her self-betrayal. "She explained she had been rehearsing with her understudy at the hotel and that she'd never even heard of this Mr. Faulkener. And the Sergeant said, 'Miss Hel——' "

She stopped and flushed.

"Miss Helman," suggested Sir Henry with a twinkle.

"Yes—yes, that would do. Thank you. He said, 'Well, Miss Helman, I felt it must be some mistake, knowing that you were stopping at the Bridge Hotel,' and he said would I have any objection to confronting—or was it being confronted? I can't remember."

"It doesn't really matter," said Sir Henry reassuringly.

"Anyway, with the young man. So I said, 'Of course

not.' And they brought him and said, 'This is Miss Helier,' and—Oh!" Jane broke off open-mouthed.

"Never mind, my dear," said Miss Marple consolingly. "We were bound to guess, you know. And you haven't given us the name of the place or anything that really matters."

"Well," said Jane, "I did mean to tell it as though it happened to someone else. But it *is* difficult, isn't it? I mean one forgets so."

Everyone assured her that it was very difficult, and soothed and reassured, she went on with her slightly involved narrative.

"He was a nice-looking man—quite a nice-looking man. Young, with reddish hair. His mouth just opened when he saw me. And the sergeant said, 'Is this the lady?' And he said, 'No, indeed it isn't. What an ass I have been.' And I smiled at him and said it didn't matter."

"I can picture the scene," said Sir Henry.

Jane Helier frowned.

"Let me see—how had I better go on?"

"Supposing you tell us what it was all about, dear?" said Miss Marple, so mildly that no one could suspect her of irony. "I mean what the young man's mistake was, and about the burglary."

"Oh, yes," said Jane. "Well, you see, this young man—Leslie Faulkener, his name was—had written a play. He'd written several plays, as a matter of fact, though none of them had ever been taken. And he had sent this particular play to me to read. I didn't know about it, because of course I have hundreds of plays sent to me and I read very few of them myself—only the ones I know something about. Anyway, there it was, and it seems that Mr. Faulkener got a letter from me—only it turned out not to be really from me—you understand——"

She paused anxiously, and they assured her that they understood.

"Saying that I'd read the play, and liked it very much and would he come down and talk it over with me. And it gave the address—The Bungalow, Riverbury. So Mr. Faulkener was frightfully pleased and he came down and arrived at this place—The Bungalow. A parlourmaid opened the door, and he asked for Miss Helier, and she said Miss Helier was in and expecting him and showed him into the drawing-room, and there a woman came to him. And he accepted her as me as a matter of course—which seems queer because after all he had seen me act and my photographs are very well known, aren't they?'

"Over the length and breadth of England," said Mrs. Bantry promptly. "But there's often a lot of difference between a photograph and its original, my dear Jane. And there's a great deal of difference between behind the footlights and off the stage. It's not every actress who stands the test as well as you do, remember."

"Well," said Jane slightly mollified, "that may be so. Anyway, he described this woman as tall and fair with big blue eyes and very good-looking, so I suppose it must have been near enough. He certainly had no suspicions. She sat down and began talking about his play and said she was anxious to do it. Whilst they were talking, cocktails were brought in and Mr. Faulkener had one as a matter of course. Well—that's all he remembers—having this cocktail. When he woke up, or came to himself, or whatever you call it—he was lying out in the road, by the hedge, of course, so that there would be no danger of his being run over. He felt very queer and shaky—so much so that he just got up and staggered along the road not quite knowing where he was going. He said if he'd had his senses about him he'd have gone back to the Bungalow and tried to find out what had happened. But he felt just stupid and dazed and walked along without quite knowing what he was doing. He was just more or less coming to himself when the police arrested him."

"Why did the police arrest him?" asked Dr. Lloyd.

"Oh! didn't I tell you?" said Jane opening her eyes very wide. "How very stupid I am. The burglary."

"You mentioned a burglary—but you didn't say where or what or why," said Mrs. Bantry.

"Well, this bungalow—the one he went to, of course—it

wasn't mine at all. It belonged to a man whose name was——"

Again Jane furrowed her brows.

"Do you want me to be godfather again?" asked Sir Henry. "Pseudonyms supplied free of charge. Describe the tenant and I'll do the naming."

"It was taken by a rich city man—a knight."

"Sir Herman Cohen," suggested Sir Henry.

"That will do beautifully. He took it for a lady—she was the wife of an actor, and she was also an actress herself."

"We'll call the actor Claud Leason," said Sir Henry, "and the lady would be known by her stage name, I suppose, so we'll call her Miss Mary Kerr."

"I think you're awfully clever," said Jane. "I don't know how you think of these things so easily. Well, you see this was sort of a week-end cottage for Sir Herman—did you say Herman?—and the lady. And, of course, his wife knew nothing about it."

"Which is so often the case," said Sir Henry.

"And he'd given this actress woman a good deal of jewellery including some very fine emeralds."

"Ah!" said Dr. Lloyd. "Now we're getting at it."

"This jewellery was at the bungalow, just locked up in a jewel case. The police said it was very careless—anyone might have taken it."

"You see, Dolly," said Colonel Bantry. "What do I always tell you?"

"Well, in my experience," said Mrs. Bantry, "it's always the people who are so dreadfully careful who lose things. I don't lock mine up in a jewel case—I keep it in a drawer loose, under my stockings. I daresay if—what's her name?—Mary Kerr had done the same, it would never have been stolen."

"It would," said Jane, "because all the drawers were burst open, and the contents strewn about."

"Then they weren't really looking for jewels," said Mrs. Bantry. "They were looking for secret papers. That's what always happens in books."

"I don't know about secret papers," said Jane doubtfully. "I never heard of any."

"Don't be distracted, Miss Helier," said Colonel Bantry. "Dolly's wild red-herrings are not to be taken seriously."

"About the burglary," said Sir Henry.

"Yes. Well the police were rung up by someone who said she was Miss Mary Kerr. She said the bungalow had been burgled and described a young man with red hair who had called there that morning. Her maid had thought there was something odd about him and had refused him admittance, but later they had seen him getting out through a window. She described the man so accurately that the police arrested him only an hour later and then he told his story and showed them the letter from me. And as I told you, they fetched me and when he saw me he said what I told you—that it hadn't been me at all!"

"A very curious story," said Dr. Lloyd. "Did Mr. Faulkener know this Miss Kerr?"

"No, he didn't—or he said he didn't. But I haven't told you the most curious part yet. The police went to the bungalow of course, and they found everything as described —drawers pulled out and jewels gone, but the whole place was empty. It wasn't till some hours later that Mary Kerr came back, and when she did she said she'd never rung them up at all and this was the first she'd heard of it. It seemed that she had had a wire that morning from a manager offering her a most important part and making an appointment, so she had naturally rushed up to town to keep it. When she got there, she found that the whole thing was a hoax. No telegram had ever been sent."

"A common enough ruse to get her out of the way," commented Sir Henry. "What about the servants?"

"The same sort of thing happened there. There was only one, and she was rung up on the telephone—apparently by Mary Kerr, who said she had left a most important thing behind. She directed the maid to bring up a certain handbag which was in the drawer of her bedroom. She was to catch the first train. The maid did so, of course locking up the house; but when she arrived at Miss Kerr's club, where she had been told to meet her mistress, she waited there in vain.

"H'm," said Sir Henry. "I begin to see. The house was left empty, and to make an entry by one of the windows would present few difficulties, I should imagine. But I don't quite see where Mr. Faulkener comes in. Who did ring up the police, if it wasn't Miss Kerr?"

"That's what nobody knew or ever found out."

"Curious," said Sir Henry. "Did the young man turn out to be genuinely the person he said he was?"

"Oh, yes, that part of it was all right. He'd even got the letter which was supposed to be written by me. It wasn't the least bit like my handwriting—but then, of course, he couldn't be supposed to know that."

"Well, let's state the position clearly," said Sir Henry. "Correct me if I go wrong. The lady and the maid are decoyed from the house. This young man is decoyed down there by means of a bogus letter—colour being lent to this last by the fact that you actually are performing at Riverbury that week. The young man is doped, and the police are rung up and have their suspicions directed against him. A burglary actually has taken place. I presume the jewels were taken?"

"Oh, yes."

"Were they ever recovered?"

"No, never. I think, as a matter of fact, Sir Herman tried to hush things up all he knew how. But he couldn't manage it, and I rather fancy his wife started divorce proceedings in consequence. Still, I don't really know about that."

"What happened to Mr. Leslie Faulkener?"

"He was released in the end. The police said they hadn't really got enough against him. Don't you think the whole thing was rather odd?"

"Distinctly odd. The first question is whose story to believe? In telling it, Miss Helier, I noticed that you incline towards believing Mr. Faulkener. Have you any reason for doing so beyond your own instinct in the matter?"

"N-no," said Jane unwillingly. "I suppose I haven't.

But he was so very nice, and so apologetic for having mistaken anyone else for me, that I feel sure he *must* have been telling the truth."

"I see," said Sir Henry smiling. "But you must admit that he could have invented the story quite easily. He could write the letter purporting to be from you himself. He could also dope himself after successfully committing the burglary. But I confess I don't see where the *point* of all that would be. Easier to enter the house, help himself, and disappear quietly—unless just possibly he was observed by someone in the neighbourhood and knew himself to have been observed. Then he might hastily concoct this plan for diverting suspicion from himself and accounting for his presence in the neighbourhood."

"Was he well off?" asked Miss Marple.

"I don't think so," said Jane. "No, I believe he was rather hard up."

"The whole thing seems curious," said Dr. Lloyd. "I must confess that if we accept the young man's story as true, it seems to make the case much more difficult. Why should the unknown woman who pretended to be Miss Helier drag this unknown man into the affair? Why should she stage such an elaborate comedy?"

"Tell me, Jane," said Mrs. Bantry. "Did young Faulkener ever come face to face with Mary Kerr at any stage of the proceedings?"

"I don't quite know," said Jane slowly, as she puzzled her brows in remembrance.

"Because if he didn't the case is solved!" said Mrs. Bantry. "I'm sure I'm right. What is easier than to pretend you're called up to town? You telephone to your maid from Paddington or whatever station you arrive at, and as she comes up to town, you go down again. The young man calls by appointment, he's doped, you set the stage for the burglary, overdoing it as much as possible. You telephone the police, give a description of your scapegoat, and off you go to town again. Then you arrive home by a later train and do the surprised innocent."

"But why should she steal her own jewels, Dolly?"

"They always do," said Mrs. Bantry. "And anyway, I can think of hundreds of reasons. She may have wanted money at once—old Sir Herman wouldn't give her cash, perhaps, so she pretends the jewels are stolen and then sells them secretly. Or she may have been being blackmailed by someone who threatened to tell her husband or Sir Herman's wife. Or she may have already sold the jewels and Sir Herman was getting ratty and asking to see them, so she had to do something about it. That's done a good deal in books. Or perhaps he was going to have them reset and she'd got paste replicas. Or—here's a very good idea—and not so much done in books—she pretends they are stolen, gets in an awful state and he gives her a fresh lot. So she gets two lots instead of one. That kind of woman, I am sure, is most frightfully artful."

"You are clever, Dolly," said Jane admiringly. "I never thought of that."

"You may be clever, but she doesn't say you're right," said Colonel Bantry. "I incline to suspicion of the city gentleman. He'd know the sort of telegram to get the lady out of the way, and he could manage the rest easily enough with the help of a new lady friend. Nobody seems to have thought of asking *him* for an alibi."

"What do you think, Miss Marple?" asked Jane, turning towards the old lady who had sat silent, a puzzled frown on her face.

"My dear, I really don't know what to say. Sir Henry will laugh, but I recall no village parallel to help me this time. Of course there are several questions that suggest themselves. For instance, the servant question. In—ahem—an irregular ménage of the kind you describe, the servant employed would doubtless be perfectly aware of the state of things, and a really nice girl would not take such a place—her mother wouldn't let her for a minute. So I think we can assume that the maid was *not* a really trustworthy character. She may have been in league with the thieves. She would leave the house open for them and actually go to London as though sure of the pretence telephone message so as to divert suspicion from herself. I must confess that

that seems the most probable solution. Only if ordinary thieves were concerned it seems very odd. It seems to argue more knowledge than a maid servant was likely to have."

Miss Marple paused and then went on dreamily:

"I can't help feeling that there was some—well, what I must describe as personal feeling about the whole thing. Supposing somebody had a spite, for instance? Don't you think that that would explain things better? A deliberate attempt to get him into trouble. That's what it looks like. And yet—that's not entirely satisfactory. . ."

"Why, Doctor, you haven't said anything," said Jane. "I'd forgotten you."

"I'm always getting forgotten," said the grizzled doctor sadly. "I must have a very inconspicuous personality."

"Oh, no!" said Jane. "Do tell us what you think?"

"I'm rather in the position of agreeing with everyone's solutions—and yet with none of them. I myself have a farfetched and probably totally erroneous theory that the wife may have had something to do with it. Sir Herman's wife, I mean. I've no grounds for thinking so—only you would be surprised if you knew the extraordinary things that a wronged wife will take it into her head to do."

"Oh! Dr. Lloyd," cried Miss Marple excitedly. "How clever of you. And I never thought of poor Mrs. Pebmarsh."

Jane stared at her.

"Mrs. Pebmarsh? Who is Mrs. Pebmarsh?"

"Well——" Miss Marple hesitated. "I don't know that she really comes in. She's a laundress. And she stole an opal pin that was pinned into a blouse and put it in another woman's house."

Jane looked more fogged than ever.

"And that makes it all perfectly clear to you, Miss Marple?" said Sir Henry, with his twinkle.

But to his surprise Miss Marple shook her head.

"No, I'm afraid it doesn't. I must confess myself completely at a loss. What I do realise is that women must stick together—one should, in an emergency, stand by one's own sex. I think that's the moral of the story Miss Helier has told us."

"I must confess that that particular ethical significance of the mystery has escaped me," said Sir Henry gravely. "Perhaps I shall see the significance of your point more clearly when Miss Helier has revealed the solution."

"Eh?" said Jane looking rather bewildered.

"I was observing that, in childish language, we 'give it up.' You and you alone, Miss Helier, have had the high honour of presenting such an absolutely baffling mystery that even Miss Marple has to confess herself defeated."

"You all give it up?" asked Jane.

"Yes." After a minute's silence during which he waited for the others to speak, Sir Henry constituted himself spokesman once more. "That is to say we stand or fall by the sketchy solutions we have tentatively advanced. One each for the mere men, two for Miss Marple, and a round dozen from Mrs. B."

"It was not a dozen," said Mrs. Bantry. "They were variations on a main theme. And how often am I to tell you that I will *not* be called Mrs. B.?"

"So you all give it up," said Jane thoughtfully. "That's very interesting."

She leaned back in her chair and began to polish her nails rather absent-mindedly.

"Well," said Mrs. Bantry. "Come on, Jane. What is the solution?"

"The solution?"

"Yes. What really happened?"

Jane stared at her.

"I haven't the least idea."

*"What?"*

"I've always wondered. I thought you were all so clever one of you would be able to tell *me.*"

Everybody harboured feelings of annoyance. It was all very well for Jane to be so beautiful—but at this moment everyone felt that stupidity could be carried too far. Even the most transcendent loveliness could not excuse it.

172

"You mean the truth was never discovered?" said Sir Henry.

"No. That's why, as I say, I did think you would be able to tell *me*."

Jane sounded injured. It was plain that she felt she had a grievance.

"Well—I'm—I'm—" said Colonel Bantry, words failing him.

"You are the most aggravating girl, Jane," said his wife. "Anyway, I'm sure and always shall be that I was right. If you just tell us the proper names of all the people, I shall be *quite* sure."

"I don't think I could do that," said Jane slowly.

"No, dear," said Miss Marple. "Miss Helier couldn't do that."

"Of course she could," said Mrs. Bantry. "Don't be so highminded, Jane. We older folks must have a bit of scandal. At any rate tell us who the city magnate was."

But Jane shook her head, and Miss Marple, in her old-fashioned way, continued to support the girl.

"It must have been a very distressing business,' she said.

"No," said Jane truthfully. "I think—I think I rather enjoyed it."

"Well, perhaps you did," said Miss Marple. "I suppose it was a break in the monotony. What play were you acting in?"

"*Smith.*"

"Oh, yes. That's one of Mr. Somerset Maugham's, isn't it? All his are very clever, I think. I've seen them nearly all."

"You're reviving it to go on tour next Autumn, aren't you?" asked Mrs. Bantry.

Jane nodded.

"Well," said Miss Marple rising, "I must go home. Such late hours! But we've had a very entertaining evening. Most unusually so. I think Miss Helier's story wins the prize. Don't you agree?"

"I'm sorry you're angry with me," said Jane. "About

not knowing the end, I mean. I suppose I should have said so sooner."

Her tone sounded wistful. Dr. Lloyd rose gallantly to the occasion.

"My dear young lady, why should you? You gave us a very pretty problem to sharpen our wits upon. I am only sorry we could none of us solve it convincingly."

"Speak for yourself," said Mrs. Bantry. "I *did* solve it. I'm convinced I am right."

"Do you know, I really believe you are," said Jane. "What you said sounded so probable."

"Which of her seven solutions do you refer to?" asked Sir Henry teasingly.

Dr. Lloyd gallantly assisted Miss Marple to put on her goloshes. "Just in case," as the old lady explained. The doctor was to be her escort to her old-world cottage. Wrapped in several woollen shawls, Miss Marple wished everyone good-night once more. She came to Jane Helier last and leaning forward, she murmured something in the actress's ear. A startled "Oh!" burst from Jane—so loud as to cause the others to turn their heads.

Smiling and nodding, Miss Marple made her exit, Jane Helier staring after her.

"Are you coming to bed, Jane?" asked Mrs. Bantry. "What's the matter with you? You're staring as though you'd seen a ghost."

With a deep sigh Jane came to herself, shed a beautiful and bewildering smile on the two men and followed her hostess up the staircase. Mrs. Bantry came into the girl's room with her.

"Your fire's nearly out," said Mrs. Bantry, giving it a vicious and ineffectual poke. "They can't have made it up properly. How stupid housemaids are. Still, I suppose we are rather late to-night. Why, it's actually past one o'clock!"

"Do you think there are many people like her?" asked Jane Helier.

She was sitting on the side of the bed apparently wrapped in thought.

"Like the housemaid?"

"No. Like that funny old woman—what's her name—Marple?"

"Oh! I don't know. I suppose she's a fairly common type in a small village."

"Oh, dear," said Jane. "I don't know what to do."

She sighed deeply.

"What's the matter?"

"I'm worried."

"What about?"

"Dolly," Jane Helier was portentously solemn. "Do you know what that queer old lady whispered to me before she went out of the door to-night?"

"No. What?"

"She said: '*I shouldn't do it if I were you, my dear. Never put yourself too much in another woman's power, even if you think she's your friend at the moment.*' You know, Dolly, that's awfully true."

"The maxim? Yes, perhaps it is. But I don't see the application."

"I suppose you can't ever really trust a woman. And I should be in her power. I never thought of that."

"What woman are you talking about?"

"Netta Greene, my understudy."

"What on earth does Miss Marple know about your understudy?"

"I supposed she guessed—but I can't see how."

"Jane, will you kindly tell me at once what you are talking about?"

"The story. The one I told. Oh, Dolly, that woman, you know—the one that took Claud from me?"

Mrs. Bantry nodded, casting her mind back rapidly to the first of Jane's unfortunate marriages—to Claud Averbury, the actor.

"He married her; and I could have told him how it would be. Claud doesn't know, but she's carrying on with Sir Joseph Salmon—week-ends with him at the bungalow I told you about. I wanted her shown up—I would like everyone to know the sort of woman she was. And you see, with a burglary, everything would be bound to come out."

"Jane!" gasped Mrs. Bantry. "Did *you* engineer this story you've been telling us?"

Jane nodded.

"That's why I chose *Smith*. I wear parlourmaid's kit in it, you know. So I should have it handy. And when they sent for me to the police station it's the easiest thing in the world to say I was rehearsing my part with my understudy at the hotel. Really, of course, we would be at the bungalow. I just to open the door and bring in the cocktails, and Netta to pretend to be me. He'd never see *her* again, of course, so there would be no fear of his recognising her. And I can make myself look quite different as a parlourmaid; and besides, one doesn't look at parlourmaids as though they were people. We planned to drag him out into the road afterwards, bag the jewel case, telephone the police and get back to the hotel. I shouldn't like the poor young man to suffer, but Sir Henry didn't seem to think he would, did he? And she'd be in the papers and everything— and Claud would see what she was really like."

Mrs. Bantry sat down and groaned.

"Oh! my poor head. And all the time—Jane Helier, you deceitful girl! Telling us that story the way you did!"

"I *am* a good actress," said Jane complacently. "I always have been, whatever people choose to say. I didn't give myself away once, did I?"

"Miss Marple was right," murmured Mrs. Bantry. "The personal element. Oh, yes, the personal element. Jane, my good child, do you realise that theft is theft, and you might have been sent to prison?"

"Well, none of you guessed," said Jane. "Except Miss Marple." The worried expression returned to her face. "Dolly, do you *really* think there are many like her?"

"Frankly, I don't," said Mrs. Bantry.

Jane sighed again.

"Still, one had better not risk it. And of course I should be in Netta's power—that's true enough. She might turn against me or blackmail me or anything. She helped me think out the details and she professed to be devoted to me, but one never *does* know with women. No, I think Miss Marple was right. I had better not risk it."

"But, my dear, you have risked it."

"Oh, no." Jane opened her blue eyes very wide. "Don't you understand? *None of this has happened yet!* I was—well, trying it on the dog, so to speak."

"I don't profess to understand your theatrical slang," said Mrs. Bantry with dignity. "Do you mean this is a future project—not a past deed?"

"I was going to do it this Autumn—in September. I don't know what to do now."

"And Jane Marple guessed—actually guessed the truth and never told us," said Mrs. Bantry wrathfully.

"I think that was why she said that—about women sticking together. She wouldn't give me away before the men. That was nice of her. I don't mind *your* knowing, Dolly."

"Well, give the idea up, Jane. I beg of you."

"I think I shall," murmured Miss Helier. "There might be other Miss Marples. . . ."

# Chapter XIII

## Death by Drowning

Sir Henry Clithering, ex-Commissioner of Scotland Yard, was staying with his friends the Bantrys at their place near the little village of St. Mary Mead.

On Saturday morning, coming down to breakfast at the pleasant guestly hour of ten-fifteen, he almost collided with his hostess, Mrs. Bantry, in the doorway of the breakfast room. She was rushing from the room, evidently in a condition of some excitement and distress.

Colonel Bantry was sitting at the table, his face rather redder than usual.

" 'Morning, Clithering," he said. "Nice day. Help yourself."

Sir Henry obeyed. As he took his seat, a plate of kidneys and bacon in front of him, his host went on:

"Dolly's a bit upset this morning."

"Yes—er—I rather thought so," said Sir Henry, mildly.

He wondered a little. His hostess was of a placid disposition, little given to moods or excitements. As far as Sir Henry knew, she felt keenly on one subject only—gardening.

"Yes," said Colonel Bantry. "Bit of news we got this morning upset her. Girl in the village—Emmott's daughter—Emmott who keeps the Blue Boar."

"Oh, yes, of course."

"Ye-es," said Colonel Bantry ruminatively. "Pretty girl. Got herself into trouble. Usual story. I've been arguing with Dolly about that. Foolish of me. Women never see sense. Dolly was all up in arms for the girl—you know what women are—men are brutes—all the rest of it, etcetera. But it's not so simple as all that—not in these days. Girls know what they're about. Fellow who seduces a girl's not necessarily a villain. Fifty-fifty as often as not. I rather liked young Sandford myself. A young ass rather than a Don Juan, I should have said."

"It is this man Sandford who got the girl into trouble?"

"So it seems. Of course I don't know anything personally," said the colonel cautiously. "It's all gossip and chat. You know what this place is! As I say, I *know* nothing. And I'm not like Dolly—leaping to conclusions, flinging accusations all over the place. Damn it all, one ought to be careful in what one says. You know—inquest and all that."

"Inquest?"

Colonel Bantry stared.

"Yes. Didn't I tell you? Girl drowned herself. That's what all the pother's about."

"That's a nasty business," said Sir Henry.

"Of course it is. Don't like to think of it myself. Poor pretty little devil. Her father's a hard man by all accounts. I suppose she just felt she couldn't face the music."

He paused.

"That's what's upset Dolly so."

"Where did she drown herself?"

"In the river. Just below the mill it runs pretty fast. There's a footpath and a bridge across. They think she threw herself off that. Well, well, it doesn't bear thinking about."

And with a portentous rustle, Colonel Bantry opened his newspaper and proceeded to distract his mind from painful matters by an absorption in the newest iniquities of the government.

Sir Henry was only mildly interested by the village tragedy. After breakfast, he established himself on a comfortable chair on the lawn, tilted his hat over his eyes and contemplated life from a peaceful angle.

It was about half-past eleven when a neat parlourmaid tripped across the lawn.

"If you please, sir, Miss Marple has called and would like to see you."

"Miss Marple?"

Sir Henry sat up and straightened his hat. The name surprised him. He remembered Miss Marple very well— her gentle quiet old-maidish ways, her amazing penetration. He remembered a dozen unsolved and hypothetical cases—and how in each case this typical "old maid of the village" had leaped unerringly to the right solution of the mystery. Sir Henry had a very deep respect for Miss Marple. He wondered what had brought her to see him.

Miss Marple was sitting in the drawing-room—very upright as always, a gaily coloured marketing basket of foreign extraction beside her. Her cheeks were rather pink, and she seemed flustered.

"Sir Henry—I am so glad. So fortunate to find you. I just happened to hear that you were staying down here. . . . I do hope you will forgive me. . . ."

"This is a great pleasure," said Sir Henry, taking her hand. "I'm afraid Mrs. Bantry's out."

"Yes," said Miss Marple. "I saw her talking to Footit, the butcher, as I passed. Henry Footit was run over yesterday—that was his dog. One of those smooth-haired fox terriers, rather stout and quarrelsome, that butchers always seem to have."

"Yes," said Sir Henry helpfully.

"I was glad to get here when she wasn't at home," continued Miss Marple. "Because it was you I wanted to see. About this sad affair."

"Henry Footit?" asked Sir Henry, slightly bewildered.

Miss Marple threw him a reproachful glance.

"No, no. Rose Emmott, of course. You've heard?"

Sir Henry nodded.

"Bantry was telling me. Very sad."

He was a little puzzled. He could not conceive why Miss Marple should want to see him about Rose Emmott.

Miss Marple sat down again. Sir Henry also sat. When the old lady spoke her manner had changed. It was grave, and had a certain dignity.

180

"You may remember, Sir Henry, that on one or two occasions we played what was really a pleasant kind of game. Propounding mysteries and giving solutions. You were kind enough to say that I—that I did not do too badly."

"You beat us all," said Sir Henry warmly. "You displayed an absolute genius for getting to the truth. And you always instanced, I remember, some village parallel which had supplied you with the clue."

He smiled as he spoke, but Miss Marple did not smile. She remained very grave.

"What you said has emboldened me to come to you now. I feel that if I say something to you—at least you will not laugh at me."

He realised suddenly that she was in deadly earnest.

"Certainly, I will not laugh," he said gently.

"Sir Henry—this girl—Rose Emmott. She did not drown herself—*she was murdered.* . . . And I know who murdered her."

Sir Henry was silent with sheer astonishment for quite three seconds. Miss Marple's voice had been perfectly quiet and unexcited. She might have been making the most ordinary statement in the world for all the emotion she showed.

"That is a very serious statement to make, Miss Marple," said Sir Henry when he had recovered his breath.

She nodded her head gently several times.

"I know—I know—that is why I have come to you."

"But, my dear lady, I am not the person to come to. I am merely a private individual nowadays. If you have knowledge of the kind you claim, you must go to the police."

"I don't think I can do that," said Miss Marple.

"But why not?"

"Because, you see, I haven't got any—what you call *knowledge.*"

"You mean it's only a guess on your part?"

"You can call it that, if you like, but it's not really that at all. I *know.* I'm in a position to know; but if I gave my reasons for knowing to Inspector Drewitt—well, he'd simply laugh. And really, I don't know that I'd blame him. It's very difficult to understand what you might call specialised knowledge."

"Such as?" suggested Sir Henry.

Miss Marple smiled a little.

"If I were to tell you that I know because of a man called Peasegood leaving turnips instead of carrots when he came round with a cart and sold vegetables to my niece several years ago——"

She stopped eloquently.

"A very appropriate name for the trade," murmured Sir Henry. "You mean that you are simply judging from the facts in a parallel case."

"I know human nature," said Miss Marple. "It's impossible not to know human nature living in a village all these years. The question is, do you believe me, or don't you?"

She looked at him very straight. The pink flush had heightened on her cheeks. Her eyes met his steadily without wavering.

Sir Henry was a man with a very vast experience of life. He made his decisions quickly without beating about the bush. Unlikely and fantastic as Miss Marple's statement might seem, he was instantly aware that he accepted it.

"I *do* believe you, Miss Marple. But I do not see what you want me to do in the matter, or why you have come to me."

"I have thought and thought about it," said Miss Marple. "As I said, it would be useless going to the police without any facts. I have no facts. What I would ask you to do is to interest yourself in the matter—Inspector Drewitt would be most flattered, I am sure. And, of course, if the matter went farther, Colonel Melchett, the Chief Constable, I am sure, would be wax in your hands."

She looked at him appealingly.

"And what data are you going to give me to work upon?"

"I thought," said Miss Marple, "of writing a name—*the* name—on a piece of paper and giving it to you. Then if, on investigation, you decide that the—the *person*—is not involved in any way—well, I shall have been quite wrong."

She paused and then added with a slight shiver. "It would be so dreadful—so very dreadful—if an innocent person were to be hanged."

"What on earth——" cried Sir Henry startled.

She turned a distressed face upon him.

"I may be wrong about that—though I don't think so. Inspector Drewitt, you see, is really an intelligent man. But a mediocre amount of intelligence is sometimes most dangerous. It does not take one far enough."

Sir Henry looked at her curiously.

Fumbling a little, Miss Marple opened a small reticule, took out a little notebook, tore out a leaf, carefully wrote a name on it and folding it in two, handed it to Sir Henry.

He opened it and read the name. It conveyed nothing to him, but his eyebrows lifted a little. He looked across at Miss Marple and tucked the piece of paper in his pocket.

"Well, well," he said. "Rather an extraordinary business, this. I've never done anything like it before. But I'm going to back my judgment—of *you*, Miss Marple."

Sir Henry was sitting in a room with Colonel Melchett, the Chief Constable of the county, and Inspector Drewitt.

The Chief Constable was a little man of aggressively military demeanour. The Inspector was big and broad and eminently sensible.

"I really do feel I'm butting in," said Sir Henry with a pleasant smile. "I can't really tell you why I'm doing it." (Strict truth, this!)

"My dear fellow, we're charmed. It's a great compliment."

"Honoured, Sir Henry," said the Inspector.

The Chief Constable was thinking: 'Bored to death, poor fellow, at the Bantrys. The old man abusing the government and the old woman babbling on about bulbs."

The Inspector was thinking: "Pity we're not up against

183

a real teaser. One of the best brains in England, I've heard it said. Pity it's all such plain sailing."

Aloud, the Chief Constable said:

"I'm afraid it's all very sordid and straightforward. First idea was that the girl had pitched herself in. She was in the family way, you understand. However, our doctor, Haydock, is a careful fellow. He noticed the bruises on each arm—upper arm. Caused before death. Just where a fellow would have taken her by the arms and flung her in."

"Would that require much strength?"

"I think not. There would be no struggle—the girl would be taken unawares. It's a footbridge of slippery wood. Easiest thing in the world to pitch her over—there's no handrail that side."

"You know for a fact that the tragedy occurred there?"

"Yes. We've got a boy—Jimmy Brown—aged twelve. He was in the woods on the other side. He heard a kind of scream from the bridge and a splash. It was dusk, you know—difficult to see anything. Presently he saw something white floating down in the water and he ran and got help. They got her out, but it was too late to revive her."

Sir Henry nodded.

"The boy saw no one on the bridge?"

"No. But, as I tell you, it was dusk, and there's mist always hanging about there. I'm going to question him as to whether he saw anyone about just afterwards or just before. You see he naturally assumed that the girl had thrown herself over. Everybody did to start with."

"Still, we've got the note," said Inspector Drewitt. He turned to Sir Henry.

"Note in the dead girl's pocket, sir. Written with a kind of artist's pencil it was, and all of a sop though the paper was we managed to read it."

"And what did it say?"

"It was from young Sandford. 'All right,' that's how it ran. 'I'll meet you at the bridge at eight-thirty.—R.S.' Well, it was as near as might be to eight-thirty—a few minutes after—when Jimmy Brown heard the cry and the splash."

"I don't know whether you've met Sandford at all?"

went on Colonel Melchett. "He's been down here about a month. One of those modern day young architects who build peculiar houses. He's doing a house for Allington. God knows what it's going to be like—full of new-fangled stuff, I suppose. Glass dinner table and surgical chairs made of steel and webbing. Well, that's neither here nor there, but it shows the kind of chap Sandford is. Bolshie, you know—no morals."

"Seduction," said Sir Henry mildly, "is quite an old-established crime though it does not, of course, date back so far as murder."

Colonel Melchett stared.

"Oh! yes," he said. "Quite. Quite."

"Well, Sir Henry," said Drewitt, "there it is—an ugly business, but plain. This young Sandford gets the girl into trouble. Then he's all for clearing off back to London. He's got a girl there—nice young lady—he's engaged to be married to her. Well, naturally this business, if she gets to hear of it, may cook his goose good and proper. He meets Rose at the bridge—it's a misty evening, no one about—he catches her by the shoulders and pitches her in. A proper young swine—and deserves what's coming to him. That's my opinion."

Sir Henry was silent for a minute or two. He perceived a strong undercurrent of local prejudice. A new fangled architect was not likely to be popular in the conservative village of St. Mary Mead.

"There is no doubt, I suppose, that this man, Sandford, was actually the father of the coming child?" he asked.

"He's the father all right" said Drewitt. "Rose Emmott let out as much to her father. She thought he'd marry her. Marry her! Not he!"

"Dear me," thought Sir Henry, "I seem to be back in mid-Victorian melodrama. Unsuspecting girl, the villain from London, the stern father, the betrayal—we only need the faithful village lover. Yes, I think it's time I asked about him."

And aloud he said:

"Hadn't the girl a young man of her own down here?"

"You mean Joe Ellis?" said the inspector. "Good fellow Joe. Carpentering's his trade. Ah! If she'd stuck to Joe——"

Colonel Melchett nodded approval.

"Stick to your own class," he snapped.

"How did Joe Ellis take this affair?" asked Sir Henry.

"Nobody knew how he was taking it," said the inspector. "He's a quiet fellow, is Joe. Close. Anything Rose did was right in his eyes. She had him on a string all right. Just hoped she'd come back to him some day—that was his attitude, I reckon."

"I'd like to see him," said Sir Henry.

"Oh! We're going to look him up," said Colonel Melchett. "We're not neglecting any line. I thought myself we'd see Emmott first, then Sandford, and then we can go on and see Ellis. That suit you, Clithering?"

Sir Henry said it would suit him admirably.

They found Tom Emmott at the Blue Boar. He was a big burly man of middle age with a shifty eye and a truculent jaw.

"Glad to see you, gentlemen—good-morning, Colonel. Come in here and we can be private. Can I offer you anything, gentlemen? No? It's as you please. You've come about this business of my poor girl. Ah! She was a good girl, Rose was. Always was a good girl—till this bloody swine—beg pardon, but that's what he is—till he came along. Promised her marriage, he did. But I'll have the law of him. Drove her to it, he did. Murdering swine. Bringing disgrace on all of us. My poor girl."

"Your daughter distinctly told you that Mr. Sandford was responsible for her condition?" asked Melchett crisply.

"She did. In this very room she did."

"And what did you say to her?" asked Sir Henry.

"Say to her?" The man seemed momentarily taken aback.

"Yes. You didn't, for example, threaten to turn her out of the house."

"I was a bit upset—that's only natural. I'm sure you'll agree that's only natural. But, of course, I didn't turn her out of the house. I wouldn't do such a thing." He assumed virtuous indignation. "No. What's the law for—that's what I say. What's the law for? He'd got to do the right thing by her. And if he didn't, by God, he'd got to pay."

He brought down his fist on the table

"What time did you last see your daughter?" asked Melchett.

"Yesterday—tea time."

"What was her manner then?"

"Well—much as usual. I didn't notice anything. If I'd known——"

"But you didn't know," said the inspector drily.

They took their leave.

"Emmott hardly creates a favourable impression," said Sir Henry thoughtfully.

"Bit of a blackguard," said Melchett "He'd have bled Sandford all right if he'd had the chance"

Their next call was on the architect. Rex Sandford was very unlike the picture Sir Henry had unconsciously formed of him. He was a tall young man, very fair and very thin. His eyes were blue and dreamy, his hair was untidy and rather too long. His speech was a little too ladylike.

Colonel Melchett introduced himself and his companions. Then passing straight to the object of his visit, he invited the architect to make a statement as to his movements on the previous evening.

"You understand," he said warningly. "I have no power to compel a statement from you and any statement you make may be used in evidence against you. I want the position to be quite clear to you."

"I—I don't understand," said Sandford.

"You understand that the girl Rose Emmott was drowned last night?"

"I know. Oh! it's too, too distressing. Really, I haven't slept a wink. I've been incapable of any work to-day. I feel responsible—terribly responsible."

He ran his hands through his hair, making it untidier still. "I never meant any harm," he said piteously. "I never thought. I never dreamt—she'd take it that way."

He sat down at a table and buried his face in his hands.

"Do I understand you to say, Mr. Sandford, that you refuse to make a statement as to where you were last night at eight-thirty?"

"No, no—certainly not. I was out. I went for a walk."

"You went to meet Miss Emmott?"

"No. I went by myself. Through the woods. A long way."

"Then how do you account for this note, sir, which was found in the dead girl's pocket?"

And Inspector Drewitt read it unemotionally aloud.

"Now, sir," he finished. "Do you deny that you wrote that?"

"No-no. You're right. I did write it. Rose asked me to meet her. She insisted. I didn't know what to do. So I wrote that note."

"Ah, that's better," said the inspector.

"But I didn't go!" Sandford's voice rose high and excited. "I didn't go! I felt it would be much better not. I was returning to town to-morrow. I felt it would be better not—not to meet. I intended to write from London and—and make—some arrangement."

"You are aware, sir, that this girl was going to have a child, and that she had named you as its father?"

Sandford groaned, but did not answer.

"Was that statement true, sir?"

Sandford buried his face deeper.

"I suppose so," he said in a muffled voice.

"Ah!" Inspector Drewitt could not disguise his satisfaction. "Now about this 'walk' of yours. Is there anyone who saw you last night?"

"I don't know. I don't think so. As far as I can remember, I didn't meet anybody."

"That's a pity."

"What do you mean?" Sandford stared wildly at him. "What does it matter whether I was out for a walk or not? What difference does that make to Rose drowning herself?"

"Ah!" said the inspector. "But you see, *she didn't*. She was thrown in deliberately, Mr. Sandford. '

"She was——" It took him a minute or two to take in all the horror of it. "My God! Then——"

He dropped into a chair.

Colonel Melchett made a move to depart.

"You understand, Sandford," he said ' You are on no account to leave this house."

The three men left together. The inspector and the Chief Constable exchanged glances.

"That's enough, I think, sir," said the inspector.

"Yes. Get a warrant made out and arrest him."

"Excuse me," said Sir Henry, "I've forgotten my gloves."

He re-entered the house rapidly. Sandford was sitting just as they had left him, staring dazedly in front of him.

"I have come back," said Sir Henry, ' to tell you that I, personally, am anxious to do all I can to assist you. The motive of my interest in you I am not at liberty to reveal. But I am going to ask you, if you will, to tell me as briefly as possible exactly what passed between you and this girl Rose."

"She was very pretty," said Sandford. "Very pretty and very alluring. And—and she made a dead set for me. Before God, that's true. She wouldn't let me alone. And it was lonely down here, and nobody liked me much, and—and, as I say she was amazingly pretty and she seemed to know her way about and all that——" His voice died away. He looked up. "And then this happened. She wanted me to marry her. I didn't know what to do. I'm engaged to a girl in London. If she ever gets to hear of this—and she will, of course—well, it's all up. She won't understand. How could she? And I'm a rotter, of course. As I say, I didn't know what to do. I avoided seeing Rose again. I thought I'd get back to town—see my lawyer—make arrangements about money and so forth, for her. God, what a fool I've been! And it's all so clear—the case against me. But they've made a mistake. She *must* have done it herself."

"Did she ever threaten to take her life?"

Sandford shook his head.

189

"Never. I shouldn't have said she was that sort."

"What about a man called Joe Ellis?"

"The carpenter fellow? Good old village stock. Dull fellow—but crazy about Rose."

"He might have been jealous?" suggested Sir Henry.

"I suppose he was a bit—but he's the bovine kind. He'd suffer in silence."

"Well," said Sir Henry. "I must be going."

He rejoined the others.

"You know, Melchett," he said, "I feel we ought to have a look at this other fellow—Ellis—before we do anything drastic. Pity if you made an arrest that turned out to be a mistake. After all, jealousy is a pretty good motive for murder—and a pretty common one, too."

"That's true enough," said the inspector. "But Joe Ellis isn't that kind. He wouldn't hurt a fly. Why, nobody's ever seen him out of temper. Still, I agree we'd better just ask him where he was last night. He'll be at home now. He lodges with Mrs. Bartlett—very decent soul—a widow, she takes in a bit of washing."

The little cottage to which they bent their footsteps was spotlessly clean and neat. A big stout woman of middle age opened the door to them. She had a pleasant face and blue eyes.

"Good-morning, Mrs. Bartlett," said the inspector. "Is Joe Ellis here?"

"Came back not ten minutes ago," said Mrs. Bartlett. "Step inside, will you, please, sirs."

Wiping her hands on her apron she led them into a tiny front parlour with stuffed birds, china dogs, a sofa and several useless pieces of furniture.

She hurriedly arranged seats for them, picked up a what-not bodily to make further room and went out calling:

"Joe, there's three gentlemen want to see you."

A voice from the back kitchen replied:

"I'll be there when I've cleaned myself."

Mrs. Bartlett smiled.

"Come in, Mrs. Bartlett," said Colonel Melchett. "Sit down."

"Oh, no sir, I couldn't think of it."

Mrs. Bartlett was shocked at the idea.

"You find Joe Ellis a good lodger?" inquired Melchett in a seemingly careless tone.

"Couldn't have a better, sir. A real steady young fellow. Never touches a drop of drink. Takes a pride in his work. And always kind and helpful about the house. He put up those shelves for me, and he's fixed a new dresser in the kitchen. And any little thing that wants doing in the house—why, Joe does it as a matter of course, and won't hardly take thanks for it. Ah! there aren't many young fellows like Joe, sir."

"Some girl will be lucky some day,' said Melchett carelessly. "He was rather sweet on that poor girl, Rose Emmott, wasn't he?"

Mrs. Bartlett sighed.

"It made me tired, it did. Him worshipping the ground she trod on and her not caring a snap of the fingers for him."

"Where does Joe spend his evenings, Mrs. Bartlett?"

"Here, sir, usually. He does some odd piece work in the evenings, sometimes, and he's trying to learn bookkeeping by correspondence."

"Ah! really. Was he in yesterday evening?"

"Yes, sir."

"You're sure, Mrs. Bartlett?" said Sir Henry sharply.

She turned to him.

"Quite sure, sir."

"He didn't go out, for instance, somewhere about eight to eight-thirty?"

"Oh no." Mrs. Bartlett laughed. "He was fixing the kitchen dresser for me nearly all the evening, and I was helping him."

Sir Henry looked at her smiling assured face and felt his first pang of doubt.

A moment later Ellis himself entered the room.

He was a tall broad-shouldered young man, very good-looking in a rustic way. He had shy blue eyes and a good-tempered smile. Altogether an amiable young giant.

AGATHA CHRISTIE

Melchett opened the conversation. Mrs. Bartlett withdrew to the kitchen.

"We are investigating the death of Rose Emmott. You knew her, Ellis."

"Yes." He hesitated, then muttered, "Hoped to marry her one day. Poor lass."

"You have heard what her condition was?"

"Yes." A spark of anger showed in his eye. "Let her down, he did. But 'twere for the best. She wouldn't have been happy married to him. I reckoned she'd come to me when this happened. I'd have looked after her."

"In spite of——"

"'Tweren't her fault. He led her astray with fine promises and all. Oh! she told me about it. She'd no call to drown herself. He weren't worth it."

"Where were you, Ellis, last night at eight-thirty?"

Was it Sir Henry's fancy, or was there really a shade of constraint in the ready—almost too ready—reply.

"I was here. Fixing up a contraption in the kitchen for Mrs. B. You ask her. She'll tell you."

"He was too quick with that," thought Sir Henry. "He's a slow thinking man. That popped out so pat that I suspect he'd got it ready beforehand."

Then he told himself that it was imagination. He was imagining things—yes, even imagining an apprehensive glint in those blue eyes.

A few more questions and answers and they left. Sir Henry made an excuse to go to the kitchen. Mrs. Bartlett was busy at the stove. She looked up with a pleasant smile. A new dresser was fixed against the wall. It was not quite finished. Some tools lay about and some pieces of wood.

"That's what Ellis was at work on last night?" said Sir Henry.

"Yes, sir, it's a nice bit of work, isn't it? He's a very clever carpenter, Joe is."

No apprehensive gleam in her eye—no embarrassment.

But Ellis—had he imagined it? No, there *had* been something.

"I must tackle him," thought Sir Henry.

Turning to leave the kitchen, he collided with a perambulator.

"Not woken the baby up, I hope," he said.

Mrs. Bartlett's laugh rang out.

"Oh, no, sir. I've no children—more's the pity. That's what I take the laundry on, sir."

"Oh! I see——"

He paused, then said on an impulse:

"Mrs. Bartlett. You knew Rose Emmott. Tell me what you really thought of her."

She looked at him curiously.

"Well, sir, I thought she was flighty. But she's dead—and I don't like to speak ill of the dead."

"But I have a reason—a very good reason for asking."

He spoke persuasively.

She seemed to consider, studying him attentively. Finally she made up her mind.

"She was a bad lot, sir," she said quietly. "I wouldn't say so before Joe. She took *him* in good and proper. That kind can—more's the pity. You know how it is, sir."

Yes, Sir Henry knew. The Joe Ellises of the world were peculiarly vulnerable. They trusted blindly. But for that very cause the shock of discovery might be greater.

He left the cottage baffled and perplexed. He was up against a blank wall. Joe Ellis had been working indoors all yesterday evening. Mrs. Bartlett had actually been there watching him. Could one possibly get round that? There was nothing to set against it—except possibly that suspicious readiness in replying on Joe Ellis's part—that suggestion of having a story pat.

"Well," said Melchett. "That seems to make the matter quite clear, eh?"

"It does, sir," agreed the inspector. "Sandford's our man. Not a leg to stand upon. The thing's as plain as daylight. It's my opinion as the girl and her father were out to—well—practically blackmail him. He's no money to speak of—he didn't want the matter to get to his young lady's ears. He was desperate and he acted accordingly. What do you say, sir?" he added, addressing Sir Henry deferentially.

193

"It seems so," admitted Sir Henry. "And yet—I can hardly picture Sandford committing any violent action."

But he knew as he spoke that that objection was hardly valid. The meekest animal, when cornered, is capable of amazing actions.

"I should like to see the boy, though," he said suddenly. "The one who heard the cry."

Jimmy Brown proved to be an intelligent lad, rather small for his age, with a sharp, rather cunning face. He was eager to be questioned and was rather disappointed when checked in his dramatic tale of what he had heard on the fatal night.

"You were on the other side of the bridge, I understand," said Sir Henry. "Across the river from the village. Did you see anyone on that side as you came over the bridge?"

"There was someone walking up in the woods. Mr. Sandford, I think it was, the architect gentleman who's building the queer house."

The three men exchanged glances.

"That was about ten minutes or so before you heard the cry?"

The boy nodded.

"Did you see anyone else—on the village side of the river?"

"A man came along the path that side. Going slow and whistling he was. Might have been Joe Ellis."

"You couldn't possibly have seen who it was," said the inspector sharply. "What with the mist and its being dusk."

"It's on account of the whistle," said the boy. "Joe Ellis always whistles the same tune—'I wanner be happy' —it's the only tune he knows."

He spoke with the scorn of the modernist for the old fashioned.

"Anyone might whistle a tune," said Melchett. "Was he going towards the bridge?"

"No. Other way—to village."

"I don't think we need concern ourselves with this unknown man," said Melchett. "You heard the cry and the splash and a few minutes later you saw the body floating downstream and you ran for help, going back to the bridge, crossing it, and making straight for the village. You didn't see anyone near the bridge as you ran for help?"

"I think as there were two men with a wheelbarrow on the river path; but they were some way away and I couldn't tell if they were going or coming and Mr. Giles's place was nearest—so I ran there."

"You did well, my boy," said Melchett. "You acted very creditably and with presence of mind. You're a scout, aren't you?"

"Yes, sir."

"Very good. Very good indeed."

Sir Henry was silent—thinking. He took a slip of paper from his pocket, looked at it, shook his head. It didn't seem possible—and yet—

He decided to pay a call on Miss Marple.

She received him in her pretty, slightly over-crowded old style drawing-room.

"I've come to report progress," said Sir Henry. "I'm afraid that from our point of view things aren't going well. They are going to arrest Sandford. And I must say I think they are justified."

"You have found nothing in—what shall I say—support of my theory, then?" She looked perplexed—anxious. "Perhaps I have been wrong—quite wrong. You have such wide experience—you would surely detect it if it were so."

"For one thing," said Sir Henry, "I can hardly believe it. And for another we are up against an unbreakable *alibi*. Joe Ellis was fixing shelves in the kitchen all the evening and Mrs. Bartlett was watching him do it."

Miss Marple leaned forward, taking in a quick breath.

"But that can't be so," she said. "It was Friday night."

"Friday night?'

"Yes—Friday night. On Friday evenings Mrs. Bartlett takes the laundry she has done round to the different people."

Sir Henry leaned back in his chair. He remembered the

195

boy Jimmy's story of the whistling man and—yes—it would all fit in.

He rose taking Miss Marple warmly by the hand.

"I think I see my way," he said. "At least I can try...."

Five minutes later he was back at Mrs. Bartlett's cottage and facing Joe Ellis in the little parlour among the china dogs.

"You lied to us, Ellis, about last night," he said crisply. "You were not in the kitchen here fixing the dresser between eight and eight-thirty. You were seen walking along the path by the river towards the bridge a few minutes before Rose Emmott was murdered."

The man gasped.

"She weren't murdered—she weren't. I had naught to do with it. She threw herself in, she did. She was desperate like. I wouldn't have harmed a hair on her head, I wouldn't."

"Then why did you lie as to where you were?" asked Sir Henry keenly.

The man's eyes shifted and lowered uncomfortably.

"I was scared. Mrs. B. saw me around there and when we heard just afterwards what had happened—well, she thought it might look bad for me. I fixed I'd say I was working here, and she agreed to back me up. She's a rare one, she is. She's always been good to me."

Without a word Sir Henry left the room and walked into the kitchen. Mrs. Bartlett was washing up at the sink.

"Mrs. Bartlett," he said, "I know everything. I think you'd better confess—that is, unless you want Joe Ellis hanged for something he didn't do.... No. I see you don't want that. I'll tell you what happened. You were out taking the laundry home. You came across Rose Emmott. You thought she'd given Joe the chuck and was taking up with this stranger. Now she was in trouble—Joe was prepared to come to the rescue—marry her if need be, and if she'd have him. He's lived in your house for four years. You've fallen in love with him. You want him for yourself. You hated this girl—you couldn't bear that this worthless little slut should take your man from you. You're a strong woman,

Mrs. Bartlett. You caught the girl by the shoulders and shoved her over into the stream. A few minutes later you met Joe Ellis. The boy Jimmy saw you together in the distance—but in the darkness and the mist he assumed the perambulator was a wheelbarrow and two men wheeling it. You persuaded Joe that he might be suspected and you concocted what was supposed to be an alibi for him, but which was really an alibi for *you*. Now then, I'm right, am I not?"

He held his breath. He had staked all on this throw.

She stood before him rubbing her hands on her apron, slowly making up her mind.

"It's just as you say, sir," she said at last, in her quiet subdued voice (a dangerous voice, Sir Henry suddenly felt it to be). "I don't know what came over me. Shameless—that's what she was. It just came over me—she shan't take Joe from me. I haven't had a happy life, sir. My husband, he was a poor lot—an invalid and cross-grained. I nursed and looked after him true. And then Joe came here to lodge. I'm not such an old woman, sir, in spite of my grey hair. I'm just forty, sir. Joe's one in a thousand. I'd have done anything for him—anything at all. He was like a little child, sir, so gentle and so believing. He was mine, sir, to look after and see to. And this—this——" She swallowed—checked her emotion. Even at this moment she was a strong woman. She stood up straight and looked at Sir Henry curiously. "I'm ready to come, sir. I never thought anyone would find out. I don't know how you knew, sir—I don't, I'm sure."

Sir Henry shook his head gently.

"It was not I who knew," he said—and he thought of the piece of paper still reposing in his pocket with the words on it written in neat old-fashioned handwriting.

*Mrs. Bartlett, with whom Joe Ellis lodges at 2 Mill Cottages.*

Miss Marple had been right again.